down on the south beach drag

down on the south beach drag

A NOVEL

Mary Kathleen Mehuron

SPARKPRESS

Copyright © 2025 Mary Kathleen Mehuron

All rights reserved. No part of this publication may be reproduced, distributed, or transmitted in any form or by any means, including photocopying, recording, digital scanning, or other electronic or mechanical methods, without the prior written permission of the publisher, except in the case of brief quotations embodied in critical reviews and certain other noncommercial uses permitted by copyright law. For permission requests, please address SparkPress.

Published by SparkPress, a BookSparks imprint,
A division of SparkPoint Studio, LLC
Phoenix, Arizona, USA, 85007
www.gosparkpress.com

Published 2025
Printed in the United States of America

Print ISBN: 978-1-68463-324-1
E-ISBN: 978-1-68463-325-8
Library of Congress Control Number: 2025905029

Interior design and typeset by Katherine Lloyd, The DESK

All company and/or product names may be trade names, logos, trademarks, and/or registered trademarks and are the property of their respective owners.

This is a work of fiction. Names, characters, places, and incidents either are the product of the author's imagination or are used fictitiously. Any resemblance to actual persons, living or dead, is entirely coincidental.

NO AI TRAINING: Without in any way limiting the author's [and publisher's] exclusive rights under copyright, any use of this publication to "train" generative artificial intelligence (AI) technologies to generate text is expressly prohibited. The author reserves all rights to license uses of this work for generative AI training and development of machine learning language models.

4th of July, Asbury Park
Words and Music by Bruce Springsteen
Copyright © 1973 Sony Music Publishing (US) LLC
and Eldridge Publishing Co.
Copyright Renewed
All Rights Administered by Sony Music Publishing (US) LLC,
424 Church Street, Suite 1200, Nashville, TN 37219
International Copyright Secured All Rights Reserved
Reprinted by Permission of Hal Leonard LLC

For my mother-in-law,
the late Irene Branislova Weislik Mehuron,
who loved me exactly as God made me.
In the process, she set me free.

"And you know that tilt-a-whirl down on the south beach drag
I got on it last night and my shirt got caught
And they kept me spinnin'
Didn't think I'd ever get off . . ."

—Bruce Springsteen

contents

Chapter 1	Growin' Up	1
Chapter 2	Born to Run	14
Chapter 3	Jersey Girl	22
Chapter 4	Does This Bus Stop at 82nd Street?	31
Chapter 5	It's Hard to Be a Saint in the City	39
Chapter 6	Girls in Their Summer Clothes	45
Chapter 7	Spirit in the Night	53
Chapter 8	The East Street Shuffle	63
Chapter 9	Tramps Like Us	73
Chapter 10	Lady and the Doctor	78
Chapter 11	Love on the Wrong Side of Town	84
Chapter 12	That Lady	91
Chapter 13	Right Place, Wrong Time	100
Chapter 14	The Angel	106
Chapter 15	I Don't Want to Go Home	112
Chapter 16	Sandy	121
Chapter 17	Backstreets	135
Chapter 18	The Sword Swallower's Blade	142
Chapter 19	Rosalita	152
Chapter 20	Fireworks Over Little Eden	159

Chapter 21	Incident on 57th Street	165
Chapter 22	We're an American Band	172
Chapter 23	Tenth Avenue Freeze-Out	177
Chapter 24	Higher Ground	182
Chapter 25	Blinded by the Light	192
Chapter 26	Thunder Road	202
Chapter 27	Long Walk Home	211
Chapter 28	Here I Am	222
Chapter 29	No Surrender	230
Chapter 30	One of a Kind (Love Affair)	236
Chapter 31	Because the Night	245
Chapter 32	Free Bird	256
Acknowledgments		265
About the Author		267

chapter 1
growin' up

I stopped whistling when I saw our parish priest sitting in our kitchen. Had someone died? But Father Murphy, hunched over a cup of coffee at our red-flecked, chipped Formica table, looked quite comfortable. Serene, even.

I wished I had my camera with me. With the late-afternoon sun pouring through the kitchen window, he looked like he was glowing. Like an angel. Not a quality I usually associated with any other priest.

Mom was fixing Father a grilled cheese sandwich. My stomach growled at the buttery-browned aroma. "Hi, Mom."

No response. Huh. Had I already done something to displease her? Every day I spent with her lately included the possibility I would have to walk on eggshells. At almost eighteen, I spent a great deal of time fantasizing about escaping the orbit of Mrs. Sheila O'Connor. I could never be the daughter she wanted. With my shock of frizzy bright red hair and ungainly height of five feet eleven, I was a walking disappointment.

"Stand up straight, Maeve," she growled over her shoulder.

I liked pants and simple collared shirts. She favored frilly dresses and blouses. I enjoyed the competition of playing sports. She wanted me to learn how to sew. And although I didn't need one—my chest was as flat as my brothers'—she forced me to wear a bra, which I thought clashed with my tomboy attire. How would I ever figure out my place in the world living *here*? But I was her only chance at producing a girly girl steeped in Irish Catholic dogma.

I had a big secret, one that turned my stomach. I wasn't like the other girls I knew. Although I didn't yet know where I fit in, I knew I wasn't cut out to be a housewife. And that was the only thing Catholic girls were supposed to aspire to. This knowledge tormented me.

Though it wasn't unheard of for the good Father Murphy to stop in for a visit, it wasn't common either. This was a special occasion, which was why Mom was making him something hot to eat even though it was past lunch and far too early for dinner.

I dropped my schoolbooks on the bench beneath the wall phone and squeezed Father's shoulder on my way by before sitting across from him. He scratched nervously at the back of his neck. It was too hot in here for him to still be wearing his priest's jacket. The standing white collar of his shirt was bad enough. I pointed to the pegs of the mudroom and lifted my hands in question. He slipped the jacket off and I jumped up to hang it on the nearest peg.

Leaning heavily on his forearms, he carefully removed his wire-rimmed glasses and rubbed the lenses with a cloth. His eyes were puffy, rheumy, and he looked exhausted—perhaps from all he had seen in his long life. My heart swelled with tenderness as I sat back down across from him.

"Father Murphy. I wasn't expecting to see *you* when I walked through the door."

"He's been *waiting* for you," Mom bleated as she flipped the grilled sandwich over on the cast iron surface. It sizzled and my mouth watered. I was always starving by the time I got home from school.

Her brusqueness made me scratch my head. "There's only one bus we can take home. It's not like I have a choice of arrival times."

growin' up

Mom sniffed loudly. "It's just like you to dillydally."

"I wasn't dillying or dallying, Mom," I protested. "Try to give me a break for once. As you always remind me—we have company, so we should be on our best behavior."

Father patted my hand and raised his eyebrows at Mom's back. He then turned and waggled them at me, one at a time. It made me giggle—and I am not really the giggling type. He floored me. How well he could work those tiny muscles on his forehead. It cracked me up every time.

Father Murphy took a sip from his brown crockery coffee cup and lightly smacked his lips. "I've come to tell you something, Maeve. First of all, thank you for the pictures you did for the monthly newsletter." From deep in his pants pocket, he took out a folded copy and laid it out in front of me.

I tilted my head, examining the layout. It looked pretty good, although the photograph in the middle of the page was disappointing. "I'm sorry about the lighting in the cafeteria," I said. "It was late afternoon, and I didn't have the right film."

"Nonsense, it's perfectly fine. And the others are wonderful."

"Thank you." I smiled. His praise warmed me inside. Father Murphy had known me for as long as I could remember, and I trusted his judgment. If he thought my work was good, that was good enough for me.

"There's something else." He fumbled around in his opposite pocket, dug a paper out, and handed it to me.

I unfolded the page with a touch of awe, and when I saw what was printed on it my breath caught in my throat and my bones turned to jelly. A photography competition for graduating high school seniors: the New York Area Photo Contest.

He winked at me. "I thought of you right away."

The existence of such a contest was surely divine intervention. A chill went through me as I made the sign of the cross.

"Maeve!" Mom scolded. "You shouldn't try to involve God

in your little goings-on. He has more important things to do."

She could say what she wanted; this little contest was going to be vital to me. My ticket out of our conservative, North Jersey, Irish Catholic suburban house. I leaned in and read some more details. You only got to submit six pictures. How to make a strong impression with only six images? If I won, I would not only be published nationally in *Look* magazine, I would also get a full scholarship to the School of Visual Arts in Manhattan. My dream school. My mother and father would never let me apply under normal circumstances. No one we knew expected to put food on the table by being an artist. It just wasn't done. But if I got a scholarship, how could they tell me no?

My heart raced as I read down to the fine print at the bottom of the page. The scholarship money was contingent on my grades being up to par. My lips curled into a contented smile.

There was no question in my mind that my permanent transcript was better than par. It wasn't even close to anything you could consider average. All through my high school years I'd made sure my grades were exemplary, because I knew that grades, SAT scores, and references were the yellow brick road leading to the School of Visual Arts. Becoming a photographer was my life's ambition. It was all that mattered.

And living in New York City? It would be the perfect antidote to my upbringing in this house. All that was so wholesomely boring about me would melt away. Yes, I would still be tall and gawky, but in the freedom of the city I could finally become the artist I longed to be. Was meant to be. I bet there was even a stylist there who could do something with my mop of hair. New York had everything.

My hands trembled. If Father hadn't brought this flyer to me, I would have missed out on the opportunity. I hadn't heard anything about it.

growin' up

I looked over the top of the paper and into his eyes. "How . . . did you know what this would mean to me?"

He discreetly reached up to wipe a teardrop away before it could escape from his eye and stream down his cheek. Everyone knew he was a wonderful painter; his work with oils was particularly masterful. Perhaps he had a good idea of the agony my aspirations caused me. Perhaps those pictures for the school and the church made him realize it wasn't just a hobby. Nuns and priests are always talking about their avocation to God. Could he have figured out that photography was *my* true calling?

Beyond that, though, I suspected he also had an idea of my big secret. Maybe had one of his own.

"You told me years ago what you wanted to do with your life," Father said. "It has always seemed like a reasonable goal. You're very gifted, Maeve. I stay in touch with some of the colleges for some of our congregation's children . . . the special ones."

I gulped in a ragged breath of gratitude. I couldn't wait to tell Cassie about all of this. Though we traveled in different circles at school—she was a popular cheerleader and prom queen—she respected my interests and loved me for me. She said that without my help in school, she never would have made it to graduation. A gross exaggeration, but it still made me feel good.

I wanted to savor the moment, but my appreciation for Father Murphy was hacked short when Mom plunked a plate in front of him with a sharp clink. The look on her face was ominous. She pursed her lips and let out an exasperated puff of air. My stomach twisted in knots.

She turned to me, her chin lifted in challenge.

I slumped in despair. She was never going to let this happen, I realized, overcome with frustration. The shabbiness of the kitchen suddenly got to me. The peeling wallpaper was especially bad over the stove and around the sink. I fantasized about ripping

down on the south beach drag

it away, and the thought made me smile. I could hear the tearing sound in my head. Satisfying, final. That would squash Mom's obvious disapproval about the photography contest. That would show her.

Plates, drinking glasses, and the baby's last bottle taunted me from the sink. Except for me, and occasionally Mom, it seemed no one else in this family of eight was capable of loading the dishwasher. I wasn't going to let this be my life. No matter what she thought about it.

Mom's narrowed eyes shifted from me to Father, and she put her hands on her hips. "You're filling her head with ideas, Father. Believe me, she has enough of her own." Her gaze returned to me, and she stared at me so long I dropped my eyes to the tabletop. Surely, she suspected my big secret. Maybe she understood my difference better than I did.

Father set his cup down. "Sheila, I have been telling you since this girl was a baby that there is something special about her."

"Yes, and we've been trying to nip it in the bud all along. With no help from you, I might add."

I gasped. To talk to a priest like that.

He remained impassive as he put the sandwich to his lips, testing the temperature of the steaming bread tentatively. "God doesn't make mistakes, Sheila. Every one of us is perfect just as we are. Everything is. Just look at that gorgeous garden of yours."

Shameless flattery; Mom was known for her gardens, and was very proud of them. She crossed her arms in front of her, a haughty expression on her face, as if she were preparing to receive more of his praise and wanted to enjoy every word of it.

"You have a magenta rhododendron," he said. "You have a white one. Both lush. Equally magnificent in their own way."

Mom smiled, picturing the blooms.

"Yes, and there's that one that is a *marvel* . . . all magenta flowers except for a single branch of white," Father said reverently.

"Just majestic. I've never seen anything like it. God's bounty, you see? All the different varieties."

Mom suddenly got where he was heading with this line of thought, and she clearly didn't like it. "More coffee?" she barked.

I couldn't believe her curt voice. My mouth dropped open. This was our priest, the shepherd of our flock. I had been taught he was literally God's representative on Earth. Mom was always pointing out my sins, yet here she was, being rude to God. Surely *that* was a bona fide mortal sin. And a whopper at that.

Father knew just as well as I did that she wasn't keen on the idea of me becoming a photographer. She'd told me many times that anybody with a camera could take a picture. She clung to this theory even though I had already been published many times in local periodicals and even once in *New Jersey Monthly* magazine, which was kind of a big deal.

Mom now stood next to Father with her hands clasped in front of her and her eyes downcast, poised like a good Catholic woman in front of her pastor. Perhaps she regretted her outburst. But no, her face was growing redder by the second. That was no look of remorse.

"You know that Maeve's willful and has a one-track mind," Mom said. In a hoarse whisper, she choked out, "I'm not sure she can make a good *marriage*."

She got me there. Marriage was the last thing I was looking forward to. I had other plans. Many of them.

Mom wanted me to go to a local college and then get what she thought of as a *real* job. One I could support myself with after a two-year associate's degree. My profession had to command a living wage that could pay my rent, as apparently I would be alone for the rest of my life.

I put my head down on the table with a sigh. She exhausted me; I was undone. But I was also scheming. There had to be a way out.

down on the south beach drag

The back door flew open and Pop walked in with Mikey, who was carrying baby Tommy. He was so sweet with him, though he was only two years younger than me—already a teenager, usually the age when boys started to become harder. He always said to the baby, "You're my little buddy, aren't you, Tom?" It was one of the few things in the world that could choke me up.

Pop's arrival was right on time. Though I didn't think for a minute he would take exception with Mom in the presence of Father Murphy, he definitely had a soft spot for my dream.

He hung his service hat on a peg and came to sit with us. He visibly swelled with pride when he spotted my photos in the newsletter, and after perusing the flyer, he patted my cheek lovingly.

Any opportunity that came my way to practice my chosen craft—the town and school newspapers, weddings, bar mitzvahs—I would take it. If someone asked me to shoot photographs, I would say yes. Pop recognized the dedication I put into it. It was a quality he admired greatly.

He ran his huge hands across the papers, smoothing them out, getting ready to tell a story. "Remember, Maeve, when you were a little girl? Just ten, if I recall. You asked me for a darkroom. I told you if you earned half of the money, I would find the rest. And you did. Just a child, but you tracked down every last cent."

Now it was his turn to wipe away a tear. As I reached out for his hand, I heard my mother click her tongue.

He ignored her. "You've done a lot of good with that camera and projector." He nodded to my mother, engaging her with his wide green eyes. "Isn't that so, Sheila?"

Mom was still standing next to Father Murphy; it was a rare thing for her to sit down when there was work to be done. She answered Pop carefully. "It's been a good hobby. It's kept her out of trouble, I'll give you that."

It was family lore that Mikey had to come down to the basement and pound on the door of the utility room where I had my equipment set up every night before dinner—"Maeve! They won't let us eat until you come upstairs! Come on!"—and Pop said the same thing every night in response to my absence: "She'd rather give up food than those pictures of hers."

He wouldn't go so far as to argue with Mom about my career goals. No one ever argued with her. That was the fact of it. Still, he made his point in his own way by telling Father Murphy about Mikey's nightly pilgrimage down to my darkroom. "It's the one thing in this crazy world you can count on, Father. We have to drag Maeve away from her pictures. She'd starve if we let her." He laughed. "And you know what a great cook my wife is." He looked at me with affection and sighed. "Still, working on those photographs is like breathing to her. She lives for it."

Mom was now at the sink, washing the frying pan. My eyes boring into her back, I considered her point of view. It might be unconscious on her part, but she definitely had her own selfish reasons for wanting me to commute to the local junior college—so I could be home most nights to help her with the kids. She *said* she was worried about the money for college tuition. Maybe that was part of it too. Apparently, it was hard raising six kids on a policeman's salary.

She put the pan on the dish rack, turned, and said something I'd heard many times before. "Maeve is still just an innocent girl—a girl who has no street smarts at all. How could she live in such a big city?"

No street smarts *yet*, maybe, but I did have smart smarts, which I knew would take me far. "I want to spend the summer at the shore," I blurted out. The idea had just occurred to me, but now I was desperate for it to happen. For that was where I could find subjects that could win me the photo contest.

I held my breath while Mom, Pop, and Father Murphy exchanged surprised looks. The four judges of the big photo

down on the south beach drag

contest were all college professors. This meant the competition was searching for much more than good composition and a competent series of prints. They were looking for artistic *vision*, a different way of looking at the world. I wasn't going to get the shots I needed here at home. Not even close.

"Maybe Cassie can go with me," I said, flailing. They loved Cassie. Everyone did.

Diane Arbus was my all-time hero. If you looked at her work and compared her subjects to the world I lived in, you would think the two couldn't possibly coexist on the same planet. In fact, the head librarian in town had made me bring a note from my parents before she even allowed me to check out any art books containing her pictures. I forged the note myself, of course, and hid the books in a box out in the loft of the garage, the only place available to me at home that was outside my mother's purview and away from my five little brothers' prying eyes.

One epiphany I'd had after spending time with Ms. Arbus's photographs was that the community I encountered in my daily life did not include a single person who acknowledged being homosexual. I'm not saying there weren't any. I'm saying they knew enough not to admit it to our conservative majority, for fear of outrage and disapproval. It was possible that such a person's parents might up and die from the shame alone. And it also struck me hard that Arbus had managed to photograph men who dressed up like women and looked very happy.

Even though I couldn't put a name to this, and had no idea what the practice would be called, her photos made me suddenly aware that the possibility even existed. It was also possible that it had something to do with my big secret. If what Ms. Arbus was showing me was truth, what else was my small town hiding?

She captured images of strippers, carnival workers, sideshow acts; as the old saying goes, the camera doesn't lie. These were actual human beings who were raising their families and making their way. They lived *somewhere*. But I sure wasn't going to find them in my town in North Jersey. Not in 1972, anyway.

Ms. Arbus opened my eyes; I had to have more. I got the library to order me some photography magazines. They even got a hold of a copy of Andy Warhol's *Interview* magazine for me— and that's where I discovered work by a young staff photographer named Robert Mapplethorpe who was becoming known for, among other things, photographing men together in a way that showcased their intimate feelings for each other. This intrigued me. I pored over his images, studying the lighting and how he framed his shots. The models in one edition were . . . well . . . *beautiful*. Luminous. They gave me a new sensation. A thrill. Stimulated me in some way I hadn't known before. Put a fullness in my belly . . . and other parts farther south, to be honest. It was exciting. Even famous people looked into his lens comfortably, as if they trusted him as a friend. As if he was loved.

With Arbus as elder stateswoman and Mapplethorpe as, to my mind, my contemporary mentor, I had inspiration enough. They were how I knew I needed to get to the shore. There was only one place I could think of in close proximity where I would find arresting, gritty, maybe even downright raunchy subjects for this contest, and that was a washed-up old seaside resort called Asbury Park.

I was sure great art and alternative kinds of lives must be gestating in plain sight. It just made sense. Asbury Park suffered from poverty, drug problems, and sporadic race rioting; it was always the decaying neighborhoods that drew original people on their way up in the world, wasn't it? Sure, there was bound to be some on their way down too. I wanted to get close to all of them and see if any of them struck a chord with me. It would be the most epic experience of my life.

Now I just had to convince my parents to let me spend the summer there.

down on the south beach drag

Though Mom and I had very different ideas about my education, I knew she loved me with her whole heart. So, I cried. Sobbed. It was heart-wrenching, even to my own ears.

"What are the chances of me winning this, Mom? If I don't try, I'm going to be commuting on the town bus to school for years. Please let me try," I begged. "Let me have the summer. Just one summer for myself."

Mom blinked repeatedly. "But where will you live?"

Father Murphy couldn't have a clue what was in my mind. Could he? Yet he jumped right in. "Why, it's practically a rite of passage around here. Lots of kids get summer jobs at the shore after graduation. Didn't you go yourself when you were a girl, Sheila?"

A little smile lit Mom's face. "To Sea Girt. With my best friend, Trish."

"Aunt Trisha?" She was still Mom's friend.

"Yes. We stayed in an old mansion. Helped with the cleaning and cooking. A very well-to-do family. They were wonderful to us." Mom nodded. She was warming to the idea.

Father felt the change in her too. "They don't call the shore 'the Irish Riviera' for nothing, Sheila," he bellowed. "We'll find a situation. Maybe as a nanny? She would be great at that. Maeve is a child that is going places. I promise you."

There was no way I was leaving the responsibility of one passel of young kids—five brothers, for Christ's sake—and trading it for another. I'd find a different kind of job.

I was too awash in a surge of other possibilities I was putting together on the fly to hear much of the discussion going on between Father and my parents. When my mind came back to the room, Father was saying, "So, it's agreed. We will allow Maeve to investigate suitable positions. If she finds something acceptable to you, she can go to the shore for the summer—just a few months, nothing to worry about." He winked at me again.

growin' up

"She'll take her pictures, and we'll see about this contest. We are in agreement there's no harm in applying, correct?"

"But we'll just *see* what happens," Mom stressed.

The good Father patted my hand. "Yes, we shall see."

I went to the kitchen sink and splashed cold water on my tearstained cheeks, then ripped a paper towel off the roll and wiped them. They were buying it. Somehow Father had folded my mother's warm feelings about her long-ago days of independence into my own quest for freedom.

To cover the smile that was now stretching across my face, I slid the towel down across my mouth and walked toward the garbage can near the pantry, lost in a dream about my summer of liberation. Where to begin?

One time, when me and Pop were on our way to the carousel pavilion in Asbury Park, we walked past the open door of an old theater called Hootch. Across the entrance, many layers of glossy paint were peeling off, revealing the colors it had been throughout the years. The sidewalk was filthy. My nose wrinkled at the distinct stench of urine. Even so, I inched closer and peeked in.

A television over a bar lit up the faces of garishly dressed women. Their makeup was caked on and their eyebrows appeared to be drawn onto their foreheads, much like you would find on a marionette.

Pop grabbed my hand. "Come now, Maeve. That's no place for the likes of you."

At the time I hadn't thought so either, but now it seemed precisely the place I should be.

Somehow, someway, I would not only go up to that doorway but walk right in. It was, in its own way, a magic portal to my new life in New York City.

chapter 2
born to run

Over the next few weeks I kept an eye on the help-wanted ads in the paper and sent letters of application through the mail as beachfront businesses would be hiring for the high summer season. All the parties and events of late spring of senior year held little meaning by comparison. Cassie was the only classmate I would miss after graduation, and though she hadn't said yes yet, I was still holding out hope that she would come with me.

We didn't have a typewriter at home, so the business teacher let me use one in her classroom—but only after school. When I stayed to write a letter, I missed the bus and had to walk two and a half miles home with my arms loaded with books. It was a schlep, but I did it.

When Mom said I was naive I bristled, but I knew deep inside it was true. I'd never lived anywhere else—hell, I'd never *been* anywhere but New Jersey and the city except for one day trip my class took to Philadelphia when we graduated from eighth grade, and that didn't count for much. Despite my bravado, the idea of striking out all by myself was daunting. Having Cassie with me would be a big help.

I talked up my idea of the summer in Asbury Park every time we hung out. What a relief it would be to go together. At least to share the burden of planning for the big move. But all she'd say was, "I'll think about it, but you know it will be hard for me to leave Bobby."

Would my parents let me go without her? Could I handle it alone?

I stomped my foot. Literally. The sheer frustration of the whole Bobby thing made me feel like a two-year-old. "He can visit."

"He won't like us having our own place. One time we were listening to that song 'See You in September,' and he said, 'What kind of guy hangs around till September? All patient and everything?'"

Ack. Be careful now. Don't piss her off. There's too much at stake. But I had to point one thing out: "He spent last summer at the shore with his friends. Doing God knows what. You waited by the phone for months."

Though Cassie remained noncommittal, I plugged away at looking for a job. Finally, the reward for my hard work came: a phone call inviting me to an interview for a waitress position in Asbury Park the following week.

This was it. Now, how to put my best foot forward?

I found a magazine article that said you could use the cylinders from orange juice concentrate as extra-large hair rollers. This was supposed to calm frizzy hair. Mom kept plenty of OJ in the chest freezer, so I force-fed my brothers juice for the next seven days, talking up the benefits of vitamin C.

"Smooth and straighten your curls," the article said. My flaming *red* curls. I couldn't do anything about the color, but surely taming the frizz would make me more attractive to the public I would be serving.

I washed my hair and coated it with Dippity-Do, then set it like in the pictures in the magazine. Bobby pins secured the juice containers in place and I left them on for ten whole hours, trying to sleep that way. My head never actually hit the pillow that night; instead, it was suspended a few inches above by the rounded cardboard. If I wasn't in exactly the right position, the big bobby pins pinched my scalp.

By morning the cylinders were crushed, and I was grouchy as all get-out.

Since the curlers were a bust, I decided to try another way of straightening that might last the whole day: I dragged the ironing board and iron into my room, locked the door, laid my cheek on the spongy cover, spread my long red hair out, and did my best to iron it flat.

It wound up looking eerily similar to my old baby doll's shiny plastic mane. Even so, it was a vast improvement on my usual self.

Mom knocked on my door impatiently. What would she make of my new look?

She handed me a pile of folded laundry when I opened it. "Your hair . . ." For a moment she hovered dangerously close to giving me a compliment, then her eyes slid to the outfit lying on my bed. "Not the taffeta?"

The blue taffeta dress had been handed down to me by my cousin. Its crinoline petticoat made the skirt stand out. *Over my dead body.* The first time I saw it, I'd told Mom that I was not a five-year-old ballerina.

"Mom."

"All right. All right. You'll look nice."

High praise.

I pressed my best outfit, one of the few dresses I owned, with spray starch. A beautiful gray linen with a U-shaped neckline, its swing skirt fell crisply to just above my knees. Looking in the mirror, I stuck my hands in the side pockets. I felt comfortable. This was the best I had. It would have to do.

I walked to the station on shaking legs and hopped on the train.

Two and a half hours later, heart pounding, I arrived at a seaside bar and grill right on the boardwalk. "On the boardwalk" meant heavy traffic. Heavy traffic meant good money.

born to run

Though Asbury Park was no longer in its glory days, the boardwalk still oozed charm: the Ferris wheel, the roller coaster, the arcades packed with frenzied customers. Its wide expanse of decking overlooked an extraordinarily white sandy beach. Way ahead of its time, the developers had included the convenience of public changing rooms. I ducked in to use the ladies' room.

I wasn't entirely surprised to see someone sleeping on the floor in one of the stalls. There were lots of homeless folks in Asbury Park. It was a little scary. Yes, it was. But the woman didn't bother me as I went about my business.

The salt air filled my senses when I stepped back outside, and a balmy humidity caressed my face. The aroma alone made me ravenous for seafood. A long stone pier stretched before me and I was a few minutes early, so I treated myself to a walk along it, out into the Atlantic Ocean.

Staring over the railing, I patted my tumbling tresses with both hands. My moment to shine. My dream to come to Asbury Park *would* become a reality. No one, nothing, could stop me now.

With a big smile on my face, I headed to the restaurant for my interview.

Dennis, the owner, shook my hand as he introduced himself. This hadn't ever happened to me before. It wasn't done with little girls. Little boys, maybe. *I guess I'm not little anymore*, I thought, and though I found it awkward I tried to look him in the eye as I shook back, the way I had seen my father do many times.

"Can we sit down for a bit?" he asked.

The café table he led me to was sticky and covered in piles of coins and banknotes.

"So, if a customer gives you a twenty and the bill is $16.75, what kind of change would you give them?" He pointed to the money.

When I handed him a quarter and three dollar bills, he went

down on the south beach drag

on with two other scenarios. He spoke carefully, like I was a child or an idiot or something. I yawned. It was pretty insulting.

"Look," I said, "I learned this math in first and second grade. I was always in the advanced groups." Though it was the truth, I hoped I didn't come across as snotty. My lips curled up in a little smile. "Let's just make this a game. You tell me how much the bill is and what they pay with and I will tell you the amount I would return and in what configuration. There's no need for me to act it out."

Our exchange was rapid-fire. He couldn't come up with problems fast enough.

Dennis was laughing when he went behind the bar and retrieved a form. He also mixed himself a vodka martini. When he pointed to his glass with raised eyebrows, I assumed he was asking me if I wanted anything. I shook my head.

"You're pretty good at math," he said. "Do you think you could be in charge of cashing out at the end of your shift?"

"Sure." I didn't have any idea what he was talking about. "What do I do?"

He handed me the piece of paper. "You count the money and you fill this out."

I read the titles of the columns. Only my eyes shifted when I glanced up at him; he was studying me. "I've never gotten less than an 'A' on any math test," I said. "My SAT score was almost perfect. I'm pretty sure I can handle this."

He scrunched his lips together and nodded, then reached behind the bar for a calendar. "But you can only work part-time, you said?"

I had to stay firm. I was coming down here to scout subjects and take photographs. If I worked too many hours, I wouldn't get it done. My cheeks flushed as I screwed up my courage. "Yes," I said. "I'm going to be very busy this summer."

"Okay, I get it. Come over here and let me show you how this works." He took me behind the old mahogany bar and pulled out some cloth-bound books.

Most of the surfaces were tacky and smelled like beer, so I tried hard not to touch anything. After looking over his bookkeeping system, I knew keeping track of his money wouldn't be hard.

We agreed on a start date and a twenty-hour-a-week schedule. I put out my hand to shake his, feeling more confident this time.

I burst out of the restaurant's front door and into the warm, salty air like I was riding on a pink cloud.

I would do my best to impress Dennis. I had a feeling the position would quickly become a bookkeeping one. Less strenuous. Better paid. The steady work would keep me from draining my savings any further than I had to.

The warmth of the late spring day caressed my shoulders. A newspaper was sitting on a bus stop bench. I swept it up and opened to the real estate section.

I needed to orient myself and look around before heading home, so I wandered across Wesley Lake on the footbridge and explored the residential neighborhoods of Ocean Grove. The quiet streets were lined with well-kept Victorian homes, though it was only a stretch of the legs from the chaos of Asbury Park.

The lilac blooms were fading, but their scent still hung in the air. Waxy magnolias were in full bloom and the heads of the peonies I spotted seemed ready to explode at any second. A small white lilac bush, planted on the north side of a white Colonial, was late in blooming. Each blossom beckoned me with its youthful innocence. I buried my face in a branch full of fragrant buds and took in their perfume with a contented sigh. I'd gotten a job! I jumped into the air and clicked my heels together.

Whistling the old song "Happy Days Are Here Again," I headed back to the bus and train station. The trip home was going to be hot and time-consuming: a bus to Pennsylvania Station in Newark, then a train on the North Jersey Line to my hometown, and things rarely ran on time.

And Newark made me nervous. Some of the fathers in my neighborhood got extra hazard pay just for agreeing to work downtown. Of all the things my parents disallowed, why did they insist I travel on mass transit alone? A mugging had happened right in front of me on one trip; I still had nightmares about it. Another time, a gang of boys had surrounded Cassie and me on the bus to the mall. The bus driver had pulled down his rearview mirror to watch what was happening, but he'd done nothing to help.

At the station, I sat down on an open bench where I could bask in the sun. A long, narrow garden separated my bench from the waiting area for the commuter trains. Several benches up, a man sat dressed to the nines in a conservative suit, his silk scarf tied in a Windsor knot.

Was he heading to Manhattan?

He sported a black fedora. The kind of hat Frank Sinatra had made famous when I was a child. While the height of glamour, it hid the man's face. He'd chosen a seat in the shadows, too, making his features even harder to see.

As a train approached, the platform shook. The man stood. He was even taller than me—well over six feet—but willowy.

"Georgie!" a woman called out, and he lit up when he saw her coming his way.

He loped gracefully, loose-limbed and so light on his feet it seemed he might break into a gliding Fred Astaire routine at any moment, to greet her. After they embraced, he took her arm and they sashayed inside the open door of one of the train cars like models would step onto a runway. Head held high, he made a dignified statement with each step. Though his manner was restrained, I couldn't take my eyes off him.

How I wished I were heading to New York instead of going

home. I would have boarded that train and made conversation with him immediately.

Maybe there's time to get on for just a second, I thought. Just to say hello and find out who this captivating fellow was. What the hell? I liked to meet new people.

A long time ago I'd learned that saying, "I'm a photographer; I'd like to take your picture," had universal appeal. I'd had my own business cards since I was fourteen. The couple who owned the print shop traded with me for babysitting hours.

I had my camera bag with me. Introducing myself would seem legit. Maybe it really was; maybe all I wanted was to capture that face on film. I ran.

It was suddenly imperative that I meet this mystery man. That I share his ride into New York so we could talk.

I could see him through the window as I sprinted. Our eyes met through the glass and my heart stopped. Blue, blue eyes. Wide but downturned. Just a trace of sadness. He waved a brief hello and smiled.

I raced faster. I was going to make it; I knew it. But just as I was about to jump off the platform and into the train car, the door snapped closed.

My heart ached. What a lost opportunity.

But I'll be living here soon, I reminded myself. *He's pretty easy to spot. We'll meet again. I'll make sure of it.*

Behind me I heard the hissing of a bus's brakes engaging. I turned. The sight of the bus was depressing. I could see that the empty front seat was torn. I would take it anyway. The closer I was to the driver, the safer I would be.

chapter 3
jersey girl

The only thing that wasn't perfectly gorgeous about my best friend was her harsh Jersey accent. Her mom was from Hoboken, and from time to time Cassie would go full-on *tawk* instead of *talk*. *Cawfee* instead of *coffee*. I teased her about it, and she didn't like that—but honestly, I was doing her a favor by pointing it out.

That was her *only* flaw. Out of the crapshoot of genetics, she'd inherited the most desirable traits of her Swedish paternal grandparents and Italian mother. Her smooth skin tanned deeply (a characteristic of which I was deeply jealous). Her eyes were Viking blue. A natural blonde, she had a habit of raising her chin and shaking her long hair so it rippled down her back.

Watching her do this now, I shook my head too—in disbelief at her bounty—and reached up and felt my curly topknot, the red mop I'd been cursed with. Life was so unfair.

"So," I said, "the meeting is set with our parents and Father Murphy at the rectory. Six thirty tonight."

Cassie had been down lately, ever since Bobby had abruptly broken up with her.

When she'd told me, I'd immediately thought, *Hurray*. It gave me a fighting chance to get her down to the shore with me. But instead of taking advantage of her newfound freedom, she'd been spending hours on end alone in her room.

jersey girl

She was wrapped in her fuzzy pink blanket, telling me about the moment, standing on the auditorium stage, when she and Bobby were crowned Prom King and Queen. How they'd hung on to each other's hands, blinded by the spotlights. "Remember, Maeve?" Tears filled her eyes.

I raised my eyes and hands to the heavens. "How can I forget? This is the third time you've brought it up this week." It was hard for me to remain patient in any given situation, let alone in the face of the endless replaying of Cassie and Bobby's dating years highlights.

I wished I could cut that pink cocoon off her. All I saw of her anymore was her face peeking out of it. It was all I could do not to scream.

Why had she put Bobby in charge of her life when she was so damned talented? She was good at everything. The sky was the limit for a girl like her.

"Let's go into the city and see a Broadway show," I suggested. "We can get standing room for five dollars. We'll see a musical. Then your mind will be filled with songs instead of all this."

She shook her head and shrugged, tears streaming down her face. "I'm heartsick," she said simply.

Our lives had barely begun. There was so much out in the world yet to explore. But she was in pain, clearly. I could at least try to be empathetic. "I guess you two were the height of cool . . . and . . . maybe it's going to be a tough act to follow . . . but you have so many options," I said, casting around for something that might soothe her. "You must have thought about what you wanted to do after high school?"

Cassie started sniffling again. "I always thought we would get *married*."

"Oh, God," popped out of my mouth before I could stop it.

She looked at me with a degree of shock that made me feel like the worst person in the world.

down on the south beach drag

They *had been* the height of cool—until this present spring of 1972, when Bobby had suddenly gotten it in his head that life was passing him by, jumped in his truck, and driven off to California. Hadn't even waited for graduation. Some said he'd been drinking the night he left, but apparently, once he'd gotten a taste for the road, he'd kept right on going. Cassie had hoped for an engagement ring, but all she'd gotten was a fare-thee-well.

I'd been pretty much the exact opposite of Cassie during our school years, working like a dog to make good grades and save money to make my escape from this town. As Cassie was the only one who ever listened to me, she knew all about it. I was on my way.

The thought of the beach bar where I'd be working this summer brought the aroma of French fries to mind. My stomach rumbled and I covered it with both hands. "It's a perfect time for you to make a fresh start," I said. "With me."

Cassie widened her blue eyes to a size that she knew from experience was almost hard for onlookers to believe. Along with hair tossing, it was one of her favorite moves. You had to laugh.

"But, Maeve, what if he comes back for me and I'm not here? What if he wants to get back together?"

The forlorn look on her face was killing me. "What would you do all summer? Wait around? Just like last year?" She had to come with me. It was important for both of us.

She picked up her guitar and started playing Joni Mitchell's "Both Sides Now," an ode to lost love and disillusionment that had become, I guess, a kind of soothing mantra for her. Cassie was born with a rich singing voice, but she was always holding back.

"This is no time to worry about tone," I told her. "Just let it out. I bet the way you sing in the church choir is a mere squeak compared to what you're actually capable of. I think you could really belt it out if you wanted to."

jersey girl

She started finger-picking the strings in the same pattern. This was followed by a soft whine.

Sweet Jaysus. If you can wince and flinch at the same time, I did. I'm as big a Joni fan as anyone, but I'd had to listen to those lines at least fifty times over the past few weeks.

I reached over and turned on Cassie's radio with a twist of my wrist and a snap of the dial. A rhythm and blues song spilled out over the airwaves from New York City into Cassie's suburban New Jersey bedroom. It made me smile.

"Learn one of these songs," I said, gesturing to the radio. "I'm begging you. It will give you some sense of empowerment, you know? It will make you feel good about yourself. And strong. Just once, it would be fun to see *you* enjoy that gorgeous voice of yours. It's a gift, Cass. A gift from God. Ask Father Murphy."

This wasn't just an empty compliment. Sometimes—when she wasn't paying attention to anyone else and she let herself go—Cassie's singing just floored me.

We sat quietly for a moment, listening to the song. Somehow, she sensed the key it was in and strummed a C chord. "You're free to leave anytime if you want to," she murmured. "Sorry I'm not in a better mood." She broke down and wept.

"Stop."

"You don't understand what we had," she wailed. "I remember in freshman year I tried to tell you about tongue kissing, and you freaked out."

I remembered it well. It *had* sounded like a disgusting thing to do.

"Over time . . . it's very gradual . . . you learn how to make each other excited," she said, trying to make me understand. "It all feels so good. Making love with Bobby? He was a part of me. I'm afraid I'll never feel that way again. A part of me is gone forever."

Grief over a boyfriend? Who had time for that?

down on the south beach drag

"Let's take a walk downtown," I suggested. "I'm kind of hiding out from my mom. She wants me to start painting the bathroom. It's the last thing I want to do."

An Aretha Franklin song came on. It made me feel energized and silly. I snapped my fingers to the up-tempo beat and leaned into Cassie, shaking my shoulders. She laughed and at first shooed me away, but she couldn't resist the fun; in short order, we were up and dancing.

When the track ended, we fell back on the bed, giggling like girls half our age.

Father Murphy sat at his desk facing us, his little poodle, Paddy, curled up in his lap. Mom sat in one of the green leather wingback chairs, Cassie's mom in the other. The rest of us were seated in folding chairs. Except for Pop, who stood, ramrod straight and still in uniform.

I caught his eye and smiled. He shrugged.

"It's wonderful that you're all here to consider the girls' idea," said Father Murphy. "Maeve, can you start us off?"

My stomach flipped. This was my new thing now—I was that anxious. What if I said the wrong thing?

"Okay. Ah . . . I've got a job for twenty hours a week. I'm pretty sure I can get more hours if I find I need them. But the important thing to me is taking pictures."

Mom groaned.

I flushed and couldn't think of another thing to say.

"Please, Sheila," Father Murphy chided. "The purpose of this meeting is to establish appropriate conditions for the possibility of their summer at the shore. It's neither the time nor place for an indictment of Maeve's interest in the arts."

Pop nodded in agreement. Encouraging.

"I'll be down by the water twice a day with my cameras, in

the morning and late afternoon—that's when the light is best," I explained. "I'll be taking pictures of people, and trying to capture the iconic landmarks too."

My face burned, and I knew it was a deep crimson color. Cassie reached out and put a hand on my arm.

The gesture made my heart ache. It would be wonderful to have her with me. The feeling gave me the strength to explain what I wanted to capture as best I could.

"I want to get everything on film: the rides in those cruddy amusement parks, even somehow try to capture the smell of popcorn, cotton candy, and fried food in the air. Get to know some carnie characters. It will be life-changing."

Father Murphy chuckled. "I'm sure I speak for all of us when I say we'd like you to be a bit careful around those characters. That would be one of the boundaries your parents would want you to have. 'Characters' is the right word. There are a lot of them down there."

While the parents nodded, I squirmed.

"Now," Father continued, "I've made a little list. Just a few things that will provide some structure so your families won't be worried about you girls."

"We're adults now," Cassie said. "What's everybody so worried about?"

"I'll consider you an adult when you are paying your own way in this world," Cassie's dad said with a scowl. "As long as I'm footing the bill, you'll follow my rules."

"She needs a change," her mom whispered to him, loud enough for all of us to hear. "It will be good for her."

Everyone stared at the floor for a few seconds, until Father Murphy cleared his throat and nodded at Cassie's dad. "What about this, Lars? At my age, I'm a senior priest. The past two years, I've qualified for a summer assignment at Holy Name in Ocean Grove. It's practically a vacation. That's where we would want the girls staying, anyway—across the town border. We all know Asbury Park can get a little rough, especially on the weekends. If we can secure a place for them in Ocean Grove, I can pop in once in a while. Give you an update."

Cassie's face wrinkled with annoyance. "You don't trust us?"

Pop's baritone filled the room. "It's not that we don't trust you, Miss Cassie. And I know Maeve is good as gold. But there's danger in the world. You'll see it soon enough for yourself. It would be a comfort to know you're looked after." Turning, he added, "Thank you, Father."

How could anybody argue with that? So now we were going to have to put up with Father Murphy babysitting us and giving our parents progress reports. That's not what I'd had in mind at all. I was looking for fringe elements. The kind of people I'd never been allowed to know. Was Father going to get in the way of that?

I could smell a pot roast cooking; it was clear Father's dinner was waiting. He spoke faster. "Of course, I expect to see you girls for Mass on Sundays. It would be a great gift to me if you'd agree to join our youth group as well."

Youth group? How will that life be any different from the one I'm living now? I raised my hand and took his nod as permission to speak. "I don't know how much extra time I'll have, Father. Between work and my project, I'm going to be swamped."

"Surely you'll have time to think about somebody other than yourself," Mom snapped.

That did it. "What I think, Mother, is that I earned all the money for this. Myself. It took me years to do it. And I want the time I'm at the shore to be my own. Just for once in my life." My voice became shrill at the end of that last sentence, causing everyone to study the carpet again.

Father held up a finger. "So, we are agreed. The girls work, go to Mass, and expect me to come by from time to time. There's one last thing. I've gone over the numbers with Maeve. High-season rent is very expensive." He unfolded a section of newspaper and ran a finger down a column of advertisements. "It might make sense to get another girl to go in with you two."

Cassie laid the palm of one hand along the length of her high cheekbone and gasped an I've-got-it gasp. "Let's call Sandra. Maybe she would come."

People had always told me that when I glowered some trick of light happened in my eyes, like molten lava simmering inside. Most found it very disconcerting, and Cassie was no exception. She quickly turned away, as did everyone sitting close to me.

"Sandra!" I fumed. "That's all we need."

While our graduating class had voted me "Most Likely to Succeed" and Cassie "Best Looking"—Sandra Katz was its most notorious sexpot.

I wanted to hear what was said on the phone, so Cassie leaned in close to me. Sandra said she was on her bed, painting her toenails and hiding out.

"Hiding out from who?" Cassie asked.

"My mom!" Sandra wailed. "Privacy is turning into a big issue around here."

Cassie giggled and flung back her perfect blonde hair. One long lock hit me in the eye, which started to water. "Perfect timing, then," she said. "I'm here with Maeve."

Sandra let out a theatrical sigh. Heat rose inside me.

"What is your problem?" I called into the mouthpiece.

"Maeve with the volcano eyes," she said without hesitation. "When you give me that judgmental look, it creeps me out!"

"It's not like I try to do it," I protested.

"I think it's exactly like you try to do it, because it always happens when I do something you disapprove of," she snapped back. "Miss High and Mighty Maeve."

down on the south beach drag

"We're talking about getting an apartment at the shore for the summer," Cassie jumped in. "Split the rent three ways, and we might be able to swing it."

That perked Sandra right up. "This could work. My mom has always liked Maeve. My dad too. Obviously. For years I've had to listen to, *Now there's a girl with a head on her shoulders.* We're talking Asbury Park, right? The possibilities take my breath away."

Sandra had a way of making anything sound dirty. I wanted freedom, not trouble. Cassie leaned her forehead against my cheek as we listened.

"I'll call Aunt Cookie at her real estate office, then come by and pick you two up," said Sandra. "I'll just be a few minutes, so wait for me outside."

"What? Now?" I asked. Mom expected me home to help with dinner. What was I going to tell her?

Sandra was insistent. "Yes, right now!"

I held the phone while Cassie put both fists up to her mouth and squealed with excitement. It would be next to impossible for me to deny her this outing. I loved her so much, I didn't have it in me to make waves. Not when she'd been in such a slump lately.

That's what I would tell Mom. That Cassie needed the outing.

In most cases a lie was only a venial sin. It wouldn't automatically send me to hell. Isn't that what the good Sisters told us? It would be a black mark on my soul for sure, but a small one—tiny, even. It was worth the risk.

chapter 4
does this bus stop at 82nd street?

With hardly a moment to think about the implications of what we were doing, I squeezed into the messy back seat of Sandra's parents' station wagon.

The last time I'd been in a car with Sandra, it was the snazzy two-seater convertible she'd been given when she turned sixteen, and within minutes of picking me up she'd screeched into a No U-turn section on the highway and proceeded to do just that. Her rear tires had skidded out, and I'd smelled burnt rubber.

Sandra knew perfectly well that my father was on the police force.

"You're going to get us arrested!" I squawked.

She just laughed, frosted lipstick marking the brown filter of the cigarette hanging from her lips, and flicked some ash at me, making me jump. "Get over it. The worst I get is a ticket. So what?"

"A *hundred-dollar* ticket," I warned her. "At least."

She shrugged and took another drag on her Marlboro.

The memory made me anxious. Luckily, Sandra started telling a story just as my stomach began to twist, giving me something else to think about.

"Get this. A couple days after my birthday party—spur of the moment, mind you, and just for an excuse to drive the car—I took off and headed down to Aunt Cookie's house to show it to her."

Sandra said she knocked at the door, but no one answered, which was strange because Cookie's Cadillac was in the driveway. Cookie took her time answering but did finally open the door a crack.

"Can you imagine how surprised I was to see she was wearing a frothy pink peignoir set?" Sandra said, laughing. "It was like something out of a movie." She took her hands off the wheel and made a big-breasts gesture in front of her chest. "I mean, it was broad daylight."

Cassie reached over and grabbed the wheel while Sandra continued.

"It was so weird. Rather than let me in, even open the door any further, she reached behind her, grabbed a trench coat, threw it on, and kind of squeezed out the front door. But I got a glimpse of a woman and a man sitting at her dining room table before she shut the door, and here's the wild part—they had on fancy peignoirs too. The guy as well. And he had on a push-up bra."

As my mind frantically tried to make a connection between Diane Arbus's photographs and Sandra's story, Cassie gaped. For her, I realized, the notion of a man dressing like a woman must seem horrific. I hadn't shared my art book discoveries with her, or any conclusions I'd come to over the past few years. How would I have explained my fascination with the subjects? I didn't understand it myself. I flipped back and forth from shame about my interest to fascination with the images.

"So that was the day," Sandra said, "I learned my aunt had a very interesting private life. Way kinkier than mine."

Sandra was the wildest girl I knew. She didn't suffer from guilt like the rest of us. "I like sex," she'd told us before. "I don't really want a boyfriend. But that feeling of being desired, the buildup and the explosion—whew! Once I discovered it, I just had to have it all the time."

Sandra turned the radio on, took a joint out of her pocket, and lit it. Johnny Nash sang "I Can See Clearly Now." As she rolled down her window and handed the weed to Cassie, she started seat-dancing along, exclaiming, "I love this song." Her sleek, dark ponytail bobbed to the rhythm as she goofily sang in a deliberately off-key voice.

Cassie broke down, giggling hysterically, as she passed the joint back to me. I waved her hand away and frantically tried to disperse the smoke. What was she thinking? When did I ever partake?

"You guys know if my father smells this on me I'll be grounded for the rest of my entire life," I whined, and sat as far back as I could in the bench seat. If it had been possible to get in the trunk, I would have crawled into it and happily braved claustrophobia.

I knew from my one attempt at inhaling pot last year that I couldn't handle it. The second it kicked in, I'd waited in a hazy panic for it to wear off. I definitely was not tempted to try it again. And Sandra's singing wasn't all that funny, either. If Cassie's high-pitched giggle was the result of the marijuana at work, it was hitting her fast. Too fast to make any sense.

She was probably just trying her level best to kiss up to Sandra, which was kind of how the whole drive down to the shore went. It got old fast.

I was sure Cassie didn't really want to be like Sandra, but she did want Sandra to think she was cool. "Cool," as far as I could tell these days, meant taking drugs and having sex.

The music drowned out their voices. I'd have had to lean really far forward, practically sitting on the center ridge on the floor, to follow what they were saying. Instead, I stretched out on the bench seat and fell asleep.

Deeply asleep.

down on the south beach drag

■ ■ ■

The car lurching to a stop jerked me awake. I rolled right off the seat into the footwell. Sandra had run into a cement curb trying to parallel park.

I bolted upright and glanced around, for several seconds completely forgetting where I was and what we were doing.

We were outside a small but jazzy little gray building with elaborate, dusty blue awnings and door overhangs and a sign with scrolling gold gilt that read KATZ REAL ESTATE. This was Cookie's place of business.

Muddled and sweaty, I jumped out and followed Sandra and Cassie inside.

The Katz family was part of a very select group of people I knew who had air-conditioning. Cookie's office, apparently, was no exception. As I stepped inside, the blasting cold air hit me like a brick wall. My sodden pink seersucker blouse stuck to my back, and I looked around for a bathroom.

When I got there, the mirror told me what I already knew. Other than flushed pink spots high on my cheeks, I was white as a ghost. Had it been offered to me at that moment, I might have sold my soul to the devil for skin that could tan.

A shiver went through me as Mom's lectures about damnation came to mind. I made the sign of the cross and said a quick prayer, then turned the gold-plated water faucet on full blast. *Forget about the tan.* I splashed water on my face, pulled a plush blue hand towel off a neatly folded pile, and dried myself off.

Returning to the office somewhat refreshed, I found Sandra standing behind Cookie, looking over her shoulder as she flipped through glossy real estate listings. They really were cute together. I wished I had a cool aunt. Mine were all pretty much like my mom: Saying their rosaries and worrying about every misstep they might take. Or, God forbid, transgressions their kids might

does this bus stop at 82nd street?

make. Every minuscule decision could be a descent in the wrong direction—toward hell instead of heaven.

Cookie's space-age desk sat atop a designer leopard-skin rug. Her modern couch echoed the dusty blue of the exterior's motif. Three mod-looking armchairs were grouped in a semicircle, all covered in bright red fabric.

Cookie must have been in her early forties, maybe very late thirties. It was hard to tell because she had smoker's lines around her mouth and the dark, leathery skin of a longtime sun worshipper. Gravity accentuated the cracks of her wrinkles as she looked down at the desk. Her dyed, brassy hair was blown dry and sprayed into a facsimile of Farrah Fawcett's iconic do, though the roots needed a touch-up and revealed a natural coloring almost identical to Sandra's.

Cookie gazed over her shoulder at her niece adoringly. I wasn't used to such open affection. The closest I'd ever experienced was the quick, satisfied look between Mom and Pop when I brought home a good test score or some such thing.

Cookie patted Sandra's hand. "Darling, I dropped everything when you called. I'm thrilled to be able to help you find a rental. Imagine, my favorite baby girl nearby? We can shop, go to the beach." She clapped with excitement. "You know what would be fun? Let's set a day every week or two and I'll take you to lunch."

Cookie used the word "serendipity" and said she had just the thing for us—one of her summer leases had fallen through. "It's in one of those huge Victorians. Some say that the glory of our town is fading, but Ocean Grove is still a good place to live. You can walk over the bridge to Asbury Park when you want some nightlife, but you can come back home to quiet. We have a good police force over here. I'm sure your father will check on that, won't he, Maeve?"

I raised my eyebrows and shot Cookie a long, grateful look. Thank the Lord she was thinking ahead.

down on the south beach drag

We rode in Cookie's huge sedan to see the house. Her enormous ring of keys jangled as she let us in through a back entrance and into a giant kitchen pantry. I was immediately smitten. Thunderstruck, in fact. I immediately took note of the tall white cabinets and the stainless steel sink set into the center of the countertop.

"Miss Katz?"

"Yes, dear."

I couldn't take my eyes off the faucet; its long spout was clearly designed with function in mind. Still staring at it, I asked, "Would I be allowed to use this area?"

She rattled her keys with what looked like joy written across her face. "Sure, it goes with the place." *Jingle, jingle.*

It's perfect. "Wow . . ." I was so excited, I was afraid I might hyperventilate. The crux of my entire summer: I could use the sink to develop film. This was, after all, my *raison d'être*. Compared to my cramped little darkroom at home, there was tons of storage and space to move around here.

I removed the pencil skewered through my topknot, retrieved my notebook from my purse, and began making a list of equipment I needed to bring. If I could get all my film processed and organized here in Ocean Grove, all I would have to do was make six prints for the contest on a visit home. That's all the competition allowed: six prints. But hopefully winning it would also lead to a show in a gallery, and the show to a photo book someday. I'd need hundreds of pictures to achieve my goals.

"Miss Katz?" I asked.

"Call me Cookie, dear."

I had never in my life called an adult by their first name, but she'd asked me to do so many times before. I was close enough to eighteen now, an adult. It was time to change my thinking. "Sorry . . . sometimes I forget. Um, Cookie . . . what's behind that door?"

does this bus stop at 82nd street?

She opened the glossy painted door and revealed a landing leading down to an old stone basement.

I couldn't have been more delighted. "I bet I can make that area lightproof. See, then I can stand down there and roll my film up to get it ready for developing."

Cookie blinked a few times, clearly not getting my excitement. "Well, that's wonderful, dear."

Without further comment, she set out to lead us through the rest of the tour.

She led us up a narrow, winding stairway to the next floor. It became much warmer as we climbed. The apartment occupied the entire third floor of the turn-of-the-century home. The heat radiating off slanting rooflines in the late afternoon sun made it clear the apartment was poorly insulated, yet the place was by no means neglected: the ceiling and walls were finished in charming tongue and groove beadboard, and every square inch of the apartment bore a new coat of white enamel. I could smell the fresh paint.

Pictures of this old place alone would be worth their weight in gold. I might be able to sell some to *Jersey Shore* magazine. I would certainly try.

The best part of the deal was that the place came fully furnished with antiques. Sure, they were a little beat up, and the couch and easy chairs sagged and smelled like dust when I plopped down to test them out, but the living and dining rooms (*Seriously, a full dining room?*) had steep double dormer windows with transoms that spanned six feet from the floor to their peak. Standing before them, you could see the Atlantic Ocean and endless sandy beaches stretched in either direction.

I opened one of the sashes wide and lay down on the couch to see if I could hear the waves. The aroma of salt spray and an insistent *crash, hiss... crash, hiss* was my reward. *When all the windows are open this summer, it will be nearly deafening*, I thought with satisfaction. Deafening in a really good, relaxing way.

The scenario running though my head immediately shifted from Sandra-is-going-to-ruin-everything to we're-going-to-have-the-best-time. Just three crazy kids together, out looking for adventure. There'd be cozy dinners, pillow fights, and lazy days on the beach, which was actually *in our backyard*.

Granted, the picturesque wraparound porch was two stories below us, but I was grateful we were allowed to use it at all. An almost unbearable feeling of delight tugged at my heart. The porch had three hanging bench swings with cushions so thick I wanted to crawl into one and take a nap. I'd lie there with a good book on a beautiful summer day. *Sigh.* I made a mental note to stock up on frozen lemonade concentrate.

Cookie took us through the dining room's French doors and onto our balcony. It ran across half of the house but wasn't very deep, only about eight feet wide. My head spun a little as I leaned over and saw two rickety flights of wooden stairs snaking their way down to the ground.

"I think they had to build these stairs for the fire code," Cookie said. "You girls can hang out here on the deck if you want, barbecue and whatnot, but if I were you, I'd stick to using the stairs to the pantry to come up and down."

I saw her point. Some of the boards that made up the treads were missing. I gripped the stair rail and took a few steps down. The entire structure shifted slightly and groaned. I shrieked and jumped back up to the landing.

Cassie nudged me. "What do you think of all this, Maeve?"

I smiled at her, and she started to sing The Drifters' "Under the Boardwalk" with something close to abandon.

Sandra and I joined in, and the three of us danced around Cookie, who said over and over again, "I just want you girls to be happy."

chapter 5
it's hard to be a saint in the city

As we drove back to her office, Cookie announced that she was going to call Sandra's father, Mordy. She claimed to have a hold over him that she said would last a lifetime.

She'd never been given the chance to go to college, she explained, while he'd been handed every opportunity in the world. "While he was away at school, I became an indispensable part of our parents' car dealership," she told us. "Most months I sold more Cadillacs than the other six people in our sales department put together. I really enjoyed the work too. Being in business with my parents was good for our family. They stopped thinking of me as a little girl once they got a look at my sales numbers. But then Mordy had to go and fall in love."

Cookie said he asked his wife to marry him on the day they both graduated with business degrees. When the fiancée, Sandra's mother, came to meet the family, she spent a weekend at their family home with him.

"I'll own up to it," Cookie said. "I was prickly. Mordy was getting set to come home and take over the family business, and I didn't know where that left me. And then the girlfriend was getting in the middle of everything. Okay—I was a bitch to her."

down on the south beach drag

Sandra's mother agreed to marry Mordy on one condition: "It's me or Cookie. I can't work with somebody who's that pushy."

Sandra gasped. "Nobody ever told me that."

"You're old enough to know the story now. It happened."

I could see Cookie's smirk in the rearview mirror. She winked at me.

"To smooth the way for the marriage, I asked my parents to buy another place for me to run." She chortled. "I totally took advantage of the moment. With tears streaming down my face, I told them, 'My heart is broken in two. I need to get out of this house for a while. I want a little place down at the shore and . . . if I'm being forced out . . . I'd like to make the move to real estate.'" She let out a big belly laugh. "I was set free. The best thing that ever happened to me."

Released from her strict religious background, from the small town where everyone knew every move she made, and from her overprotective parents, Cookie learned how to have some real fun. But Mordy had no idea this was the case and still felt guilty about hurting his sister, his only sibling.

"He still carries that guilt like a bag of boulders around his neck," Cookie said, snickering, as she ushered us back into her office.

She dialed him on her desk phone. The three of us stood in a C shape behind her and leaned in as she told him about the apartment. I, for one, was holding my breath.

"They came down in price for us, Mordy. They'll take five thousand for the whole summer." I could hear his raised voice, but not exactly what he was saying. "Sure, it's a lot of money, but there will be three of them in a two-bedroom. And it's a screaming deal. You should see what some of these places go for." She turned and locked eyes with Sandra. Her eyebrows shot up and she had a silly little smile on her face. "I hear you, Mord . . . she needs to learn a better work ethic . . . don't you think, darling brother,

it's hard to be a saint in the city

it may be better for her to learn it away from home? She's not a little girl anymore . . . uh-huh . . . uh-huh. Okay. Bye."

Cookie hung up the phone and stretched out her fingers, studying her bright red fingernails. The phone rang less than five seconds later.

"Ummhumm?" she murmured. She listened quietly for a bit, and then said, "Uh-huh. That sounds great. But, sweetheart, there is one problem—the other girls can't foot a full third of the money . . . that's what I was thinking, yes—let Sandra have a bedroom of her own . . . only for the summer, very good. You are a good Abba. I'll see you for Shabbat. Love you."

After putting the receiver back in the cradle, Cookie fluffed the back of her brassy hair with both hands, a satisfied look on her face. But when she swiveled around to face us, her look changed suddenly.

She stared at Sandra with one eyebrow arched and her lips pressed together. As much as she had cajoled her brother into renting the apartment, she was surprisingly blunt with Sandra. "That man adores you. You are his princess, but you need to grow up. He will sign for the lease, pay the first and last months' deposit, and cover three-fifths of the rent." Her expression softened when she turned to me and Cassie. "Girls, that means you'll each pay a thousand. Mordy's making this offer because he wants Sandra to have her own room. Good deal, right?"

Is it good? Will Cassie's father agree to pay this kind of money up front? He wasn't sounding so excited about the shore idea when we met with Father Murphy.

I held my breath once again as Cassie called her parents. Her mother was totally on board. Her father said no. An argument ensued, with all of us listening—Cookie's phone had a speaker, which I had never seen before.

"She needs a chance to spread her wings. To start fresh."

"On *my* dime? She can start fresh in her own room."

down on the south beach drag

My knees nearly gave out. So much was riding on this argument.

"I will pay you back," Cassie yelled at the phone. "I'll get a job."

"Doing what?" her father demanded. "You're lucky if you can make enough to feed yourself."

"Okay. Okay." Her mother sounded upset. "I have some savings. I never wanted you to get married young the way I did, Cassie. Sorry, honey, but it's true. I know you're sad about your breakup with Bobby, but I think this is your chance to get past it. Cassie, will you agree to pay back half of the rent? I will pay the other half. Can we all agree to that?"

"No," her father said, "we cannot."

"We will work this matter out," Cassie's mother said firmly. "Please go ahead with the rental." Then she hung up.

Thank God I had money in the bank. And it was my money. I didn't have to ask my parents for permission.

Cookie pointed at Sandra. "And you . . . you have to agree to get a job too."

To Sandra's credit, though she rolled her eyes, she didn't disagree with her aunt.

Cookie must have worried she'd been too harsh; she gently pinched Sandra's cheek with an expression so exquisitely tender Cassie and I looked away.

Sandra still pouted.

"What is it, Sandy?" Cookie asked carefully, like the girl might break in two.

"This was supposed to be my summer to party hearty." She sniffled and wiped a drop that escaped from one eye.

"Isn't that what you've been doing your entire senior year?" Cookie cooed. "Except you went to all the trouble of getting your real estate license. Your father and I are both very proud of that accomplishment. Time to use it now."

it's hard to be a saint in the city

"But I'm gonna be away from home for the first time. I kinda wanted to go nuts."

Cookie held Sandra's face in her hands. This level of endearment—this entire interaction, in fact—was a shock to my system. I would never speak to my parents about partying. Mom would smack me good.

But Cookie just said, "Darling, you can have a wonderful time and still have a job. Your father wants to see that credit card bill come down a bit every month. Is that really too much to ask? You'll come and work for me. You're going to learn that financial security feels better than anything else." She looked Sandra straight in the eye. "Better than anything, trust me." She pinched her one more time before releasing her niece from her embrace.

The desk phone rang again. Cookie stepped back over and picked it up. "Katz Real Estate."

I was perplexed when she stretched the coiled cord out and handed the receiver to me, saying, "He wants to talk to you."

"Who? Mr. Katz?" I asked.

She nodded as I took the phone.

"Hello, Mr. Katz," I squeaked.

He and Pop had gone through elementary and high school together. They were super friendly with each other. When Pop bought our family car, I was told Mr. Katz had given it to him at cost, and when the Katz dealership was burglarized, my father single-handedly tracked down the perpetrator.

Mordy cleared his throat on the other end of the line. "Maeve, just tell me one thing. Why are you doing this? This whole summer-at-the-shore thing."

"Why . . . ?"

"The other girls, sure. I can see why. But what are *you* trying to accomplish?"

I smiled at the idea that my ambitious reputation preceded

me. With one hand I reached up, checked the position of my top-knot, and grasped onto the pencil I'd returned to its place.

"I'm getting ready for a big photography contest," I told him, "and part of the prize is a college scholarship—to the School of Visual Arts in Manhattan."

He chuckled. "Only part? What's the other part?" I heard his desk chair creak and pictured him leaning back.

"Some of my pictures would be featured in *Look* magazine."

Mordy let out a low whistle and laughed appreciatively. He was always asking me about my schoolwork and grades. More than once, when my father and I ran into him, he'd told Pop what a lucky man he was to have me as his daughter.

"All right," he said. "I'm gonna talk to your old man . . . and Cassie's too. They had the big meeting, right? Malky told me about it." Malky was his nickname for Pop. "But, Maeve, you have to agree to be the voice of reason here. Who knows what the other girls will get up to. We all need to know we can count on you."

I went stiff with apprehension. "Count on *me*?" How was I going to control anyone else? Just getting these photos done was going to take everything I had. "I'm going to put Sandra on," I mumbled, and handed her the phone.

Whatever he said when she got on the line made Sandra red with fury. "What do you mean, *she's* in charge?"

chapter 6
girls in their summer clothes

We could have just walked over one of the footbridges that stretched across Wesley Lake, or even down along the beach—it would have been fun to stroll and watch the sunset. But it was our first Saturday night living on the shore, and Sandra had it in her head that she wanted to cruise around the Circuit in her fancy Stingray. I always referred to it that way—with "fancy" in front of the name. Most kids my age didn't even own a car, let alone a Corvette.

But Sandy did—so, instead of the leisurely walk on a beautiful summer evening I'd been hoping for, I was perched on the back of the two-seater convertible, hanging on for dear life. The gathered top was rolled down underneath me.

I'd brought my camera so I could get in a few shots if we came across something really interesting. I was terrified I was going to drop it.

Between Sandra's orange dress and her flashy car, it couldn't be more obvious she was outright hunting for a man. She waved to every guy who smiled at her like she was the queen of a parade. Mid-wave to the fourth guy, she caught a glimpse of me in the rear-view mirror, swaying back and forth. "Watch the paint, Maeve," she shouted.

down on the south beach drag

Easier said than done. It was lumpy, and the metal frame stabbed at me. The only place to stretch my ridiculously long legs was the narrow space between the driver and passenger seats, which was next to impossible. I had to stack them on top of each other, and with my narrow ass and all, whenever we hit a bump I was thrown to one side or the other.

I screamed, desperately grasping for something to hold on to.

Sandra and Cassie passed a joint between them. This, on top of the acid they had dropped earlier in the evening! They didn't give a damn about my comfort. All I heard out of them was a series of complaints about my shoes touching their clothing.

"Watch it—that's couture," Sandra complained as she checked her lipstick in the rearview mirror.

"Pardon me. I'm so *sorry*, Sandra."

Sandra went to Hoboken to shop because that was where *real* designers manufactured their clothing. You needed to make an appointment and spend a lot of money. Not something I was ever going to get to do.

The Circuit here in Asbury Park was famous. Four intersecting streets where thousands flocked on the weekends—a parade of young people out to impress the opposite sex. I needn't have worried about Sandra looking like a big orange neon sign in her tight dress—she actually fit right in. The streets were packed with greasers, hippies, and superflies on their motorcycles, in hot rods, or in their parents' cars, driving around and around pointlessly.

I looked at the street in front of us through the viewfinder of my camera and zoomed in, framing what looked like a sea of cars. I waited and waited, only clicking when the people in the shot were positioned just right. Shooting behind me was tricky. I balanced precariously on one hip bone, snapped my picture quickly, and turned back around.

One of these might be one of the select six pictures for the contest—who knew? The Select Six—my new nickname for the

girls in their summer clothes

project. I'd have to tell Cassie about it later. It could be part of our secret code.

Along with the rest of the crowd, we looped around the Circuit all night. Talk about boring. When a muscle car pulled up next to us and revved its engine, I burst out laughing. All four lanes were backed up with traffic, and we were barely crawling along. Where did they intend to go?

The driver pushed the gas pedal once more and yelled, "Come on, baby."

I gestured to all the vehicles around us and gave him an exaggerated shrug.

In return he gave me the finger. Lovely. I shook my head at him.

Having exhausted anything interesting around us, I was anxious to get out and move around. But then a voice reached out to me. And it captured my full attention.

I turned toward the music clubs. Many had open front walls, and you could see and hear the bands inside. Every single place was jammed. I wanted to hurl myself off the car, run toward the riotous sounds, and join in with the revelry. It was only loyalty to Cassie that held me back.

That near-irresistible urge to dance became even stronger when some twist of the forces of physics made a line from a song shoot out to me clearly. It was plaintive. Urgent and raw. The singer said he was coming for me. How I wished that it were true.

Come and get me, whoever you are.

I reached down and put my hands on Cassie's and Sandra's shoulders. When they looked back, I yelled over the engines, "I want to hear some music." *And take some photos of the bands*, I added to myself. They nodded noncommittally, both looking pretty zonked.

We made the requisite drive up Ocean Avenue and over to Kingsley, then headed south till we saw the Palace Theater and started all over again. It was slow, the rumbling engines competing with the roaring sea. Though the tang of the salt air was ever present, the gasoline fumes were overpowering, making me want to gag.

At the farthest end of the loop were two large, dusty parking lots. As we crept up to them again, I saw a fortune teller's wagon tucked away in the far back, near a bluff of trees. A real wooden wagon with a hand-painted sign. The horse next to it was tied to a guardrail. The whole thing could have been a prop on a movie set.

I called down to Cassie and Sandra, "Why don't we park?"

Sandra slid into the lot immediately and found a spot not far from the wagon. As she rarely listened to a word I said, I was pleasantly surprised.

She stared at the wagon in a wistful way. "This is fantastic. I'm going to get my fortune told."

Though I wanted to check it out, too, I worried that Sandra looked incredibly stoned.

I clenched my camera securely as I made my way off the top of the car. Even for me, it was a long step down. With a groan, I managed not to damage anything, photographic or otherwise.

"Girls," I told them, "I'm going to walk back to our apartment later. It's just too uncomfortable up there."

Cassie, walking ahead with Sandra, tossed me a concerned look over her shoulder. "I don't think that's a good idea. We should stick together." She stopped, gathered us up in a little circle, and put one hand on my arm, the other on Sandra's.

A middle-aged woman wearing a long peasant dress made of coarse, off-white material came down the wagon's steps and sat on the short riser. Auburn hair streaked with gray escaped from the colorful scarf wrapped around her head.

Cassie cast a doubtful eye her way. "Are we sure she tells fortunes? Isn't that, like . . . a cultural stereotype or something?"

girls in their summer clothes

"I've been to fortune tellers lots of times," Sandra said. "They all dress like that. It's expected, I guess."

Cassie fidgeted as she glanced around the lot. "Why would she be all the way back here, then? If she wanted customers, she'd have parked closer to the street."

I longed to find out more about the woman. So, when Sandra strode straight toward the wagon, I followed, just a few steps behind.

Sandra was busy fishing around in her pockets for money as she shot ahead, so she barely looked where she was going until she was directly in front of the woman.

"How much to tell my fortune?" she asked brusquely.

When the woman didn't immediately answer, Sandra peered into her face—and startled me by staggering backward.

Was she having some kind of seizure? I caught her by both arms before she fell, then gently sat her on the ground, stroking her dark hair. "Are you all right?"

She shook her head.

"What is it, Sandra?"

She was gasping. It took her a while to answer.

I was kneeling behind her now. I put my arms around her, hoping to soothe her.

"Maeve. Jesus," she finally hissed. "Her eyes . . . her eyes."

She pulled away and struggled to stand. As I helped her up, she was shaking. What on earth?

The fortune teller put a cigarette between her lips. She had a box of wooden matches in her hand. When she struck one against the box, the sound of the head igniting was somehow amplified, sustained for longer than seemed right. Though the woman remained calm, the head of flame flared so high it lit up the night. She leaned in and lit her smoke, sucking greedily, then held the flame up like a torch. The harsh light illuminated the crow's feet near her eyes—and their color.

down on the south beach drag

Sandra hid behind me, clinging to the back of my jumpsuit with both hands, her breathing ragged.

Unlike Cassie and Sandra, who were both cowering in fear and clinging to each other, I felt drawn to the woman. From deep inside me—from my gut, my heart—something pulled me in her direction.

The flare must have been some kind of magic trick. Cassie and Sandra were tripping. Not figuratively—the LSD was intended to make them see things. I was sure that's what made the woman so frightening to them. *I* found the flare impressive, not scary. Though I wasn't drugged, I wasn't feeling entirely myself either. Everything seemed surreal, different. Like gravity had released me. Walking felt like gliding. As I was no longer rooted to the earth, nothing seemed certain.

"I think you must be an Irish Traveller," I said to the woman. "I saw some of you here in Asbury Park when I was younger, and my father told me about your culture."

The Traveller stood and straightened up to her full, regal height. When she spoke, it was with undeniable authority. "They say my name Or-leh."

I nodded, awaiting her wisdom. She scanned me with curiosity.

"Is it spelled O-r-l-a-y?"

She shook her head. "No. Do you know about all the vowels in the Irish language? It's O-r-l-a-i-t-h."

My eyes and Orlaith's were the exact same color. She was the only other person I had ever seen with amber eyes. The familiar liquid quality in hers made me shiver. For my entire life, everyone had described my stare as penetrating. Even as a baby, I could make adults uncomfortable just by watching them. As I grew up, I'd learned to be more careful. It usually wasn't advantageous to put people off. Of course, sometimes it worked in my favor too.

"Your people are from Limerick," she told me. Not a question.

"Yes," I whispered. So, she really was psychic. The nuns had taught me that such people drew their power from the devil, and anything to do with the devil frightened me. The Sisters seemed sure that clairvoyants could release demons upon us. Evil incarnate.

Yet *The Gift*, to be born with a second sight, was widely talked about in our community. Revered, in fact, despite the good Sisters' warnings. It was always said that we Irish were more intuitive than most, that we had unspoken ways of communicating, and that once in a while a child was born with a powerful sixth sense. A child who could see the future—and the past.

"Are you androgyne?" Orlaith asked me.

"I'm not sure what you mean."

She put her hands on my shoulders and closed her eyes. "I feel both male and female in you." Orlaith's power came off her in waves that swept through me. She nodded, folded her hands in front of her, and cast her eyes down as though in prayer. "My cousin." She lifted her gaze. "So."

As I lost myself in her eyes, she took both my hands reverently. "Take heart, young one. Tonight will turn out well . . . but . . . this . . ." She let go of one of my hands and gestured toward Cassie and Sandra. "This will not. You are not one of them." Her trembling voice hung in the air.

Orlaith pointed at Sandra in an accusatory fashion and glared. We all gasped as her face darkened and she shouted in a strong, deep voice, "*This* will not."

With that, Orlaith scooped up the hem of her skirt and royally ascended the three steep steps that led to the curved back of her wagon.

I was shaking from head to toe. "Orlaith?" I squeaked out. "Do I owe—"

She cut me off with a frantic wave of her hand, and shook her head as she prepared to close the curtains behind her.

down on the south beach drag

The last thing she said to me was, "My cousin—beware."

Sandra. A walking instigator of trouble. She was harmful, and I'd known it all along. When I got home, I'd say a rosary asking God to forgive me my transgressions. I'd wanted to win the contest so badly, to get that damn scholarship, I'd forgotten an important lesson. Nothing wrong ever turns out right.

Turning away from the wagon, I couldn't believe my eyes—Cassie and Sandra were jumping into a car with two guys.

Before I could even begin to react, they were gone. Left alone in that dark lot, I wondered who else was out there.

In a panic, I ran.

chapter 7
spirit in the night

I made my way to the beach and headed back toward Ocean Grove. But, drawn once again by the music, I wound up in front of the bar where I'd heard that song lyric booming out to the street.

I peeked through the door. It was smoky inside. A tall man with a saxophone was climbing onto the stage. I could have walked in and gotten to work with my light meter right then, but I didn't have the nerve to penetrate the crowd. Not yet. Not when I was feeling so deflated by Cassie's abandonment.

Instead, I wound up exploring parallel streets farther back from the shoreline. There were fewer people, but it was still busy. I pushed in, block by block, and the crowds grew thinner and thinner until I found myself under a streetlight on an empty street, panting.

I stopped and looked around. A dense fog had rolled in. Where was I? Though I was disoriented, I was also kind of taken with the bluish circle the streetlamp cast around me in the gathering mist. With my camera hung around my neck, I figured I stuck out like a tourist, if there was anybody around who cared to look my way. But there wasn't and I remained relaxed.

I studied the blue circle through my viewfinder. When I shifted the camera up to check the framing of the entire street, a dark-haired man wearing a fedora appeared, leaning against the

down on the south beach drag

doorframe of an establishment called Hootch, smoking a cigarette. The line of his jaw was strong, and he looked like a member of the old Rat Pack, in a very well-made slim suit of shining black sharkskin fabric. A showman of some sort?

Hootch. This was the very place I had dreamed of revisiting—my imagined portal to New York City. Perhaps the night was looking up after all, though the deserted street was spooky with the swirling fog. I inhaled and exhaled deeply, trying to calm my racing heart.

"What are you doing out here, doll?" His voice was laced with concern, and higher-pitched than I'd expected.

I walked toward him, unafraid. There was an ease in his manner, an amused smile on his face. With each step I took, the hard heels of my shoes on the pavement echoed sharply. The clicks bounced off the walls of the brick buildings that surrounded us and carried ahead of me like they were announcing my arrival.

I did a little tap dance to play with the phenomenon, and he laughed—and then, to my delight, returned the same tap pattern back to me on the cement stoop, swinging his arms, imitating me.

Gauntlet thrown down and accepted.

The ten years of dance classes Mom had insisted on to make me more graceful were finally paying off. I easily executed a triple-time step, staring into his eyes the whole time. Take that, Mr. Man.

He gave it right back to me, cigarette stuffed into the corner of his mouth.

Draped in both the oncoming vapor and his cigarette smoke, the entry lights to Hootch created a halo around him. Perfect for a moody photograph.

Breathless with excitement, filled with relief instead of the tension that had haunted me all evening, I envisioned an eight-by-ten print of this man secured to white mountboard. Hanging in a gallery. A picture for the Select Six.

"Well, hi," I said to him with the widest smile I could muster.

He put one finger to his lips and batted his eyelashes, as if saying, "Who, me?"

I laughed, just as he expected I would. When he spoke again, it was in a voice that was almost feminine. For me, I suddenly realized, that was all the more beguiling.

His symmetrical features meant he'd be a perfect subject to photograph. Handsome in a refined way. Not rugged; slight, instead. Thank you, God, not a hulky All-American boy. And that black hair with those light blue eyes—the contrast was breathtaking.

Though I hadn't known it until I laid eyes on him, he was just what I was looking for. He was tall and striking. He moved with grace.

More importantly, he was the epitome of what had so long intrigued me—male, but also female. He seemed to take up less room than many men I had known. A self-amused look was in his eyes. What some might call quirky, I found unique. And comfortable, to be honest. He reminded me of the Mapplethorpe photographs I had studied for hours and hours. Only here he was in living flesh.

"I like your suit," I said, and motioned with my head toward the sign on the door that said BURLESQUE. "Are you supposed to be . . . what? Frank Sinatra?"

He tsked, and though he was smiling, shook his head. "Gene Kelly, fool."

Ha. Of course.

"Can't you tell the difference?"

I tilted my head and leaned in. Those sooooo blue eyes made me a bit dizzy. Yet they also felt familiar, somehow. Since when was I the coquette? "No. Obviously, I can't tell. Though I do get it now that you say it. What details make the difference?"

He ran the fingertips of both hands up and down his lapels. "Satin, baby."

"It looks very nice." Better than nice.

"Thanks so much." He clicked his heels together like a European count. "I'm George. Georgie Bello."

"I'm Maeve O'Connor." I fought the urge to curtsy.

He never took his eyes off me as he drew smoke between his sensuous lips with great relish, like he wished I was that cigarette. But not in a creepy, over-the-top way. More like he couldn't hide how strong the spark was between us. When he exhaled, he looked up at the sky, threw his arms wide open, and smiled. "Who knew I'd meet a girl like you out here?"

"Bello," I said. "That's . . . an Italian name, isn't it?"

"Obviously. But I'm Irish on my mother's side."

"And are you Catholic too?"

He raised an eyebrow.

I took that as a yes. "Do you know I was almost ten before I found out that you could be of Irish descent and have a different religion? That it was even possible?"

He nodded and chuckled. "I've been baptized, had my First Holy Communion, and Confirmation. Do you want to check the certificates?"

We both let out a long belly laugh that left us out of breath.

"No!" I managed through gasps for air. "I don't want to see anything about the Sacraments. I'm trying to leave some of that behind for the summer. It *is* comforting to have similar backgrounds, though, to know that you understand. You have to admit it—we have a jump start on getting to know each other. Are you a dancer?"

He puckered his lips. Had I offended him?

"No. I'm a singer."

"But you dance." I did a quick shuffle. "I've seen you." I bounced on the balls of my feet; I was that excited to find out more about him.

"I'm a good mimic. In between the dancers' acts, I sing the

spirit in the night

hits of famous divas—Diana Ross, Gladys Knight, Aretha, all the greats. But then . . . you know . . . given who I am . . . I put this suit on and do Frank, Gene, and Dino too. Hell, I can even kill an Elvis impression. It just depends on how much time they give me. And how much they're willing to pay."

This wasn't what I'd expected. What did he mean by "given who I am"? I didn't know whether or not to believe he could imitate all those famous men and women. I shook my head. "You must be really talented."

He exhaled smoke again. "I am. I work a lot in different clubs, but the Hootch most often."

I was spellbound. I just gazed at him, hands cradling my camera. Damp and encrusted with a layer of sand, I was smudged and sweaty. I wouldn't even think about what the humidity had made of my hair.

In contrast, Georgie was a cool cat, expertly put together. He even wore makeup. His sequined shirt sent a thousand points of reflection into the dim night. His shoes were exquisite. I couldn't begin to imagine where one could buy shoes like that. I stared at them, open-mouthed.

"We got some rough characters in this neighborhood. What are you doing out here alone?" His frown fixed on me, he pushed his lips out, making his cheekbones even more defined. Though he seemed suspicious of me, he was engrossed, nonetheless.

In the silence, I thought about his question. What *was* I doing out here?

I held the camera up higher for him to see.

He laughed softly. "Oh, I see. I see. A little girl from the suburbs trying to go all Diane Arbus on the half-man, half-woman."

The term "half-man, half-woman" jangled in my head. Was that what he was? And I was stunned that he knew about the great Diane Arbus. That in itself was thrilling, but his characterization of me as a little girl stung.

"I'm eighteen," I said, lifting my chin high. "How old are you?"

He let out a thin whistle that ricocheted around the neighborhood, gathering power in the fog that was growing thicker by the moment. "Well. I'm only two years older than you. Twenty. Look at you, a big girl out searching for trouble."

"Am I?"

He put a hand to my cheek and stroked it. "Yes, miss. You surely are."

He had my number. There was no point in denying it. Where might honesty take me?

"Diane Arbus is my hero. She just is."

"Why?" He stared.

"I don't know if you can imagine where I grew up. You sure as heck aren't going to find a burlesque house in my hometown. Whatever I know about the real world, I have found out from books. And Andy Warhol."

That got him. He put a hand to his heart and fell back laughing. "Warhol? Well, yeah. He's a trailblazer for sure."

"But Arbus," I pressed. "What's your problem with her? How would you describe her work? What do you think about it?"

He flicked his head to one side, like he was cracking his neck. It was an ultra-masculine gesture, at odds with his king-of-smooth persona. He crossed his arms, cigarette held high, and closed his eyes. I assumed he was thinking my question over.

"She was an artist who liked people on the edges, the more *bizarre* the better," he said bitterly.

"What if I want to know people on the edges?" I demanded. "My whole life I've had to pretend to be something I'm not—at the risk of hell and damnation, I might add. God made me this way, but I'm supposed to act like a prom queen or something. Ugh." I was sorry Georgie didn't see Diane's images in the same way I did. I would have liked to have that to share with him.

spirit in the night

"As someone who lives on the edges whether I want to or not—or, more precisely, lives in the *middle* whether I want to or not—I don't want a photographer trying to paint me as a freak. I think you can tell I'm not a regular boy. Or girl, for that matter."

"But you're gorgeous." It popped out before I could stop it.

He was tall, and his skin was so smooth. His high coloring made him glow.

"The pictures I'm working on are for a contest, and it's a big one. I could wind up in *Look* magazine."

He let out another whistle, lowered his chin, and leaned in. He was clearly prepared to listen.

Now that I had his full attention, I just hoped I didn't sound like an idiot. "The thing is . . . I'll never win if I just copy Arbus . . . you know, if my work is derivative. I have to do something new, but I think it could be an homage to her."

Silence.

"The critics say she took the time to know her subjects," I continued. "Running into you tonight is a fantastic coincidence."

"How so?" he asked through an exhalation of smoke.

"What I'm hoping to do is approach similar kinds of people like . . . well . . . you know . . . maybe the same types of populations that she captured but bring out their innate glamour." Nervous about how he'd react to all this, I shifted on my feet.

"So, I'm in one of her 'populations'?" He looked around and shrugged. "What would you do with me here?" He stared over his cigarette and into my eyes. The boldness in his gaze made me tremble.

"Idealize you, in a way. I mean, look at you! I'd want to capture your glamour against this cracked and peeling old town. The scene that frames you will be edgy because, let's face it, Asbury Park has seen better days. But I want *you* to look dazzling."

He bent over and stubbed his cigarette out on the cement

step. When he rose back up, his eyes were sparkling. "How are you going to manage all that?"

"It's all about the lighting, and the lenses too," I explained. "I brought a bunch of studio lights when I came down here for the summer. But I'd love to do a couple of pictures out here, right now. Just using the ambient light."

He took his pack of cigarettes out of his pocket. "Now? It's pretty dark."

"I've got fast film for just that purpose. It will be grainy, sure, but that goes great with the fog and your tux and all." I was talking so fast now I was almost tripping over my words. "Can you light up another smoke? Let me shoot this roll, and I'll come back again tomorrow. I'll have to show you the negatives on a light box because I can't print till I get back home. That's where my full darkroom is."

"I usually get here by four for work. You can come by then, but not tomorrow. Sunday's my one day off. How about Monday?"

Georgie smoothed his jacket down in preparation for being photographed. He was going to give me a chance, and I was grateful.

"What do you want me to do?" he asked. I laughed when he put a hand on one hip and the other in the air as if saying, "Ta-da."

My head swam. I ached to touch him. How could I find a way?

He watched me studying him and smiled.

"You don't have to do anything special," I said. "I'll move around you. You look like a star already." I prowled around him until I found the right position. "You are so compelling, especially standing next to this cheap little bar. Nice. Love the pose; let me get up higher than you." I climbed the short stairway. "Can you walk over under the streetlight? I want to get a long shot." I sighed. "These are going to be great."

He started singing and dancing around the light post. His demeanor changed entirely when he shifted from mimicking one famous performer to another. Sheer talent, the power of it, filled

spirit in the night

the block. I heard windows slide open and saw the silhouettes of neighbors listening to him quietly. I couldn't advance the film and shoot fast enough to keep up with him. In a thrilled daze I shot, shot, shot, and the next thing I knew I was out of film.

He dangled his cigarette down by his side and raked the hair on the crown of his head with his other hand. "We're done?" He sounded disappointed. But when he came over and put an arm around me, he laughed softly. "All right, little sweetheart. I am going to walk you over to the bridge and we'll say our goodnights."

Though my obvious youth and uncoolness embarrassed me, I was grateful to be watched over. The street was completely socked in by the thick fog now. If I had been pressed to find my way home, I wasn't sure I could have.

Still, I said, "I'm fine. You don't need to bother."

"Little girl, you don't even know what you don't know."

I *was* like a child next to Georgie, needing protection. Once again, something about him seemed familiar. Longing to make an impression, I asked, "You afraid I'm going to run into a werewolf?"

"It would *not* surprise me. On a night like this? Man, I have seen everything on this street." He chortled. "Since you're going to make me famous, I'm not taking any chances. Let's just take a stroll over to the bridge. You'll be safe once we cross you over to Ocean Grove. Everybody knows me here; nobody is going to hurt George Bello. Not on purpose, anyway."

"How come?"

"Let's just say . . . my grandfather is an important man." Georgie put his hand on my arm and squeezed it to emphasize his point, his face glowing.

His confession, the vulnerability he showed in that moment, connected us. I longed to know how his cheek would feel against my lips. What he would smell like very close up. I leaned over and caught his scent, and was relieved that he didn't wear some kind of cheesy cologne. The boys in my class at home all reeked of Old

down on the south beach drag

Spice. Yuck. At school dances, it would get all over me. I'd have to shower twice to get the smell out of my hair. It bothered me so much I stopped saying "yes" to a slow dance. The hell with peer pressure. I didn't want them that close anyway.

A dreamy smile spread across my face. I bet Georgie was fun to dance with up close.

What was going on with me? In an attempt to pull myself together, I tried to be funny and put on a British accent. "Werewolves, you say, Governor?" and followed with my best imitation of a wolf howl—"*Ahhhhwhoooo*."

We collapsed against each other, laughing.

When we reached the other side of the footbridge, I put my hand on his arm. "Georgie, have we met before?"

"I don't think so, Miss Girl."

"I know I've seen you somewhere. At the train station?"

He picked my hand up and held it for a moment, searching my face. "Maybe. I go into New York a lot."

Don't push your luck, Maeve O'Connor. I dropped my eyes. "Goodnight, then. I'll see you on Monday at four."

He nodded and slid his hands into his pockets as he turned on his heels to walk away. I tried to interpret the meaning of the nod he had given me. Was he being curt? Cool? Dapper?

As I watched him, he whistled, then called over one shoulder, "You better be on time, Girl. I am a busy man."

As I scurried home, I saw Sandra and Cassie zoom by in the car with the two guys. All the windows were rolled down. I hollered out but neither one turned my way.

I was supposed to be in charge. Me being the boss wasn't turning out very well at all.

Worse, tomorrow was our first Sunday here. Cassie and I had to show up at Mass in the morning.

Where the hell were they going?

chapter 8
the east street shuffle

My processed roll of film from the night before hung to dry on a piece of string stretched across the top of my window frame. Both my memory of taking those pictures and the current roar of the surf made me smile.

Even though it had been late when I got home, developing the film couldn't wait. I'd mixed the chemicals, rolled the film into my stainless reel, and processed it right then, breathless all the while. I didn't want to make a single mistake.

By the time I hung it to dry, I was so beat I fell asleep in seconds. But I kept having a nightmare that meeting Georgie was merely a dream. Twice I sat up and felt for the reassurance of the container of film on my bedside table. Even when I found it, anticipation gnawed at me. I tried to remember every single frame I'd shot. The thought of examining the pictures was more exciting than waiting for Christmas morning when I was a kid.

Somehow, I'd eventually managed to doze off again. Now I'd awoken midmorning, with nerves buzzing and drool on my pillow.

Cassie had one arm flung across her face and was snoring lightly. She'd come home and gone to bed even later than I had. God knows what kind of shape she'd been in. Or would be in this morning, when she woke up.

down on the south beach drag

A letter of introduction from Father Murphy, as a "visiting" priest, looked up at me from my beside table. I was to take it with me to Mass and hand it to the local priest at Holy Name. If he wasn't there, I was to give it to the nuns. This was a firm condition of my parents allowing me to come here. I had to offer my help to the parish.

"I am not working with kids," I'd said clearly, multiple times. They'd finally gotten the message. But I'd taken lots of pictures for Father Murphy's church over the years, saving them a substantial amount of money. He thought I could do the same at Holy Name.

Mass was every Sunday morning; missing it was a sin. A war waged inside me. I drummed my fingers on the surface of the envelope. I'd have to hustle to get there on time—I wouldn't be able to shower or make myself presentable. Most importantly, if I attended Mass, the negatives would have to wait.

Father would just have to understand. I couldn't make Mass today. Not when there was much to be done with these negatives. If called upon to defend my absence, I could claim it was that time of the month. In my limited experience, men never argued with that sort of thing.

I threw on my robe and slipped out of the room with the light box and negatives, heading for the deep brown velveteen chair in the gable of one of the living room windows.

It was stuffy in the living room; I opened a few windows. The ocean breeze blew hard at the skirt of my ankle-length nightgown, almost tripping me, as I searched for an electrical outlet. There were hardly any in the old house, but I found one hidden behind the chair. I plugged in my light box and mentally crossed my fingers.

Thirty-five-millimeter images aren't very big. It took a moment for my eyes to get used to the magnifying lens.

My breath caught in my chest.

The swirling mist. Georgie, so debonair, contrasted against

scraps of paper blowing in the wind, caught midair by the snap of my shutter. The sparkle of his sequins against the darkness. Him wearing a most marvelous expression: delight at being the center of attention, a powerful joy. I could see his very essence in those blue, blue eyes.

I sat back hard with a gasp. Though I had always fought for my right to take pictures, I was often hit with moments of crippling self-doubt. Father Murphy was the only adult I knew who consistently encouraged me. Other grown-ups rolled their eyes when they asked what I wanted to do with my life and I gave them an honest answer. Was I driven? Yes. Confident that I could make it? Not even close. Yet here was undisputable proof of my talent. These photographs of Georgie were nothing short of inspired.

As I studied my work, the surging of the ocean's waves picked up outside. I paid it no mind. Even when the wind blew to the point that it made a whistling sound as it swept along the eaves, I was too absorbed to care. When my hair whipped around, I simply raised one hand to tuck the tendrils out of my eyes.

I craved more time with Georgie. Craved it like sugar. My pulse quickened at the thought of seeing him again.

After studying three-point studio lighting in textbooks, I'd bought my own key, fill, and backlights the previous winter to practice with. I went down to the pantry and, one by one, carefully hauled them up the narrow stairs.

Back in our huge dining room, I scanned the polished floor for a spot to put them all. If Cassie and Sandra didn't like my equipment set up in here, they could say so. Better to ask forgiveness than permission.

I pulled one of the chairs over to an interior wall and positioned the lights around it. My subject being absent, I grabbed a large china doll out of a curio cabinet as a stand-in. With three clicks, the lights blazed.

down on the south beach drag

I pulled the ever present pencil out of my hair and found my notebook. As I moved the lights around, I estimated their distances from the doll and the resulting shadows that were produced. Nuance. Mood. Effects. Exposure. It all went down in my journal.

I was going to convince Georgie to come over and sit for an old-fashioned portrait. I had to; he was my first important discovery in Asbury Park, and I wanted to explore him in a variety of different settings. Studio next, definitely, under the control of my lighting.

Then, maybe some pictures on the boardwalk. How about in the pool hall? I could shoot him cueing up a ball, leaning over the table with the stick in his hand like Paul Newman in *The Hustler*. Georgie's eyes blazed every bit as bright as the famous actor's. More so.

Huh . . . Georgie did imitations for a living. Photographs of famous celebrities? Now that was a great idea. I could do some research on iconic shots and try to duplicate the gist of them. Cary Grant in a heavy silk scarf, stepping out of a restaurant; Tom Selleck with his thick mustache, caught in the act of buttoning his shirt; Warren Beatty with his hair sticking up in cowlicks like in *Bonnie and Clyde*; Clint Eastwood with those sideburns. I wondered if Georgie would like to be photographed in his diva costumes as well.

It had already occurred to me to ask him to introduce me to the women who worked at Hootch. I might ask a whole group of them to dress as Marilyn Monroe and capture their skirts blowing up at the same time in the ocean breeze. What a shot that would be.

Life was suddenly filled with possibilities. *Wheee!*

But I was getting ahead of myself. First things first. I needed to get Georgie over here under my lights.

Surely, when he saw these negatives and I told him about my ideas, he'd be convinced. For starters, I wanted to take the kind of black-and-white pictures that were worthy of a movie star from the 1940s, capture that same drama with the use of strong, direct lighting. Just for fun, I would play with exposure—underexpose a few, deliberately overexpose others.

If I opened my lens two stops more than normal exposure, it would blow away the background and make a soft white cloud for him to float in. The notion of Georgie floating made me happy.

Technique would be crucial. Should I use filters on my lenses? And which lens would be best to capture his fine features?

I wanted to do a candid in the velveteen chair too. I could picture him without his hat, his long legs thrown over one arm of the chair, head thrown back, laughing. Did he own blue jeans and a simple white shirt?

Georgie had said to come by the Hootch at four on Monday. I'd be there on the dot, begging him to set a time to come on over. In the meantime, the lighting would stay put. I'd tell my roommates, in no uncertain terms, not to move anything.

My confidence suddenly evaporated, like air being let out of a balloon. How would I tell Sandra and Cassie about Georgie? He was different from anybody we knew in Bergen County, where the mores were so narrow and prescribed. They might take exception to my friendship with him. Would they be able to handle the fact that he wasn't overtly male or female but some marvelous mix in between? The world was starting to see this androgynous quality in rock stars—Mick Jagger and David Bowie, for example—but it was one thing to see it on a concert stage and another to see it in our apartment in South Jersey.

Although neither Cassie nor Sandra exactly followed the rules of their religions, they did each have one—respectively, Catholic and Jewish. I feared they would get on a moral high horse about Georgie.

Between the two, Sandra might be more welcoming. She didn't seem to care at all what others thought of her. And she had often been the subject of vicious gossip, given her wanton ways. Maybe she would be less judgmental. But she was so hard to predict.

Cassie had been a cheerleader and prom queen. She might look down on Georgie. But she'd been in all the plays and music ensembles in high school too. The boys in those groups weren't usually ultra-masculine. And she'd been friends with *me* all these years. I was certainly a social outlier, with my height, red hair, and attitude. Still, the thought of them all meeting made my stomach clench. *I would die of embarrassment if they turned their noses up at him.*

Georgie was so much fun. And I wanted more. More of the way he put me at ease in a way few did. I couldn't allow Sandra and Cassie to put a wedge between us and our possible relationship.

As if Sandra could hear my thoughts, her door squeaked open. But instead of her, a tall man wearing nothing but a towel around his waist appeared. A statuesque man. The part of him that was straining against the towel was clearly enormous. I snapped my head away from the sight of it.

With the exception of his face, the parts of his body I could see were entirely covered by tattoos. His face was only half covered. His face—Jesus, Mary, and Joseph, I'd never seen anyone with a tattoo on their face. It just wasn't done. Was I more shocked by his nakedness, or the ink carved into his skin?

I wanted to get away from home and meet different types of people. I sure got what I asked for. Thank God Father Murphy is busy early mornings, so I know he won't be popping in anytime soon.

"Hey," the tattooed man said. "Where's the . . . uh . . . facilities?"

I pointed to a door behind him and stared at his back as he walked away. The thought of all those tiny needles piercing him many thousands of times made me wince. How did he bear the pain? And why?

the east street shuffle

Before he closed the bathroom door, he called over his shoulder, "I'm Rickey, by the way. Rickey Travers."

An innocuous enough declaration, but the edge in his voice surprised me. So unnecessary. Yet he was deliberately quiet as he shut the door behind him. Funny that he thought it was the noise of a door slamming that might bother me, not his brusqueness, his nakedness, or his carnie-guy appearance.

He would be very interesting to photograph, no doubt about that. Talk about arresting subject matter. But my gut was telling me to be cautious. There was a brutality about him. A kind of caveman maleness that I generally shied away from.

Of course, I'd only just met him, and I shouldn't judge a book by its cover. It could be that his entirely unfamiliar look was causing me to make assumptions. I should give him a chance. Plenty of men my father's age who'd served in World War II had gotten tattoos. An image on their forearm or one shoulder. But this guy was *enveloped*. Both his arms, his torso, and his legs had drawings on them. And the half of his face that was inked was etched to resemble a skull—not something you could cover with clothing so you could join polite society when it suited you.

The skeleton face raised many questions for me. What restaurant would serve him? Where could he shop for groceries?

Transfixed, I remained in the chair in a dull stupor, not even glancing at my negatives, as I waited for him to come back out.

A flash of light and loud thunderclap made me jump. Giant tear-shaped raindrops hammered against the roof in a chaotic roar. I scrambled to shut the windows.

Even as I flew from one to the next, Rickey filled my mind. What does it say about a person when they chose to be so far out of the ordinary? Georgie was out of the ordinary, too, but he'd been born that way. At least I assumed he had. Not exactly a regular guy, but he was adorable. A breath of fresh air.

down on the south beach drag

But this Rickey? He struck me as trouble. The dark and broody kind.

I turned my focus to my light box and studied my negatives intently. Hopefully he'd just go straight back into Sandra's room when he was done with his business.

The swoosh of the old toilet signaled he'd soon open the tall oak door.

I heard a creaking sound and knew he must have emerged. I wanted to peek at him out of the corner of my eye, but I didn't dare draw his attention.

Finally, I gave in and snuck a look at him. I felt awkward when I realized he was watching me. How many hours a day must he work out to maintain his muscley size? He had to be using steroids too. No regular person could get that big. I'd read about steroids. They produced results physically, but one side effect was a hair-trigger temper. All the more reason to discourage him.

But he didn't budge, just stared. Waiting. Both his bearing and his body loomed, taking up more cubic footage than anyone else I'd ever met. It would be impossible to overlook him, even in a large crowd. Was he used to being the center of attention at all times?

Added to that, he looked like a character out of a horror movie with that skull face. I found it intimidating that he'd chosen to cover his skin by painting it one agonizing step at a time. Masochistic. Might he be sadistic as well? My heart fluttered. A range of emotions roiled through me.

Sandra's father had put me in charge. What was I supposed to do about Rickey Travers? Call Mr. Katz and say, "I don't want to bother you, Mordy, but your daughter is sleeping with a sideshow freak"?

Despite my cold shoulder, Rickey tiptoed toward me—a caricature of shy, like you'd see in a cartoon. Hard to believe the timid act when he was so scantily clad. I considered the possibility that his towel might fall, and my face twitched with worry.

"I'm an early riser," he said. "Whatcha doin'?"

You couldn't compare his body to, say, Burt Reynolds. That didn't do it justice. I scrambled for the right descriptor. He wasn't just in shape . . . he was an Adonis. I felt a jumble of confusion. Many of his muscles appeared jacked up, especially his pectorals and biceps. I was flabbergasted by their size, the cut of them. Fear shivered through me too. I felt certain the man could crush me with his bare hands if he wanted to. Confronted by the thought, I wanted to run.

The area bulging from inside his tightly wrapped and much-too-small bath towel once again got my attention. It curved to one side like a banana, but larger. A truncheon of manhood. A veritable club. I tried very hard to avert my eyes, but they kept wandering back as if they had a mind of their own. And he noticed every time it happened. The smirk it put on his face was unbearable. Couldn't he see how uncomfortable I was?

To gain some control, I looked him right in the eye and glared. It was my superpower, after all. The simmering-molten-liquid thing made him jump back. I still had it. Thank God.

"Oh! I'm sorry," he exclaimed. "I should put something on." Like it had only just occurred to him. He theatrically scurried into Sandra's room, kind of hopping onto each leg as he did, his knees coming up higher than they should.

I had to admit, it looked pretty funny. Physical comedy must be one of his schticks.

I escaped to my room the second he was gone and—as quietly as I could, so as not to wake Cassie—threw on a bra, T-shirt, and a pair of shorts.

I was looking for my flip-flops in the kitchen when he found me again. His excessively short cutoff jeans and tank top still revealed plenty of the artwork on his skin.

down on the south beach drag

I noticed a book in his hands. "Where did you get that?"

"Off one of the shelves in the living room. It's one of my favorites."

When I went back to my velveteen chair to try to get back to my pictures, he followed me to the living room, casually lay down on one of the couches as if he owned the place, and opened the volume. Though the move was invasive, I have to say I was curious about what a tattooed man might read in his spare time.

He appeared totally at home, even though he'd only met Sandra last night. *He better not get too comfortable.*

"Are you going to wait here for her?" I demanded.

"Just so I can say goodbye. It's the polite thing to do. Don't worry, I won't be moving in anytime soon." He chuckled and the book blocked his face from my line of sight.

I was too far away to read the title. I didn't want to ask, but it just popped out of me. "What are you reading?" I still had the light box on my lap and the magnifying lens in my right hand.

"*Great Expectations*," he said, laying the book across his chest and giving me his full attention.

"Dickens?" This was a surprise. I loved Dickens with all my heart. The fact that we shared the love of a book quickly changed things, turning our little scene into something approaching cozy. He pulled an afghan over his legs and propped his head up on a throw pillow, facing my direction. The safety of being deep in my chair on the other side of the room made me bolder. You know how they say what makes us good makes us bad? I am nothing if not curious.

chapter 9
tramps like us

"You really love Charles Dickens?" I found it hard to believe.

"He's my favorite, really," Rickey said. "I read it about ten years ago and I reference it all the time, so when I saw it on the shelf, I thought I'd go through it again with a different eye."

Whatever I'd expected from the Tattooed Man, it wasn't this. My mind quickly zeroed in on the look in his eyes and his facial expressions. It was amazing how quickly what I had originally thought of as his disfigurement faded away.

I had strong opinions about *Great Expectations*. "Miss Havisham. Who would spend their whole life sulking because the groom doesn't show up on their wedding day? Just sitting around the house in a broken-down white dress and a veil in tatters? How boring would that have to be?"

"His betrayal drove her mad," he said sadly—and he was quite serious.

"Please!" I crossed my legs, balancing my equipment across them.

"Maybe you've never been in love before. Maybe that's why you can't imagine it." He batted his eyes at me playfully.

I made a face back at him. "You sound like my friend Cassie. With her, it's all moon and June."

He fanned the pages of his book, obviously thinking over my comment. "So, how old are you?"

down on the south beach drag

"Eighteen. We all just graduated. How old are you?"

"Twenty-three. I can't remember how I felt about love at your age, but I met somebody very special two years ago, and I lost her. It turned out she wanted somebody more"—he let out a hard laugh—"somebody more average, I suppose. I'm not sitting around my house in an old wedding dress, but it still hurts pretty bad." After a long sigh, he shrugged and motioned with his head toward the light box. "So, what are the pictures about?" He did have some charm.

Within seconds, I was happily telling him all about my project, my family, the contest, how I wanted to go to school in New York, and, most importantly, meeting Georgie the night before.

"And he knew about Diane Arbus," I said. "That floored me. Do you know who she is?"

Rickey looked offended. "I don't live under a rock. Of course I know who she is. There aren't many artists who've made it their business to explore the disaffected in our society. My family has a long history of following Miss Arbus, God rest her soul. She's particularly important to us because both my parents are little people."

I shook my head in confusion. "Like midgets?"

"Well, yeah. But that's not the correct term anymore. It's little people."

My face flushed. I certainly didn't mean to disparage his family. "I'm sorry. I didn't know."

"I have to correct people all the time. Don't sweat it. I'm a second-generation sideshow performer here at the shore. But in New York City I'm considered a performance artist. I've been getting some work lately in Greenwich Village. I'd love to move there full-time."

Perhaps it was empowering to choose one's own title. I was suffocated by my own—just an Irish Catholic Jersey girl. So ordinary. Such a cliché. Maybe one day I might be able to change that too. In a time when people formerly known as Negroes had chosen to be called Black and those long referred to as Indians had claimed the term Native American, it made perfect sense to give myself a new label. What did I want to be called?

Rickey smiled at me in a way that set alarm bells ringing in my brain. Too smooth, practiced, like he was ever so impressed with himself.

"I'm going to start putting in for some acting jobs," he said. "I could use a good headshot."

Oh, so he wanted something.

"Can I hire you to do that? I don't have much money, but I really need pictures to get started. Just the way you study the negatives, I can tell you're good at what you do. And obviously, you're very smart."

He postured for a few moments, his teeth flashing, deeply indented dimples held in position. His charm had degenerated into smarmy. Unsettling, I must say. Still, he was way too good a photographic subject to simply pass over. And he had upped the ante by asking for pictures.

I remained silent, thinking his proposal over.

"I'm not the only one," he added. "I can get you others to photograph."

"Uh-huh. What others?" My poker face was masterly.

"I work at the sideshow tent, remember. We have a sword swallower, the Monkey Girl, the Fat Lady, a guy who's a contortionist—all great subjects. All of them need headshots. Just the kind of people Arbus liked to take pictures of. I could get them to sit for you."

"When?" He was the slippery kind, so I wanted to nail the offer down. Secure tangible commitments. And do sittings as soon as possible.

"The show's open on Sundays. We can go this afternoon. Meet me over there at three o'clock?"

down on the south beach drag

"Yeah? You don't think they'll want advance notice?"

"Customers take pictures of them all day long. The difference is, you'll be with me, and you can go backstage. I'll talk you up; don't worry."

I very much wanted to take those pictures. Wanted those contacts. But I had to make it clear to Rickey that this was strictly business, and had nothing to do with his fake charm, easy compliments, or ridiculously dimpled smile. He was a caricature, nothing more.

I put my things down on the floor and stood up, arms crossed. Definitely a better position to negotiate from. My hair was back up in its usual topknot. I reached up for my pencil, my touchstone. "How about this? You sit for some portraits now and I'll shoot . . . ten headshots for you. You can pick from them."

"Now? But I'm kind of a mess; my hair's all over the place."

This had to be done now—before I chickened out. Over and done with. I didn't want to bring him back here again, and hopefully Sandra wouldn't either.

"Go take a shower, then. Sandra's not going to be up for hours, I promise you that. There's a stack of towels in there; a hair dryer, too, if you're so inclined. I'll just turn the studio lights on and get ready."

I honestly couldn't believe what I was about to say. I hesitated. My face flushed. But if I was really going to do this, I was going to do it right.

"There's just one thing . . . I'd like to do the shots . . ." I could barely get the words out. "I'd like to take them without your shirt . . . if that's okay with you."

Rickey sat back and grinned in that smug way that made me blush even harder than I already was.

"Of course," he said, already swaggering toward the bathroom. "That would be best."

He had the wrong idea. I just wanted to capture the artwork.

There was nothing remotely sexual about my request. But he disappeared into the bathroom before I could explain.

I heard the spray of the shower start up, and my hands began to shake. If the good Sisters of St. Joseph could see me now, they'd be shocked. *Looking at the naked chest of a man isn't a sin—is it? Not a mortal sin, anyway.* Though I experienced a squirming sensation at my core, I pushed away the dawning realization that the nuns would consider this yet another mark upon my soul.

Perhaps you couldn't be an artist with a perfectly clean slate. Maybe that was my problem. I looked out at the churning ocean. Maybe God had a special place in heaven for artists, one where he allowed some transgressions. It would be an interesting discussion to have with Father Murphy one day. Perhaps he knew how to give me special dispensations in such matters. After all, much of the great art historically commissioned by the Catholic Church showed plenty of skin.

I would keep the shoot with Rickey professional—I would. But a gnawing feeling in my stomach told me Rickey might not. He was so full of himself; guys like that were always trying to win girls over. Some might be stupid enough to fall for it. Not me.

I pushed my concerns aside, already framing the shots in my mind.

He was back in a jiffy, wearing only his scanty shorts.

From behind my lens, I asked him to turn this way and that. The topless Tattooed Man. His bulging muscles looked even bigger when I created deep shadows with my studio lights.

Father Murphy and my mother might as well be a million miles away. I was finding it easy to ignore their teachings, especially when they got in the way of my photography contest. Winning the contest was the only way forward.

The end justifies the means. Doesn't it?

chapter 10
lady and the doctor

"License and registration, please."

The policeman stood by Sandra's door with a pad and pen in his hands. With the top down and him standing over us in the low riding car, he looked like a giant. I was sweating bullets in the passenger seat.

This was a moment I'd always dreaded when spending time with Sandra—the moment she inevitably got caught. Would I be somehow implicated in her latest crime? Would Pop find out about it from the state police log? I'd bet anything he was missing me by now. And Mom? She probably couldn't wait to have her Cinderella back home to cook and clean again. This one little mistake—volunteering to accompany Sandra after she got the news about her aunt's accident—could get me swept up in a parental tornado.

If it came to it, I wouldn't agree to leave Asbury Park. I'd dig my heels in if I had to.

Other than the speeding, which wasn't my doing, I'd done what I was asked since arriving at the shore—except for missing that first Mass. But I knew that wouldn't matter if my mother and father found out about my being an accomplice to a ticket of any kind.

I had to act. I leaned over as far as I could toward the cop. "Officer, may I ask a question?"

lady and the doctor

"Just the license and registration, miss."

Out of the side of her mouth, Sandra hissed in a stage whisper, "They're in the glove box, Maeve."

I found a small leather folder and flipped it open to check its contents. The documents looked right. I passed it to Sandra, who handed it to the policeman.

Leaning over again, ignoring Sandra's sour expression, I said, "Officer, I've never been in a car that got stopped before. It's making me nervous. Do you have to take my name down too? I mean ... I wasn't driving."

He squinted at me. "No, miss. When there's a traffic violation, we're only concerned about the driver of the vehicle. Unless we suspect that drugs or other contraband is in the car. You carrying illegal drugs, miss?"

Who knew what Sandra had in her purse? "No, sir," I squeaked, sinking back into my seat.

I was in the free and clear from the traffic violation, so I let out a deep exhale and allowed the scene around me to sink in. Hopefully, Sandra didn't have a stash of pot on her.

I tried hard to put that thought out of my mind. I wouldn't think about it. Instead, I would think about how, after my many warnings, Sandra was finally getting her comeuppance. A self-satisfied smirk spread across my face. Not my finest moment, but now that I wasn't scared, I was enjoying this immensely.

The officer scanned Sandra's documents with a scowl. His eyes shifted up and down. Down, then up. *Snap* went the license against the leather folder. *Crack* went her registration as he pulled it out and gave it the same treatment. He scrutinized the insurance card last before he barked, "Wait right here."

Sandra watched his every move in the rearview mirror. As soon as he made it to the patrol car, she made a miffed sound. "Shiiiiit, Maeve. Why did you get him talking about drugs? What if he frisks me?"

down on the south beach drag

It would serve her right to get busted. The smug look dropped from my face. Fell right off. To be replaced, for maximum effect and good measure, with cartoonishly widened eyes—the visual equivalent of small children torturing each other with *Na-na na-na goo-goo*. I knew it would infuriate her.

In response, Sandra stuck her tongue out at me.

We both turned to watch the police officer, who was talking into his radio.

"Sandra," I said, "he's checking to see if you have any outstanding tickets or warrants. You don't, do you? That will make things much worse."

She put the fingertips of one hand to her lips. "Not that I know of . . . but I don't always . . . remember . . . everything."

This was news to me. I'd seen her take pills now and then, and there were lots of times when she'd seemed pretty stoned, but I'd assumed these last few years were just a phase, that she would one day grow up and get over her teenage rebellion. Only now did it occur to me that she might have a serious problem. Nobody else I knew took things as far as she did. Maybe she just couldn't control herself. And that tendency caused trouble for the rest of us.

The policeman sauntered back toward us, stopping to wave at a passerby who honked along the way. Why was he taking his sweet time?

An eternity passed before he once again stood next to the car door.

Sandra put on her best damsel-in-distress voice. "I'm so sorry, Officer. I'm on the way to the hospital and I'm so upset."

"You were doing sixty-two in a fifty-mile-an-hour zone."

Sandra bit her lip and tears pooled in her eyes. Was she truly distraught, or just good at acting the part? It was hard to get a read on her.

I leaned toward them once again and butted in, which had so often proven effective for me in the past.

lady and the doctor

"Officer, my father is a police officer too. This is my friend Sandra. The thing is, sir, her aunt just had a terrible accident. We got the call and headed right out. Please, could you let us go with a warning just this once? We have to get to Cookie and see if she's all right. We'll be sure to stay under the speed limit the rest of the way, I promise."

Hopefully my intentionally higher tone sounded young and frightened.

He shifted his weight to one hip and his hands dropped down to his sides. "Did you say Cookie?"

"Yes, that's my aunt," Sandra said. "Cookie Katz."

I was surprised when he leaned onto the car on one elbow. "From Katz Real Estate? Jeez, I hope she's okay. Ya know, she sold our starter house in three days. And she found the house we live in now. We wanted a better school system and more elbow room, and she found it for us. Cookie's a go-getter." He laughed, like it was some kind of a private joke. "A real pistol, too, that one."

Relief swept through me and across Sandra's face as well. "Yes, she is," she said. "Thank you. We're very close; she's my only aunt."

He stood back up straight, and his posture led me to believe he now had a different purpose. "You be sure and tell her Officer Barbieri let you off with a warning." He reached in his back pocket for his wallet and handed Sandra a card. "Can you let me know how she's doing when you get a chance? My wife and I think the world of her."

Sandra hesitated and stared at the card for a moment. I knew exactly what she was worried about, but in the end she managed to tuck it in her purse without revealing its contents.

Officer Barbieri's eyes shifted over to me. "You know what? I think it's better if you drive her to the hospital, ah, miss..."

"Maeve. My name is Maeve." *Now why did I have to tell him*

down on the south beach drag

that? It's an unusual name; he'll remember it. I wanted to kick myself. This kerfuffle might come back to haunt me one day if he ran into my father at an official function of some kind. My pride had gotten the better of me once again.

He nodded. "Well, Maeve, Sandra's bound to be shaken up by her aunt's accident. Do you have a valid license in your possession?"

I did, so there was no point in arguing. I handed it over to him and he radioed my information back to the station.

After a few more minutes, he said, "You check out."

Without any discussion, we got out, walked around the car, and switched places. As I adjusted the seat for more legroom, Officer Barbieri moved back a few steps.

He waved us toward the flow of traffic. "Be careful pulling out!"

He was done with us.

I exhaled slowly. "We have to be more careful, Sandra."

As I pulled away, she took my hand and interlaced her fingers with mine. "I just want to say how grateful I am, Maeve. And sorry. I got us stopped because I was speeding, and you were kind enough to jump in to help me. I know how that kind of thing bothers you. I didn't put myself in your shoes, and I'm sorry."

Just when I thought I had her all figured out, she could be so sweet it was disarming. "It's . . . okay. It's okay, because it all worked out."

She let go of me, rooted around in her purse, and found a pack of cigarettes and some matches.

As we had promised, I didn't speed at all on the way. We did get lost, though, and I had to pull off the highway and ask for directions at a delicatessen in a strip mall.

Sandra just sat in the convertible, smoking her Marlboro, and didn't lift a finger to help.

By the time I returned, she had slid back into her red leather

lady and the doctor

driver's seat. As she shifted gears and looked back over her shoulder, she asked, "Are you working tonight?"

"No. Things have changed. I'm doing all the books now and I make my own hours."

I reached up to feel my new hair accessories. Cassie had finally surrendered to my quirk of pencil-in-hair. "Instead of fighting you about it," she'd said the previous day, presenting me with a small box, "I've decided to find you beautiful pencils from now on. They'll be more like hair ornaments than for writing."

I was wearing the two she'd presented me with now. The first was glittering red and topped by a replica of the ruby slipper from *The Wizard of Oz*. The second, crossed over the first, was orange with a beaded tassel. They were sort of Japanese-looking—like kanzashi sticks.

Sandra fished around in her purse until she located a lipstick. When she twisted the mirror down and started to apply it, I gasped and grabbed the wheel.

"You're doing *sixty-five*, Sandra. We've been over this." She turned, made a face at me, and reclaimed the wheel. She was just so frigging reckless.

Just as I wondered if I might be overreacting, she cut across two lanes of traffic at breakneck speed and turned left at the last possible second of a yellow light.

"This accident thing is going to work out well for me," she said casually, like she hadn't just almost killed us both. "Cookie's going to need me at the office. With both arms and her leg broken, she'll be completely incapacitated. Daddy will be so happy that I'm helping out. On my days off, I can get away with murder."

Like she wasn't getting away with murder already? What was she planning now?

chapter 11
love on the wrong side of town

The Hootch was dilapidated in the light of day, but Georgie was fresh as a daisy in a light blue Cuban shirt. He reached out to embrace me. "There's my girl."

Glowing at the idea of being his girl—I'd have settled for him just remembering me—I hugged him back. Yes, I did. You betcha. "I was worried you were just a dream I'd had," I admitted. "The negatives turned out to be my anchor. They proved we'd really met."

He giggled. "Can I see them?"

He took me through a grimy back door and into a room with a round table. I put my light box down on it but eyed the black fake-leather seat cover of my chair with suspicion. Who knew who might have sat there? But Georgie dropped into the chair opposite without hesitation.

I found a power outlet, plugged in, and pushed the box in front of him. For several minutes he appeared hypnotized as he looked through my magnifying lens at the film. I watched every move on his face: how the corners of his mouth turned up, the way his eyes widened, the way they sparkled. Clearly my pictures were every bit as good as I thought they were.

love on the wrong side of town

When he finally put the lens down, he reached out and took one of my hands in his. His deep sigh made me smile.

"Oh, Girl," he said, tears spilling down his cheeks.

I scooted my chair closer to him and wiped them away with my fingertips, clucking with concern like my grandmother used to do, like I did with my little brothers. He was even more moved by my comforting. That was all I needed to know.

"Will you come back to my apartment and sit for me?" I asked eagerly. "I've got my lights all set up for you."

"Do you think you can help me with headshots?" he asked. "Do you know how? Some good pictures might get me more chances to audition in the City."

So Georgie, like Rickey, had ideas about trying to get better work in New York. That wasn't a surprise. There were myriad of theaters in Manhattan. Film and television studios too. Artists who needed models. In the Big Apple, the sky was the limit, or at the very least not filled with barriers every time Georgie turned around. And good photographs could open doors.

He glanced around the room, then leaned toward me, as if to tell me a secret. "I got to get out of this place," he whispered. With a laugh, he changed like a chameleon—stood and started to dance and sing the chorus of "We Gotta Get Out of This Place."

The Animals. His vocals were spot-on. I sang with him about getting out of this place until abject silliness took hold of both of us and we were laughing too hard to finish the song.

"Sit here a minute; let me see if someone can cover me," Georgie said.

He left me sitting in the dim light while he quickly made a call on the clunky old pay phone outside. It turned out to be one of those lucky moments in life where everything falls into place: another entertainer needed the extra money and her daughter was with her father for the night, so she was available. It was a short exchange and quickly decided.

"I still have to make my later shift," he warned me. "It's at a different club."

"We'll work fast," I promised.

He went into a dressing room and came back wearing a T-shirt that said CLAPTON IS GOD.

"Do you imitate Eric Clapton?" I asked.

"I do a better job with his voice than the tone of his guitar," he said.

I added guitar playing to my mental list of Georgie's many accomplishments.

He slung the long strap of his large bag over his head and across his shoulder. I cut shy glances at him. His black hair, cut in a short, chic style that worked with his natural curls, was so shiny I longed to run my fingers through it.

I put both hands up to my own hair and patted it. "Who does your hair? It looks great. Do you think they can do something with mine?"

He took me by both shoulders and made me turn around for him. "I can tell you aren't using the right shampoo. You don't want to strip the oils out. If anything, you need more. I'll make an appointment—in fact, I'll go with you."

The fact that he cared put a silly grin on my face.

As we made our way toward the bridge together, he swung his bag back and forth.

"Your outfit is great for a candid," I told him. I had my heart set on the glamour shots. "But I was . . . uh . . . hoping you'd wear your suit for the studio pictures."

It appeared he was pouting. "I can change when we get there," he said. "I brought two with me, black and white, but I can't walk into Ocean Grove dressed up like that."

"Why not? Whatever happened to 'They won't mess with

love on the wrong side of town

Georgie Bello'?" I asked, though I was secretly relieved he had toned himself down a bit.

"Things are different in the daytime. And what I said was, no one would dare to really hurt me. Big difference."

Maybe it was because he was wearing sneakers instead of dress shoes, but his gait was different right now too. He wasn't moving with his usual swagger. I waited for him to say more.

"The cops might hassle me," he said. "I used to have a girlfriend over that way. I wound up getting arrested twice because, well, they didn't believe I was really a boy. Not my best days."

I stopped dead in my tracks. The police were supposed to be the good guys. My face screwed up in thought. "In my hometown—no offense—we don't have, well, I never met anybody like you . . . before."

"You mean because I'm not your average regular guy or girl?"

"Well, yeah. I think you would kind of stand out in my hometown. I know I do. I'm never girly enough for my mother—that's for sure. And I didn't fit in with many of the kids at school."

He let out a sarcastic chuckle that reverberated through his whole body, rich and low. "Somebody-like-me lives in your town and every town in the United States. I don't care where it is. They are just hiding in plain sight—because we have to."

My mind spiraled and I massaged my temples. I met his eyes and reached up to my hair—my nervous habit. "You know, we're mostly Catholic where I come from, and people are pretty strict about things. Maybe we don't have, you know . . . I don't know how to say it."

He nodded solemnly. "Androgynous people. It's tricky, because dressing as the opposite sex is illegal. No one understands that better than me. But I already told you, I'm Catholic too."

"But not like us. I went to church every Sunday. And I had to wear the frilly dresses my mother picked out for me. To try to blend in."

"I still go," Georgie retorted. "With my parents, when I can."

That particular notion nearly knocked me off my feet. How could that be? It seemed so improbable, my face flushed and I thought I might cry. Inclusion wasn't exactly encouraged in the congregation.

I stammered, "It's not that I don't believe you that somebody in my town might be . . ."

"In between male and female."

"Okay. I—in between male and female. You sound so sure about it. That makes me believe you, but it also makes me wonder who it would be in my town. Mr. Queally who owns the hardware store? My high school history teacher? Since I didn't know it could be widespread, I feel like it might be anybody."

The Diane Arbus books I'd studied ran through my head once again. Sandra's revelation about Aunt Cookie's "costume party" followed. These were bewildering enough without Georgie adding more food for thought.

It seemed there was a person's gender—male, female, I guess even in between—and then separately, there was who you picked to love. Not in my wildest imagination had I considered this. I'd always been taught it was supposed to be men who loved women. And not women like me. Husbands and wives. That was how I'd been raised. I hadn't begun to accept otherwise.

Yet it didn't seem right that Georgie could go to jail because of the kind of clothes he chose to wear.

"I don't understand how this works," I said. "Did you used to be a regular girl or boy? And then you wanted to be in between? Or were you always this way?"

He snorted. "What kind of question is that?"

My ignorance was a barrier. I was going to get myself into hot water here. "I mean, you look really handsome now. But different."

"A specialist told my parents that the best thing they could do was raise me as a girl," he said. "They didn't know what to do, so they followed his advice."

"Why haven't I heard about something like this before?" I asked.

"Parents hide it. It's embarrassing. And let's face it, most people hate the idea and wind up hating us."

"But what about the kids? Where does that leave them?"

"I think my parents did pretty well, considering. They didn't like the advice they were getting from doctors."

We were approaching a bench at a bus stop. I took his hand and pulled him down to sit next to me. "I guess that was pretty brave of your parents."

"My mother and father decided to wait and find out what I thought about my gender. Whether the doctors liked it or not. When I was twelve, I shot up in height. I didn't feel like a girl at all."

We heard the hiss of bus brakes and the hydraulic sound of the door opening. A man and a woman climbed down the steps and swept by us. We were silent until they were halfway down the block.

A shiver went through me. The safe little world I'd grown up in had a shadowy side where some people had to hide to escape condemnation. Even though I was tall and muscular and got teased about the hair on my arms, I was ashamed that the condemners had, up to now, included me. I wasn't brave at all. I didn't tell anybody about my desires as I was growing up, about who I was drawn to. I saw my friends get in a tizzy when a boy paid attention to them and knew I wasn't the same, but I was too afraid to discuss it with anyone, even Cassie, so I just tried to avoid the subject altogether.

A mental inventory of people I knew flashed through my mind. I tried to see them in a different light, so intently I was sure I must be going pale with the effort. I, myself, was often accused of being a tomboy. We had a dress code at school that dictated

down on the south beach drag

girls wear skirts each day. Never pants. Yet I wore pants anyway, and got away with it. Was I one of the people he was talking about? What exactly did that make me?

I looked down at my brown leather walking shoes and linen pants. It occurred to me that I had a very particular sense of style. I'd always admired the great actress Katharine Hepburn. The way she mixed men's and women's clothes in her outfits. I didn't think I was mimicking her, exactly, but in that moment I recognized that I did the same thing.

The glow of Georgie's ruddy skin drew my attention. His lush lashes. As the changing angle of sunlight flared, I became aware of a chorus of birdsong too. They sounded like they were rejoicing.

Georgie would photograph like a dream under my lights. Maybe I would use some of the warm-tinted bulbs I'd picked up to make him glow just like he was now.

"You know, even in regular clothes you look great," I told him. I had studied many series of black-and-white photographs of Gene Kelly. One of him wearing jeans on the shoot of *Singing in the Rain* came back to me now. Georgie was easily as glamorous and charismatic as the movie star—no exaggeration. For me, to know this guy was to love him.

We rose, and he went bouncing down the street just ahead of me, though it was hazy, hot, and humid. *So much energy*, I marveled.

But then we passed a group of young men lining the boulevard, and one of the guys put two fingers in his mouth and let out a shrill, "*Wheet-whooo*." Georgie visibly braced himself as the group tried to outdo each other with their jeering and whistles. How I hated attention like this. Attention . . . if that's what you call it.

"Hey," one of the men shouted, "what have we here?"

chapter 12
that lady

Georgie took my arm and groaned.
I heard a loud "Yo!" and turned to see a guy grabbing the fly of his pants in a pointed way.

Wonderful. Nothing like a little class.

"Nobody wants to be with a perv like you, Felix," Georgie yelled at him. "You may be getting hard, but nobody else around here is."

Felix barked a laugh. "Not even a freak like you, Georgie? I think you're out looking for some. Don't you, guys?" He put his hands to the sides of his mouth like a megaphone to amplify the sound of his voice. "You got a nice ass, baby."

Georgie hollered back over his shoulder, "I do have a nice ass. I also have your mother's phone number. I'm gonna call her and ask how come her son turned out so stupid."

All the men guffawed. They were enjoying the banter.

Another one joined in, "I heard you used to be a girl, so which is it? Boy or girl? Why don't you come over here and show us?"

The others became a chorus of questions. Rude. Challenging. I was afraid for both of us, and terrified by the thought that they might really force Georgie to pull down his pants and show them. Might that rile them up enough to turn on me?

"And who's the giraffe you got with you, Georgie?"

Though Georgie wore an openly defiant look as he took my arm and strode away, I could feel he was shaking. Men I knew back home would sometimes make crude jokes to each other that they thought I wouldn't understand, but the black looks on the men's faces here on this street were by far the worst thing that I had ever witnessed. They were treating Georgie as if he were less than human. And I guessed that, by association, I was considered such as well.

For two or three seconds all I could hear was my shoes clicking against the pavement. But then another man from the group decided to get in on the action before it was too late.

"Eh! BABEH!" he called out and burst into laughter.

I grimaced. It seemed he thought he was brilliant. His voice hung in the air until we reached the end of the block and turned the corner.

I snuck a final look back at the men. From what I could see behind us in the distance, they were getting ready to harass a girl who was coming toward them. Poor thing. But I was too terrified to consider going back to help her.

Georgie's shoulders slumped. I assumed this was the least of what he put up with every day of his life. His haggard expression made me well up. I thought about my photographs. My collection. The contest. The Select Six. Maybe my mother was right about one thing: I really did have a one-track mind. While I should be thinking about Georgie's feelings, I was letting myself get sucked back in by my ambitions.

"If you ever meet my parents, please don't tell them about that," he said. "My dad is furious that I didn't go to college. Dartmouth accepted me, and he would have liked nothing better than to have me up in New Hampshire, where he could believe I was safe from stuff like this."

"I would kill to go to college," I said. And I felt I almost would. Anything short of kill.

He stopped. "But I was born to be a performer. You can see that, can't you?"

that lady

In that spirit, I projected my own dreams onto him. "Do you think things would be better if you were living in New York City?"

"Better? Maybe, in the sense that the teasing is usually more playful there. More open-minded. But there is something that always stands in my way. It's like we're all supposed to aspire to the roles of either quarterback or cheerleader. Ultra-male or ultra-female. How many can attain that? It's hard to find your place in the world when you're like me. And the hostility we provoke is plain dangerous. I just want to mind my own business, but guys like the ones back there can easily snap. It's happened to me before." He held me by the arm protectively as we walked, his fear palpable.

Once we crossed over the bridge to Ocean Grove, I stopped clenching my fists and jaw. Finally, peace and quiet. I could only see two people out in their yards on this side of the bridge, and they barely looked our way. Relief flooded through me; I was within striking distance of getting the sitting I'd been obsessing about all day. The deep, shaded porch of my house beckoned to us.

"Is this it?" Georgie asked as we slowed. "Oh, it's nice, Maeve." He held the palm of his hand up like he was asking me to do the minuet. Would he bow next? "Can we have tea on the veranda later, and sit out in one of the porch swings? Mademoiselle?"

"Sure," I said. "I've got some of that Constant Comment tea. You know, with the little pieces of orange in it?"

He shook his head.

"You'll like it. It's different."

We walked up the stairs from the pantry and through the front door of the apartment and found that Cassie was finally awake, sitting in what I thought of as *my* velveteen chair. She'd made a nest for herself with the dreaded pink blanket.

Georgie spotted her over my shoulder. "Who is this?!"

You couldn't beat him for sheer enthusiasm. I laughed.

"You look like a princess in a movie," he told her, sounding sincere.

down on the south beach drag

My laughter died as jealousy swept through me.

Cassie playfully dove under the pink blanket—to show Georgie that she was shy, I assumed. Which she was, of course.

"Cassie's just a regular girl, believe me." The harshness of my tone made me wince. "Gorgeous, though, I know. I've had to listen to everyone telling me about her gorgeousness since we were little kids. Georgie, this is Cassie. Cassie, this is my new friend and photographic subject, Georgie."

Cassie emerged from the blanket and I scrutinized her face, looking for any reaction to his shape-shifting appearance. I also searched Georgie's for further telltale signs that he was bowled over by her beauty.

Cassie seemed unfazed. Maybe she hadn't figured him out yet, hadn't realized. She still seemed half asleep, truth be told. Georgie, meanwhile, let out a low whistle of concern, elbowed me, and said, "This little beauty is feeling low."

Since the pink wrap was usually a sign that Cassie was mooning about Bobby, I stiffened. I did not want to get into that sad old story just as I was about to take some great pictures.

Georgie obviously felt differently. He dragged a chair close to where Cassie was sitting, straddled the seat, and folded his arms across the back. "Tell me what's the matter, Beauty."

While I was "Girl," Cassie was "Beauty." Terrific.

Cassie stared at him silently for about two seconds, then burst into tears. She sobbed for so long she wound up gulping the way a baby does after it's had a long cry. Georgie moved from his chair to perch on the padded arm of hers and stroked her back.

I squirmed with impatience. And possessiveness. When would Cassie's pity party ever end? Georgie noticed my fidgeting and shot me a cold stare. Under his scrutiny, I thought, I should at least pretend to be a concerned friend. Perhaps I could take control of the situation.

"What's wrong, Cassie?" I asked.

that lady

She leaned into Georgie's embrace, put her hand over her eyes, and wailed, like it was the end of the world. "I cheated on Bobby!"

Given the fact that I'd seen Sandra and Cassie jump into a car with two guys on Saturday night and I knew they had been tripping at the time, it hadn't surprised me. What was it that boys usually wanted from girls, anyway? And she was with Sandra. We'd all known right from the start of the evening what Sandra was hoping to find.

"He's my high school sweetheart," she explained to Georgie. "We were together all that time. He went to California, but friends told me he's coming back. He's already got a place down here lined up with friends. I just know he'll want to get back together."

I grunted loudly. Georgie turned to me with a frown.

Cassie knew better than to look to me for sympathy, so she bawled to him, "I was high. We tried acid two nights ago."

"Well, of course you did." He patted her hand as if this made perfect sense. "When you have a big breakup, you have to try different things to get past it."

I raised my eyes to the ceiling. "So, tripping is a good solution?" I said in a sarcastic voice. "Drugs? How about picking up a different musical instrument for a change of pace? Maybe studying a new language?"

Georgie glared at me with one hand on his hip. "Must be you have never fallen hard before. It isn't that easy to get over."

This was the second time today I'd heard that assessment. Was it so obvious?

Georgie turned his attention back to Cassie. "What's done is done," he cooed, stroking Cassie's blonde hair. His voice fell into the register of a throaty whisper. "How was it?"

They both cracked up.

I didn't get it until he added, "The sex, I mean."

down on the south beach drag

I was steaming. Why was he asking her that? Only seconds ago, Cassie had found it hard to talk through her tears, and now she was struggling to talk through her laughter.

She managed to gasp out, "It was *fantastic*."

They just about fell apart laughing.

Since I'd never had any kind of sex at all, I couldn't figure it out. "So, you enjoyed it, then you were sad . . . and now it's funny?"

"Oh, Girl." Georgie shot me a disgusted look. "What goes on in that little mind of yours, Maeve?"

What exactly was I doing to deserve his reproof? I'd thought befriending Georgie was going to teach me something about myself, something I didn't have a prayer of learning at home. Now he was siding with my oldest friend, and she was positioned a little too close to him for my comfort.

Both of them were against me. A united front. But if Cassie thought she was going to win him over without a fight from me, she was sadly mistaken.

Georgie was different too; given that, you'd think he'd be more sensitive to my feelings. If I needed to do it, I could blend in with some of the girls I knew, with some effort. Obviously, Georgie could not. Not with the guys *or* the girls. No way. You'd think that general lack of acceptance would make him easier on me right now. I felt uncertain, and outnumbered. He was supposed to be *my* friend.

The next thing I knew, he was rooting around in the kitchen to find food to make Cassie something for breakfast.

"We just got to get you a bite to eat and you're going to start feeling a whole lot better," he called out. "Let's see what we have." I heard the refrigerator door open. "Toast and eggs? How's that, Ms. Cassie?"

My resentment, combined with the urge to start my photo session, drove me to pace back and forth. On my sixth circuit, the phone on the desk near the front door rang. I ran to answer it.

"Hello?"

"Hi, Maeve, it's Rickey." He sounded lively, though he went on to tell me he'd hardly slept the night before. "That cocaine I scored was strong. I don't think I closed my eyes at all. And Sandra snores. Did you know that?"

"Not always." I looked back toward the kitchen for any sign of Georgie. Cassie caught my eyes. I gathered the fingertips of one hand to an imaginary point and shook them at her. It was an Italian gesture I had seen. I was using it to question her sanity at the moment.

She giggled. Much to my dismay.

"Well, she sure snored last night," Rickey said.

I assumed he'd called for her. "Sandra's at work this afternoon. She said she'll be late tonight. Shall I leave a note for her to call you?" I didn't know if he'd heard about Cookie's accident, but I wasn't about to be the one to fill him in.

"Yeah, I know she's at the office," he said. "I just talked to her. But now I'm calling to talk to you. I wanted to bring some people by to meet you. They need headshots too. Seems like everyone I know wants to go on auditions. I thought I'd throw you the work."

Today? I rubbed the bridge of my nose with my thumb and forefinger. How many rolls of film did I have stored in the freezer? I'd shot several at the sideshow tent yesterday. I reached up to feel for my pencils. "I've got a client here already and we haven't started shooting yet. I'm going to need an hour and a half with him. At least."

"Him, huh? That will be fine. Perfect. We'll stop by with some beer and snacks. It'll be fun. We'll make it a party."

I shrugged. "Okay." I was never one to turn away good money.

In order to focus and turn my attitude around, I shifted to the view of the waves outside our tall windows, reminding myself how fortunate I was to be here. Scented salt air billowed in. If

down on the south beach drag

only I could live here forever. The splendor of the ocean filled my senses and people were clamoring for my photographs—I should be on top of the world.

Cassie wandered into the kitchen and came back carrying a plate of scrambled eggs. She was shoveling in food as she padded back toward the chair.

"Cass, there's some other people coming over to get their pictures taken. You're going to have to get dressed. I don't mean to interrupt your—"

She tittered, swallowed, and took another big, greedy forkful. "The food is helping. I'll take a shower after this and then help Georgie with his makeup. He has such beautiful skin."

"He does. That high coloring." I nodded to her. "Thanks for helping. I'm really thinking hard about how to capture that skin on film." It would be fun having Cassie assisting a shoot. It had been a long time since we'd worked on a project together.

"We have to set a time limit, though," she said. "Remember, you're coming with me to the open mic night tonight. I'm a nervous wreck." She must have thought I was going to disagree, because she added, "Don't worry, it starts late. We can get it all done."

What a whirlwind of a day this was going to be.

Georgie came in from the kitchen, wiping his hands on a dishcloth. "What's going on?"

"I'm so proud of Cassie," I said. "She's singing later. She's really good too." Not as good as Georgie—or, I supposed, good in a different way. "You two should sing together sometime."

Georgie smoothed his hair and yawned. "I wish I didn't have to work. I'd love to see her. We better get going, Maeve. I have to get back."

He used the mirror in my bedroom to get himself ready while I turned on the lights and tacked up a black background. He sat down and I shot a roll of medium format film slowly, playing

that lady

with my fill light. First, I placed it as far away as I could; then I slid it closer and closer for a sequence of six shots. Dramatic shadows traveled across his face.

I was already dreaming of framing those six pictures and hanging them side by side.

chapter 13
right place, wrong time

"It's amazing," Georgie said. "It's like that camera becomes part of you. I feel like I'm sitting here watching a one-eyed cyclops or something."

He'd changed into one of his suits.

"Please don't wear your fedora in this series," I said. "Let's not hide your face." His gorgeous face. And that luxuriant hair. Thick and so damn shiny. His perfectly shaped eyebrows. No, no hat; we wanted all of this out on full display for the camera.

He tied his silk cravat as he sat down in front of the lights. He leaned back with one elbow on the arm of the chair.

I gestured to his jacket. "Do you mind?" I felt awkward. I had already asked one man to disrobe in the last two days. Still, there was an urge to pull it off him. I'd thought I wanted him in a full suit, but now I longed to make him look more casual. But it felt too intimate to insist.

"Go ahead," he said. "Do what you want."

Overcoming my reticence, I slipped the garment off his shoulders. Then, my face flaming . . . God help me . . . I unbuttoned his shirt all the way, pulled his tie so it was loose, and coaxed the coral-colored cravat to flow down across his chest muscles.

"Cassie," I called. I knew she had all her makeup laid out on the top of our dresser. "Come look."

She popped her head in.

"See how his lips and cheeks kind of bloom with color? You got anything to accentuate that? This is black-and-white film. We're going to lose some of the natural effect in grayscale."

Cassie brought a tube of bronzing gel and a jar of rouge that she blended and massaged onto Georgie's cheekbones. She used face cream to fan the color toward his ears. Georgie accepted her touch-up like a pro, staring straight ahead as she worked on him.

It hadn't occurred to me that he'd done all this before. I'd been fantasizing about how I was going to coach him and draw him out. Ha! Georgie already knew how to work with a camera. As I moved around, his eyes followed me like a wild cheetah, my camera his prey. He was ravenous. He even roared at one point, making me guffaw.

He stared eye-to-eye with me through the viewfinder. You'd think the camera would create some distance, make me feel removed, but it had the opposite effect. My stomach ached with awe. We were locked together, soul to soul. I had never been closer to another human being in my life as we were at this moment. I suddenly understood the passages in romance novels that spoke of throbbing loins and heaving bodices.

When I wound the film to the next frame, I felt a tug on the handle that I knew from experience not to force any further. Tearing myself away from him took discipline, but I just managed it. "It's time to switch out rolls of film. You want to change clothes?"

"Yes, I've got a white tuxedo. I'll put it on."

End of discussion.

He slipped on his dress shoes and walked, step by careful step, toward the bedroom. I quickly grabbed my 35mm camera and snapped away—*click, click, click*—catching his strutting backside before he disappeared behind the door. Georgie would be forever captured in the light pouring through my bedroom window, his tall, lithe form enveloped in fairy dust.

Minutes passed. Both Cassie and Georgie were in our bedroom now, and they had shut the door. What were they doing in there?

A knock on the front door startled me. I pushed all my equipment aside and carefully stepped over the electrical cords to answer it.

"Father?"

Father Murphy stood at the threshold, his dog Paddy on a leash next to him. "I thought I'd pop in. Can you spare a cup of coffee for an old man?" He appeared delighted with himself, with a twinkle in his eye and a smile at the corners of his lips.

"Oh, gosh, I've got a client here. And more coming. I'm sorry, it's just not a good time."

Just then our bedroom door opened, and Georgie spotted him. Loose-limbed, brimming with energy, he strode over with his hand outstretched. "Father Murphy! Long time, no see. So, you're back for the summer?" He seemed genuinely pleased. It hadn't occurred to me that they might know each other.

Georgie looped his arm across my shoulders and pulled me closer. A natural enough gesture, given that we were both squeezed into the doorframe.

Father stared at Georgie's hand on me, long enough for me to take in a sharp breath and hold it. A rush of guilt followed. The pressure of his censure was more than familiar to me. It was ingrained. I felt knee-jerk shame mixed with fear, though I wasn't sure what we'd done wrong. When Father got on to the subject of sin, he was like a dog with a bone.

But, in the end, he scanned our faces with a pleased smile on his face. I decided he'd just been surprised.

right place, wrong time

A racket rose up the stairwell. Rickey and an older couple appeared, looking up at us curiously. Their arms were filled with grocery bags, and they were all dressed to the nines in what I assumed was their Sunday best. Since the couple were little people and Rickey looked a bit like both of them, I assumed they were Mr. and Mrs. Travers.

Flustered, I gestured toward them and said, "Oh, Father, you see? I'm booked this afternoon."

He appeared flummoxed. "You said you were taking pictures of the beach. That you might show them to me. Who are all these people?"

"I will show those pictures to you. I discovered some unusual shells that I got some great shots of." I nodded rapidly, cheeks burning. "That's only part of the collection I'm working on. We'll discuss it, but another time, please, Father. We have to get the shoots done and then Cassie and I have a commitment afterward."

Father reached down, picked up Paddy, and stepped into the apartment—he had to in order to allow the other three to come inside. It was clear he would have liked to stay. I could have invited him to, but I didn't want him cramping my style. All these photos had the potential to make the Select Six for the contest, as far as I was concerned. I couldn't spend precious minutes treading on eggshells, worrying about what Father might think.

"I'll show you out," I said politely.

Before we exited, he hollered, "Goodbye, Cassandra," toward our open bedroom door.

Cassie didn't answer.

As soon as I shut the door, he put a hand on my shoulder. "I'm going to ask you again, who are these people?"

Where did I begin? "Performers. It's a separate project."

His nostrils flared. "I know that Georgie is quite a talented musician. I've known him since he was a child. But the others . . . they are . . . ?"

down on the south beach drag

"Part of the carnival life on the boardwalk. My new interest." It rushed out of me unbidden, and I was surprised that it sounded perfectly plausible.

He coughed into his fist. "I'm not sure your father would want you congregating with these sorts. People like that aren't always . . . savory."

An interesting choice of word. "I'll be careful," I promised. "They just need headshots. I'm getting paid for it." I didn't say how much I was getting paid. My bargain basement prices might make the work seem less credible. They get photos cheap and I get to use them any way I want to.

He muttered goodbye and clung to the railing as he made his way down. Paddy barked at me over Father's shoulder, making it known that he was annoyed too.

I eased the door open and slid back into the room.

Rickey's mother was a vibrant redhead with a porcelain complexion. Her curly hair was piled high on top of the crown of her head. I felt like a giant version of her. As I usually did when I felt much bigger than another person, I slumped to the point that I probably looked like the hunchback of Notre Dame. I couldn't help the posture, though. It was something I'd done since first grade.

My mother's voice rang in my head, telling me to stand up straight. With a self-loathing click of my tongue, I did so—mostly because I didn't want to provoke a round of jokes about me ringing church bells. Cassie was more than capable of getting that going. It had happened many times before.

Mrs. Travers had a huge grin on her face and seemed delighted to meet me. She giggled, hitched her head toward her husband, and winked my way. "Of course, she's another redhead." She looked up at the hulking Rickey and beamed. "He's already told us so much about you."

My gaze shifted to her son, with a question in it. He smirked.

right place, wrong time

Georgie moved closer to me and took my arm. Staking his claim? Or was I only hoping he was?

He made me walk him to the door when we completed his final shoot with the Traverses looking on, and he kissed my cheek in front of everyone before leaving. But he'd kissed Cassie, too, so I tried not to make too much out of it.

"You watch out for that Rickey," he whispered in my ear. "He's got a bad reputation around here. With the ladies, in particular."

I whispered back, "I'm just taking his picture. He's a customer."

He pulled back and patted my cheek. "He doesn't get that, Maeve. He thinks you're into him."

Georgie was going too far. Rickey was a big flirt, that was true. But I wasn't special to him; he probably did it with everyone.

"See you soon, Georgie?"

"Before you know it."

chapter 14
the angel

As soon as the door shut behind Georgie, Rickey moved right in. But so what if he was talking to me? It was safe enough. His parents were there, after all.

Throughout their session, he asked me all manner of questions: "What kind of film are you using? Do you prefer any particular brand? Can you get everything you need locally? My dad often commutes into Newark if you need anything special."

At that last comment, his father beamed my way.

I'd never been so popular in a given day. I guess I was, maybe, feeling a little full of myself. Like Rickey was admiring my overwhelming talent, only interested in my brain.

Cassie watched as I went out on the deck with him and he lit a joint. When he passed it to me and I accepted it, she came to the window and shook her head. I thought it must be my smoking she disapproved of, though during the photo shoot there had been significant talk about marijuana. All the Traverses, and Georgie, too, thought anyone who considered themselves a real artist should, at the very least, try it to free their mind from conformity. They thought certain drugs worked well to achieve just that.

Even Cassie had chimed in. "Oh, yeah. Learning to play the guitar was hard, but after I started smoking pot, the chord changes just came to me."

Raised with a dogma that still clung to me like a bad smell, I

the angel

longed to free myself too. Their reasoning and unanimous agreement had convinced me. I'd decided I would try it one more time.

I held the joint with my elbow pointed away from my body at ninety degrees, like an actress from a very old movie. Uncertain how to do it properly, I channeled the Bette Davis films I liked to watch on Channel 9. I knew it was possible that I looked like an idiot. Even probable. I took the tiniest puff possible, and handed it back to Rickey.

I studied him as he placed the joint at the corner of his skeleton mouth, sucked the smoke way in, and held his breath. On my next drag, I tried it his way—and coughed so hard he patted me on the back.

Lord, he was strong. It actually hurt a bit. Cassie laughed at me from the living room.

I'd consumed two beers during this impromptu photo party, as well as the smoke. Cassie had made a point of telling everyone I had a warmer glow than usual. I wasn't at all sure what she meant by that, other than that it didn't convey high praise about my usual attitude. I did feel quite happy, though.

"You are just my type," Rickey whispered hoarsely. "I couldn't believe it the first time I laid eyes on you."

Well, this was a shock. "How so?"

"I like big girls. Strong ones. And the hair on your arms is a turn-on. I'm guessing the rest of you is . . . natural too. That's my thing."

Over-the-top BS. I snorted. "What do you really want?"

He lowered his chin so he had to stare up at me. "You, babe. Just you."

"That's unfortunate, Rickey. Never going to happen." Did this actually work on other girls? I fidgeted. Georgie had been right.

I saw Cassie glance up at the wall clock and begin to tap the heel of her shoe nervously on the wooden floor. Grateful for an excuse to escape Rickey, I popped my head in.

down on the south beach drag

"After taking my last few shots of this group, my film is mostly gone," I told her. "I'm sorry, but I won't be able to take many photos of your open mic debut."

"Hurray," she said. "For once you can pay attention to me instead of what you see through your viewfinder. I need you tonight."

I smiled. It felt good to be needed.

"I'm sure you'd like nothing better than to disappear into the basement right now to start rolling up all that film," she added. "I can just picture you hunkered down in the dank darkness, only leaving to process your negatives in stages in the pantry sink."

"That's a little dramatic, Cass." She was right. But I'd promised her I would go to the open mic night, and I would. Say what you want about me, but I am as good as my word.

The big problem for Cassie was always the getting-on-stage-solo part. She said it was easy to sing confidently as part of the chorus because she was just part of the crowd. Even in school plays it wasn't so bad, since she had cast members to share the burden with. But being onstage alone? It terrified her.

Remembering this, I gave her a soft look. "You're gonna be great."

She grimaced. "It makes my stomach sour just thinking about it."

"You're ready," I told her. "You've been practicing like crazy since Bobby went away. Singing was like your magic weapon to get you through the breakup."

I was trying to be supportive, though I suspected the actual truth was that this effort was all part of an elaborate plan to get Bobby back. Most of the kids from Bradley Beach, where Bobby was supposedly living now, wound up hanging out at the Osprey nightclub at some point or another. If she could get a regular spot at the open mic nights, he was bound to see her eventually. And it had occurred to me more than once that she was probably

the angel

determined to be so good that, when he did finally see her, he'd fall in love with her all over again.

"I feel a little swoozy," Cassie said.

That was no surprise. All the beer was gone, and she'd consumed her fair share. I looked back at Rickey. "We'd better wrap things up. Cassie and I have to get over to the Osprey."

We gathered our things and came back in from the deck. A pungent cloud followed us through the French doors.

"Hey, this was great, but, Cassie, Maeve tells me you two have to get going." Rickey made pointed eye contact with his father. "Cassie's going to play music tonight over in Manasquan. Can we give them a ride?"

His mother put one hand across her bosom. "What? So soon?" It seemed she'd settled in quite nicely. But when her son nodded solemnly, she scrambled to her feet and looked around at the mess we'd all made. "Can I help you girls clean up?"

"Please don't worry about it, Mrs. Travers," Cassie said. "We'll pick up in the morning."

I squinted at Cassie. She knew perfectly well she would still be sleeping; I always got stuck tidying up. Presumably to change the subject, she pointed one thumb toward the deck and, out of the corner of her mouth, whispered to me, "What got into you out there?"

I shrugged. "If I was ever going to try pot again, this seemed like a good time."

I then took a gracelessly wrong step and grabbed the back of a chair for support. Cassie shook her head, giggling.

The drive to the club was short but cramped. The five of us, Cassie's guitar, two coolers, and a variety of boxes were all jammed into the Traverses' little blue sedan. The moment we arrived, Cassie jumped out.

down on the south beach drag

Rickey hoisted himself out of the back seat after her, and I wiggled out right behind him. A streetlight flooded the skeleton-inked side of his face in yellow light. While my mom and pop wouldn't even allow me to get my ears pierced, Rickey's parents didn't seem to think anything about his tattoos. Or his muscle mass.

He was lingering. Was he was holding out for an invitation to join us? I sucked in my breath. I'd had enough of him for one day. Cassie was nervous enough about performing; she didn't need to make a grand entrance with the Tattooed Man from the carnival.

Then there was the matter of Sandra. I'd gotten the impression this morning that she was much taken with Rickey. For him to spend the evening clubbing with Cassie and me would inevitably brew trouble. The last thing I wanted was to lead him on or, more importantly, piss Sandra off.

So, when he took my elbow, I turned on him. "It was *your* choice to sleep with Sandra. You don't get to switch around roommates at your convenience. Sandra and I have been friends since we were kids."

Cassie stared at the ground, clearly not wanting to get involved. The reality was, neither she nor I would have ever given him the time of day if he came calling, Sandra or no Sandra. That much was a given, but I didn't want to be overly cruel.

The sudden thought of bringing this guy home to meet Pop, the honorable Officer O'Connor, made me yelp with laughter. I put a hand over my mouth to stifle the sound. The very idea was side-splitting. And Mom?

Cassie noticed. "What?"

When I whispered to her what was going through my mind, she, too, cracked up. "Picture your mother's faaaaaaaaace," she managed to get out between convulsions. Cassie knew my parents almost as well as I did.

Whatever Rickey was thinking, despite the blessing his parents kept smiling my way, we were never going to happen.

the angel

"What's so funny?" Rickey demanded.

Immediately, I sobered up. I was being horribly rude. It was not my finest moment, and I was sorry about it. I'd been raised better.

I ducked my head into the car through the back door and said, "Thank you, Mrs. Travers, Mr. Travers. I'll bring those shots to the local lab and have a contact sheet for you by the end of the week. The only thing I can process myself is black-and-white film."

They answered in chorus, "Thanks, honey. You're a doll."

There was another indisputable barrier between me and Rickey that no one but me knew about: I simply didn't want to be with a masculine boy. It was only a few years ago that I'd seriously dreamed about becoming a nun.

I guess I hadn't acted like a nun earlier, though; I should never have gone out on the deck alone with Rickey, or accepted his marijuana. It turned out to be such an intimate thing, the careful passing of the rolled joint, our hands touching, then sucking on the very end that had just been between his lips. Big mistake. Plus, I wasn't used to being mentally dulled, and being high rattled me.

It took every ounce of concentration to make myself turn and head toward the entrance of the Osprey. But it was a good thing I did, because it was the kick in the pants Rickey needed to finally reach into the trunk and hand over Cassie's guitar case.

He did it with a heavy sigh, then stood with his hands in his pockets, glowering at the ground. The expression on the skull side of his face gave me a queasy feeling.

"Thanks for the ride," I said. "See you later."

"Sure," he muttered.

Cassie and I waved goodbye over our shoulders as we rushed in. We couldn't get away from him fast enough.

chapter 15
i don't want to go home

The Osprey was a smoky old roadhouse. Neon beer signs, a sour smell, and a pool table in an adjoining room—even from my limited experience with bars, I could tell it was your average dump. A small stage was wedged in one corner, its platform less than two feet off the ground.

A larger wing of the building contained a theater, and there was a crowd now emptying into the bar. Rock legend Bo Diddley's gig had just ended. I hollered at Cassie over the noise. "I wish you'd told me he was playing. I bet it was a great show."

A young man with a craggy face and a black leather jacket overheard. "It *was* great," he said. "You missed out."

I hoped he and his buddy wouldn't keep trying to talk to us, but they turned away and settled onto a couple of nearby barstools. Cassie wore a worried look, too, as she spotted a young man in a tan zoot suit and Panama hat heading her way. She sucked in a breath, clearly bracing herself for just another jerk trying to get in her pants.

"Surprise!" he said. It was Georgie. So this was the job he'd been heading to.

He gently took the guitar case from her. "It's usually busy here on Thursdays, so I help out. The open mic draws a lot of

i don't want to go home

performers and their friends. I'm not exactly a bouncer—more like a greeter. Though I do call for security at the first sign of trouble."

I had one hand over my mouth. "But what's with the outfit?"

He tugged at the lapels of his long jacket as he turned around to display it. "It was my father's. Like it?" The shiny wide-leg pants cut in sharply at the ankles.

"Is there a reason you're dressed up?" I laughed.

"Yeah. I'm going to do 'In the Mood' later." I knew that song. Glenn Miller and his big band had made it a hit in the '40s.

He picked up Cassie's right hand and kissed it. Under any other circumstances I would have considered it corny, even creepy, but the gesture seemed entirely natural coming from him. His eyes crinkled good-naturedly when he gently pinched one of her cheeks.

Enough with the Cassie-touching, already.

"You want a drink?" He leaned against the bar and looked at her through his eyelashes in a way that was impossible to resist. Incredibly suave for someone so young.

Cassie had never looked better. Her blue eyes and blonde hair shone, and her short skirt revealed the length of her tanned legs. "Sure, Georgie. Thank you."

He put up one finger, as if to say, "Wait a minute," strode across the room to the stage, and slid the guitar underneath it. As he walked back toward us, he pulled a roll of bills out of his pocket, licked his thumb, and started sorting the money into denominations. "What are you girls having?"

"How about a scotch and soda?" I asked without having any idea why. I'd never had one before and I wasn't sure how it would taste, but I was on some kind of roll this evening.

Cassie grabbed my shoulders and peered into my eyes suspiciously, pulling me closer, like she had when we were little girls, so that our noses were touching. "Are you sure? You're not used to the pot. And you already had a couple of beers."

down on the south beach drag

"Scotch and soda it is." Georgie snapped his fingers and pointed at me. The move drew my attention to two chunky gold rings on his right hand, the one on his pinky sporting a ruby. A gold chain arced downward from one belt loop and back up into his pocket. He had an amazing attention for detail. While Cassie was concerned, Georgie was encouraging me to drink more. Either he didn't understand Cassie's meaning, or he wanted me to hang around and be his wingman. Woman. Whatever. He wanted me to support him in his flirtation with her.

Cassie rolled her eyes at me and asked for a gin and tonic. With a satisfied expression, Georgie put an arm around her waist and waved to the man in black who'd spoken to me earlier. When the man waved back, Georgie leaned into the center of our little circle and shot each of us a crooked finger. "Come closer. That guy's a musician," he whispered. "He's huge down here. Everyone says he's going to get a record deal."

Cassie stretched up to her full height, eyes sparkling. She sent a blazing smile his way. He chuckled and laid one hand over his heart. What man wouldn't?

This was the first time I'd ever seen Cassie flirt with a boy—or man, in this case. Besides Bobby, that is. But here she was, flirting with an almost famous musician. She had never struck me as ambitious before. This was interesting.

Georgie peeled a twenty off his roll, handed it to the bartender, and held up the palm of his hand. "Keep the change."

The bartender shouted, "You're the best!" They slapped their hands, palm side then back side, in a practiced move.

Obviously, Georgie was some kind of big shot around here.

"Hey, man," he called to the musician, then pointed to Cassie. "She's gonna play tonight."

He gave a thumbs-up, though I couldn't tell if it was because Cassie was going to sing, or he was indicating that Georgie was lucky to be hanging out with a knockout like her.

i don't want to go home

"You are one beau-ti-ful girl." Georgie sighed at Cassie and stroked her hair with such an affectionate look on his face it was impossible to be offended.

Normally such an invasion of her space would have made her shrink away, but she blossomed under his attention. "Thanks for the drink, Georgie. You're pretty cute too." Cassie clinked the rim of her highball with Georgie's rocks glass. "But you know I've already got a boyfriend."

He pursed his lips and wrinkled his nose dramatically. Cassie and I laughed.

"Where is he, then?" Georgie teased.

I was surprised when Cassie's eyes filled with tears. Surely she was over Bobby by now. Or maybe I just prayed for her to be. She shrugged and wiped them, but the tears spilled out and down her cheeks.

Georgie put his drink on the bar and shook his head, clearly disgusted with something. "A girl as pretty as you, as nice as you, he probably thinks he can find another one just as good. He's wrong. Believe me, he really doesn't know what he had with you. And I'll tell you something, Cass, he's gonna live to regret it."

It was endearing to me that he called her Cass. I wished he'd give me a nickname. One besides Girl. He put his hand to her cheek and patted it. They say people can turn green with envy. They're wrong. They turn red.

When the house band started their sound check, Georgie went up to the stage and handed the front man a folded bill held between his index and middle fingers, finishing with a twist of his arm. The musician returned the gesture with a handshake, and they shared a few words.

Georgie came dancing back to us. "He's going to get you on first. Then I'll do my number—and I'm going to take you girls out for midnight breakfast."

down on the south beach drag

I held my hands up in the direction of the growing crowd. "What about your job?"

He winked. "Let's just say I know the owner."

I guess we were leaving when he decided we should leave. Presumptuous. Yet I actually had no objections at all. There wasn't a doubt in my mind this spontaneous adventure would be fun—except for the part where I'd be subjected to his apparent attraction to my best friend.

Cassie eyed the stage and then me with panic in her eyes. "You know I can't go up there alone. Come up with me. You've been singing harmonies with me for days now."

Being the eldest child in my family had shaped me into a natural problem solver. I wasn't at all surprised by this turn of events, but I was realistic too. "My voice, by itself, isn't going to help much . . . I'm not very good. Wait—I got it."

I handed my glass to Georgie and marched over to Mr. Gonna Get a Record Deal—it must have been the marijuana that made me so brazen. He looked like he was in a terrific mood; he met my approach with a wide smile. Georgie and Cassie followed behind me.

"I just had my first drink ever. Can you believe that?" he asked.

I shook my head. "You must not be Irish, then."

He doubled over laughing. "No. But my friend here is—they call him Big Danny Gallagher. He knows a thing or two about being Irish."

I looked Big Danny over—a fellow redhead and a lion of a man—and lit up at the sound of his familiar surname. I had cousins who were Gallaghers. He'd be on my side from the get-go, I was sure. So I got right down to business.

"Danny. This is my best friend, Cassie. Her voice sounds as good as she looks, I promise. She plays guitar too. But she's nervous."

i don't want to go home

How to dig deep for a convincing amount of blarney? Flagrantly. I opened my eyes as wide as they could go, blinked at him three times, and grinned. "We just graduated from high school, Danny. This is all pretty new to us . . . and pretty scary. Cassie wants me to sing harmony with her. She doesn't want to be alone up there. I want to be a good friend, but I'm going to need your help."

Cassie put a hand over her mouth to cover the giggle that escaped her. She couldn't believe what a smooth talker I was turning out to be. The marijuana, the beer, the scotch—why hadn't I done this before?

Danny took my hand. He downed his shot of tequila and so did his friend. A determined scowl on his face, he pushed off the barstool, put his arm around me, and leaned in toward Cassie. "What song are you singing, girl?"

Cassie's voice came out small. She practically whispered, "Al Green. 'Let's Stay Together.'" She flushed and leaned into one hip. I could tell she wanted to lower her gaze, so I inwardly applauded her for maintaining eye contact.

"Nice," Danny and his buddy said at the same time. "Jinx," they added, elbowing each other.

All of us laughed as Danny pushed through the crowd and we followed him onto the stage.

He pulled one of the microphone stands to the back and assembled his friend, me, and himself around it, with me in the middle. Georgie had paid one of the band members on the sly to tune Cassie's guitar, so it was ready to go. He seemed to think of everything—at least when it came to her. He handed the guitar up to Cassie like it was made of gold. She smiled down at him when he blew her a kiss. Aargh.

The house band's front man announced over the microphone, "Ladies and gentlemen, our first singer tonight is Cassie . . . ?"

"Olsen!" I shouted, startling myself and jumping back. The

volume of my voice had come out way too high. The men on either side of me widened their eyes.

"Cut her off," Danny joked.

The front man barked a laugh into his microphone. "Okay. Cassie Olsen. Miss Cassie Olsen, everyone. And friends."

I'd been gifted with a heightened sixth sense—a simple fact that anyone with a drop of Irish blood accepted as part of our genetic makeup. This, in addition to my long history with Cassie, meant that I knew she believed this was her one chance to earn a permanent spot at the open mic night. A spot where Bobby would one day find her again. For all she knew, he was out there in the crowd right now. It was packed. She inhaled deeply, her intent to make this song count painted across her face.

She glanced back at me and nodded confidently. A phrase started to repeat in my brain like a mantra: "soul music, soul music, soul music . . ."

In that exact timing, Cassie began to strum a percussive rhythm unlike anything I'd ever heard her play at home. I didn't know she could hammer out a beat like this. The other musicians exchanged a satisfied look, confirming that this was a very, very good way to start, and they began to play along.

By the time she reached the third line of the song, we backup singers were dancing and snapping our fingers along to the music and the backup guitar players were rocking back and forth exuberantly.

And the audience? There was a mad rush to the dance floor.

Cassie blew that room away. The ovation she received when the song ended made it clear she couldn't leave the stage before she did another.

Somehow, she'd had the wherewithal to prepare one. She counted down—"a one, and a two, and a three, and a four"—and started her own unique version of Rare Earth's "I Just Want to Celebrate."

i don't want to go home

What a joy it was to watch her. She was totally in command. I'd heard singers on television say that in their everyday lives they were very shy, but when onstage they turned into someone else. That's what happened to my friend. Even strapped with a guitar, she moved like Tina Turner—maybe even better. Her alto voice was as steady as could be, and clear as a bell. I didn't know when I'd ever been so inspired.

I took advantage of an instrumental break and took a couple pictures from my spot on the stage. My heart skipped a beat as I started to envision the whole next phase of my work through my camera lens. I was going to jump down stage left and get some from the audience in a minute. Everyone said the guy next to me was going to make the big time. Well, nobody was thinking about him right now. Tonight, Cassie ruled.

It was going to be my time too. I had an inroad here—a chance to photograph her, Danny, and everybody else riding their coattails. I already had the sideshow pictures. This was phase two: The Music Scene.

When Cassie reached the chorus and the *yeah, yeah* backup part of the song, Danny went crazy. He sang the lyrics in a voice that emanated from deep inside him. He stomped and waved his hands in the air. Back to back with his friend, he switched positions several times in a little do-si-do. I moved back a few paces and got a shot of them. If two people could have more fun than they were having, I just didn't know how. It sparked the entire audience to keep dancing. *Click.* I was careful not to waste a shot.

The number was another showstopper, but even showstoppers must end. Cassie and I both had tears in our eyes when we hugged at the back of the stage afterward.

"They are going to have to ask me back next week. Aren't they?" She sounded desperate.

I laughed so hard I bent forward. "Cassie, after this I think

down on the south beach drag

you can play here any time you want. In fact, you'll get plenty of invitations to play at other places too."

Each song for the rest of the set started with a different singer making a joke about how hard it was going to be to follow Cassie's triumph. One guy who got up to play said, "Cassie, you got to take mercy on us . . . next time, you go on last. You can be the grand finale—I'm fine with that." The audience applauded and hooted.

Even Georgie couldn't upstage Cassie, though his zoot suit number was great fun.

When it came time for the band to call for a customary break, he appeared with both our purses and Cassie's guitar.

"Breakfast, girls."

chapter 16
sandy

Cassie sat next to Georgie in the passenger seat and I sprawled out in the back as he drove us to the local open-all-night diner.

As we spun away from the Osprey, I shouted from the back seat of the car, "I don't know where you found the chutzpah, Cassie. I've never heard you play like that."

"I don't know," she said. "I think if you work hard enough, put enough hours in, your natural style just takes over. It was pretty cool." She lit up a joint. "I don't want this night to ennnnndddd."

I didn't know what was up with me, but I accepted the joint when she passed it back. Even though I was just starting to come down from the first round of pot earlier in the evening, not to mention buzzing hard from my scotch and soda.

We pulled into the parking lot of a 1953 Jerry O'Mahony Diner car—a big deal because it was an original, built by the guy who invented the Jersey Diners. This was another great photo opportunity, but I'd need color film, the place was so vibrant. *Just look at that huge lemon meringue pie in the display case.* It would photograph beautifully.

We settled into a red leatherette booth. I was definitely bringing my camera here when I bought more film. The diner struck me as more authentic than the amusement park, filled with locals instead of tourists.

down on the south beach drag

We all ordered omelets with hash brown potatoes.

"Can you bring us hot sauce?" I asked the waitress when she set down our plates. None of us could stop smiling. Sure, it was the grass that made us squinty and cheerful, but it was also the fun of reliving the high points of our night. And we had the munchies, bad. Eggs had never tasted so good.

"What *kind* of eggs are these?" I asked. "They must be super fresh or something."

Both Georgie and Cassie laughed at me.

"Seriously," I insisted. "Do you think we can buy some locally?"

"You're just high," Cassie told me. "Everything tastes extra good on pot."

"So, listen to this," Georgie said. "I've got something to tell you." He sipped his lemonade and scanned the diner suspiciously, as though someone might be listening in. "A guy comes over to me after your set—he's serious, now—and wants to know if I'm your *manager*."

Cassie and I squealed like little girls.

"Of course, I said yes." He shrugged with his hands high in the air. "What else could I say? '*No, she's just some girl I met yesterday*'? I gave him my card and he said he'd be in touch. I sure wasn't expecting this. Meeting you two. Having the time of my life. You know, girls, I always wanted to get into the business side of music."

Cassie looked away. I wondered if she wasn't ready to make a commitment.

"No offense, Georgie, but Cassie might want to speak to him herself," I said. "Why would you want to be a manager?"

"It can help me get through lean times as a performer. Given who I am, I'll never get the kind of bookings Cassie can. You could do worse than me. I'm good at . . . getting things done, let's just leave it at that. Music management would be a good complement to my other investments. Something fun to do in my spare time."

Made sense to me. "If you're her manager, I want to be her official photographer," I said. "The only one who gets close to her."

"Aren't you two getting ahead of yourselves?" Cassie said. "Nothing has happened yet."

"But it will." I hit the table with closed fists; however lightly, I made my point. "This is important to me."

Cassie nodded.

Georgie tilted his head and made eye contact with me. "You got it."

Cassie's face lit up. "Maeve, tomorrow I'm going to make you a lanyard to hang around your neck. We'll make a press pass, and you two will be like an entourage. My first entourage. I'll feel more confident having you around."

Elbows up on the table, I studied my friend closely. Though my mouth suddenly felt dry, I was full and satisfied. Gone was that morose sad sack wrapped in a pink bedspread. Cassie had fully bloomed tonight into the girl she was meant to be.

It gave me hope. Hope for both of us and our futures. Cassie had said it well. I fully believed that succeeding in photography, or in any of the arts, took hours and hours of practice and preparation . . . and the magic of being in the right place at the right time.

There was going to be a right time for me here, too, and I was going to be out and about with my eyes peeled looking for it.

If only she would keep her hands off my guy.

Over the next weeks I became friendly with two young men at the Osprey, Todd and Martin, both sharp dressers who were aspiring fashion designers. They commented on the pencils adorning my hair and the heavy silk Chinese pajama tops I'd taken to wearing lately, pairing them with jeans.

As Todd looked me over, he put a fingertip to his lips and made a smacking sound.

"The hair doesn't *not* work," he said to Martin. "But if you're going to stick with this hybrid look, Maeve—is that a fantastic name or what?"—Martin nodded solemnly—"you'll have to take it further."

He obviously knew what he was talking about, so I asked, "How so?"

"You need to collect other hair ornaments too. And I'm not saying you shouldn't wear Asian stuff at all—it's a signature; I get it. Very original. And cheap, too, am I right?"

I nodded.

He waved a hand in my direction. "You're built like a flat-chested model. You can wear anything—but become the expert. Buy some really nice pieces to show off."

"I don't know where to go shopping for that."

Martin gently pushed me and giggled. "You leave that to us."

They took me to Manhattan, to shops in Chinatown that sold intricate hair ornaments, silk robes, and pajamas, and shirts that felt like heaven next to my skin. My bookkeeping job at the bar had me flush with cash and I indulged myself with items that they picked out.

When we stopped in a café for lunch, they kept discussing me and my style. As if I were a celebrity.

"Each of these pieces is powerful," said Todd. "You have to be careful not to overdo it, or it will come off as corny. Like those big barrettes you got, with the fans and trailing flowers? You can only wear one at a time, and only at night."

"But what about—"

"The pencil, the pencil—we all know about the pencil."

We laughed so hard we had our heads down on the table.

Then Todd got serious. "It's okay to have it tucked in there— it's part of your mystique. The rest of us are thinking you must be a genius or something—you have to have a pencil ready to write down all your important thoughts. But you don't want it to be the first thing people notice about you."

I listened and took their suggestions. They were so much fun; I was glad we'd become friends. I met them when the open mic night changed from Monday to Thursday; I was sure it was to draw more customers in to see Cassie. The boys stuck close by me. Them on one side, Georgie on the other.

The series of photographs I did with them under my studio lights made me choke with emotion every time I looked at the pictures. They were kindness incarnate. Glowing angels. As if the love they held for each other oozed out of every pore, and they had to share it with the world. It gave me hope about the very notion of love.

Could it ever happen to me?

I froze when I heard someone moving around in the living room. It was barely daybreak, and I was in the kitchen making myself a cup of tea. I tried not to breathe so I could listen, but the sound of my heart drowned out everything else. I knew both Cassie and Sandra were still asleep, so who the hell was creeping around out there?

Cassie had been seeing a lot of gentlemen callers over the past few days. Ever since her big show, the phone had been ringing off the hook. But the ones I'd met were more like puppy dogs than potential boyfriends or sexual partners. As for showing up here without permission early in the morning . . . no, they weren't pushy like that. Not yet. They wanted more from her than sharing a cup of tea, I was sure, but they didn't dare insist.

Of course, Sandra having an overnight guest wouldn't be anything out of the ordinary.

I stood at the swinging door, my fingertips resting lightly on opposite sides of the doorjamb, paying close attention to every creak of the old house, every sound of gusting wind sweeping across the eaves.

The door started to swing open and I jumped back, heart racing.

When Rickey popped his head in, I was startled but not entirely fazed—maybe I was even a tad relieved. Better than dealing with a complete stranger. What was that old saying? "Better the devil you know than the devil you don't know."

Though his state of undress was, as always, an issue for me. He was wearing the skimpiest shorts and had his thumbs in his pockets, so the waistband pulled low under his chiseled abdominal muscles. He thought he was God's gift to women.

I turned back toward the stove.

Admittedly, as strictly a work of art, Rickey was both physically fit and a fine balance of artistic tattoo composition. What kept me from admiring him any further was the cocky grin plastered across his face.

"Hey, good looking," he said.

I snorted. *Good looking? He couldn't do better than that?* Dealing with Rickey was no way to start my morning.

He leaned against the counter next to me. "I know you like me. I can always tell."

"In this case you are mistaken."

When he moved in for a kiss, I jerked away, my heart racing.

Egotistical, entitled jackass.

"Get the hell off of me."

When he pointedly looked me up and down, I shuddered. He couldn't have missed it. But I was learning that a lot of different people got off on a lot of different things. Maybe disgust was the kind of reaction he wanted. What he craved.

I shook my head and attempted to make my feelings clearer. "I'm hardly awake. I don't want you all over me." I held up my cup to show him, as if the cup explained everything. "And, just to be clear, I like someone else."

He stepped toward me again. Though he wasn't yet close enough to touch, I pushed at the space in front of me like I was pushing him away.

Undaunted, he dropped into one of the benches of the breakfast nook, lounging backward on one arm as he did. Posing for me. Was I supposed to find him irresistible? Had this worked for him in the past?

"We were drawn together from the very first moment. You're exactly my type. Tall and strong, with that narrow little ass." He licked his lips as he said it.

Surely, he was joking. His face was carefully composed into a caricature of sincerity. He was a walking cartoon.

The skeleton side of his tattooed face was his essence. He emanated selfish intentions, mostly sexual in nature. It turned my stomach. Yet there were other times when I could focus on his regular just-human side—when he was acting like a decent guy. He flipped back and forth like that in my mind, like a switch activated by his body language. During Mr. Skeleton moments, like I'd been experiencing since he walked in this morning, I got the creeps.

I made myself look into his eyes. His arrogant stare was infuriating. I needed something to deflate him. "Didn't you just spend the night with Sandra?"

He mugged at me. "Yeah? So?" Still, my bluntness must have caught him by surprise, because he changed the subject. "Ya know, I went to the library the other day." A sly smile lifted the human side of his face. "The big one in Newark."

The kettle screamed.

I had to turn back toward him to grab a teabag, and though my nose was crinkled, he mistook my movement for an opening. He stood and came over to me, so close that we were almost nose

down on the south beach drag

to nose as I dunked my teabag several times in and out of the steaming water.

He stared into my eyes with . . . what? Longing? I heard a peculiar puffing sound. Was he panting?

"You take my breath away," he said, his voice catching on the words.

He released me by shifting his gaze. Clasping his hands behind his back, he sauntered over to look out the window. Shifting his strategy.

"So, what's next for your photography show? For the contest?"

He knew my weak spot, sure enough; I was always willing to talk about my work. "I met an Irish fortune teller named Orlaith. I'm going to track her down."

"That's a great idea. There's a whole group of them around here. They call themselves the Travellers." His voice sounded fake and coaxing. Smooth to the point of oily. "You've got your shots of Georgie, my sideshow friends, my parents' and my headshots." He wasn't fooling me at all by showing interest. He was trying to worm his way into my good graces, and my bed.

"And torso shots," I reminded him. "The first time we met."

Looking pleased that I'd remembered that morning just weeks ago, he moved closer to me again and batted his eyelashes.

I groaned. He was reading way more into my remembrance than I'd intended.

Looming was his specialty—I could feel the heat coming off his body, both frightening and exhausting.

"Yeah, but there's so much more to discover about me than just my midsection and face," he said. He ran the palms of his hands down both sides of his body, starting at his rib cage and finally resting on his butt cheeks. So clearly in love with himself.

"At the library I had an idea as I was going through the art magazines. There was a shot of a guy's backside, lit so I didn't even know what it was at first. He was lying on his side and the

sandy

focus was the curve of his hip. It looked like a marble sculpture."

Rickey had guessed right that this would intrigue me. He was good at reading my artistic interests, I had to give him that. Though I didn't like him hanging around and I prickled at his attempted seduction, I could picture the photograph perfectly. It was so clear I got lost in my thoughts. The texture could be luscious with the right exposure and chemical development.

"Black-and-white photograph?" I asked.

"Yep. But I thought two things about that. First, we've already done the grayscale thing with me. I'd like to do some pictures in color and, if we're going to do it, I want to reveal more of my designs."

"More of your skin, you mean." Because my mind was racing, I pushed away the warning bells that had gone off just seconds ago, though my breath quickened.

The idea of a new shoot gave me a thrill. I had never seen tasteful nudes of tattooed men before, or even read about them. This could be new territory. Something original. By using close-ups, I would avoid falling into the territory of being gratuitous or lewd.

Pushing away my many qualms, I nodded and said, voice squeaking a bit, "I have color film." It felt terribly important to me to get started immediately. Before I changed my mind. Both Sandra and Cassie were in the house. How bad could things get?

I slammed my cup down on the counter. Rickey had already blown into the living room, headed toward my studio lights. I followed after him.

Without a moment's hesitation, he unzipped his shorts and let them drop to the floor.

I stopped dead in my tracks. Paralyzed. I couldn't even draw a breath in.

He turned toward the open window and chortled. "The wind feels good on my dick."

His *tattooed* dick. I was in deep now. Either I committed to this series of photographs completely now or I had to turn and run. There was no in-between.

He put his arms up in the air and swung his penis back and forth with his back arched. As he did so, he became erect.

Now or never. Yes or no. Hell or heaven? The contest. My scholarship. New York. A gallery show. God help me.

His genital area had started out looking like a plant—a shrub perhaps, or something akin to a hosta. But as it grew, it became an apple tree. I was transfixed by the novelty of such a thing.

"Here's my forbidden fruit, Maeve," he teased. "The Garden of Eden. Get it while it's hot."

"Is there a way to make it small again, to capture the change of growth in stages?" Where on earth had I found the nerve to say that? I was shaking, but a sequence of pictures like this could be groundbreaking.

He shot me a wicked grin. "Sure . . . there's a way."

I watched his whole process from behind my lens. I was surprised by how rough he was with himself, but I kept perfectly still. With my camera in front of my face, flanked by my lights and folding equipment table, I was protected.

He talked to me the whole time. "You like it, don't you? I know you want it." He pointed it toward the lens. His tone rather frightened me; it was almost the opposite of loving. Not hate, exactly. Domination?

He asked over and over again, "Do you like this, baby?" But I felt sure he didn't really expect me to answer. Or to like it.

Given the chance, I felt he'd like to jerk me around the way he was doing to his privates. It was in no way appealing. Compelling, yes. The expression on each side of his face. His frenzied movements. The tension in his hunched stance. It was riveting.

The sound of Sandra's steps startled me. By the time she

sandy

entered the room, he had just finished climaxing, though he still held his penis in his trembling hand.

I felt the blood drain from my face.

"What have we here?" she asked.

I felt sheepish, but when I could bring myself to look her way, she seemed amused. She raised her eyebrows at him and made a smooching noise.

I, however, was floored. Literally. I sank to the ground. I hadn't anticipated getting caught in the act. What was there to say, really?

For better or worse, I had started something. Something dark. I hoarsely whispered, "That was . . . very dramatic . . . Can you get ready to start all over again?"

Sandra laughed. "You two are demented." And she went to get herself a cup of coffee.

She's not mad? Or will there be hell to pay later?

Rickey went to the bathroom to wash up and prepare for the next roll of film.

Maybe this photo shoot *was* demented. Maybe I had lost my good sense. But it was a challenge I couldn't walk away from. To capture the Tree of Forbidden Fruit as it grew. I had my zoom lens at the ready, though my hands were shaking.

He stood before me. Through the viewfinder, I looked at his penis from every angle. "How long did it take for the tattoo artist to create this?"

He laughed. "Oh, God. Hours."

I winced. "That must have hurt like hell." Ugh.

"Yep." Hands on his hips, he looked down. The size of him was as close as a real human could get to a comic book superhero. Including that private part. Yet all the energy had gone out of him. It seemed he couldn't summon any more strength. No one had ever appeared more vulnerable to me. I raised my camera and caught the defeated slump of his shoulders, then a close-up of the discouraged look on his face.

down on the south beach drag

I'd learned a little about his Tattooed Man persona when I visited the sideshow tent. Similar to a professional weight lifter, he'd learned to flex isolated muscles of his body. The movement helped the drawings on his skin come alive. It took great focus, that much I could see. Once he started, he was unaware of anything but his sequence of poses.

He must have felt the heat of the lights as I shifted the beams across and up and down his body, for he automatically turned in the direction I wanted him facing.

Down below, he was coming alive again.

From time to time, I would adjust the position of his arm or leg. At one point, I stretched his arms out and closed his fingers over the back of a spindle chair. When I gently pushed him to lean forward, a groan came out of him.

I knelt down on one knee and hurried to capture his phallus from the front. Next, I plopped down on my bottom and scooted around on the ground, dragging a light stand behind me, to the different angles I wanted. It was important to seize the moment.

By the time I was out of film, I was breathless. Rickey looked dazed when I told him I was done.

I, too, had trouble coming back to the here and now. As I pushed myself up from the floor, I heard the shower in the bathroom start up. Only then did I remember that Sandra had come in and watched us intently for a while. I'd heard her breath quickening while she stood there, and the sound had made my pulse surge. It was disorienting to discover she was now gone. I hadn't even noticed her leaving.

Rickey sat in a chair with his head in his hands. His naked ass on the padded fabric seat upset me. What did we do now? How would I get rid of him? I didn't know what he might expect from me after the intensity of what we'd just done.

Sandra had to open Aunt Cookie's office this morning. She'd been working long hours at Katz Real Estate, because Cookie was still in bad shape. The poor woman was stuck in an extensive system of casts that left her pretty much bedridden. Surely, she must be lonely with so much time on her hands. I'd go by and visit her. What a great excuse to get away from Rickey.

"Hey," I said, "I'm going to ride with Sandra to Katz Real Estate. I have to see Cookie. Then I am going to look for the fortune teller. Late afternoon I have to get to work too."

He sat up. "What, you are leaving now?"

I nodded.

His face darkened with undeniable fury. "Okay. Just use me and leave. Nice."

As I packed up my film and wound the cords out of the way, he stood slowly.

Luckily, Sandra came out of the bathroom just then—one towel around her and another wrapped and twisted over her hair. It seemed I was the only person present who found the moment incredibly awkward, with the two of them basically naked.

The phone rang. When she jumped to answer it, Rickey stormed into the kitchen.

Sandra had been given far more responsibility at the business because of Cookie's injuries than she otherwise would. What was a shock was that she was consistently rising to the occasion. Even when home, she was always on the telephone talking to clients.

When she hung up, she shifted gears. The sexual tension that had filled the room moments before was gone. She was no longer a beautiful woman dressed only in a bath towel; she was a businesswoman.

"Maeve! I didn't tell you. It looks like I'm going to close the sale of that big house over in Sea Girt. Their financing came off without a hitch. Can you believe it?" She looked so pretty standing there in the morning sun. So young. I was happy to see her using her talents.

The wash of feeling made me relax for a moment. I turned

away from my equipment and beamed at her. "That's great, Sandra. That place is huge. It's like . . . a mansion. What commission do you make on a place like that?"

She grinned and threw her hands in the air. "*Thirty-five thousand!*" Her towel opened and threatened to fall to the floor as she celebrated; she yelped and grabbed for it.

"Thirty-five?" My mouth fell open. I didn't think my father made that kind of money in a whole year.

"Yeah. I can live on it for a long time. Maybe buy a place of my own." She unwound the towel from her head and used it to dry her hair. "My aunt was right—money is power, and right now I feel supercharged. I've decided I'm staying here at the shore. Why would I go back home?"

Rickey came out of the kitchen with a cup of coffee in hand and headed toward Sandra's room. He shot me a look over his shoulder and pointed at me before closing the door, mouthing, "See *you* later."

chapter 17
backstreets

Orlaith was no longer in the dusty parking lot where I'd first met her. After asking around, I was told she'd moved her wagon to the outskirts of town. I called Georgie and he agreed to drive me out there, but was hesitant to just drop me off.

For some reason, leaving a woman alone in the middle of nowhere didn't seem like a good idea to him.

Orlaith was standing at the bottom of her steps, arms crossed, as if awaiting my arrival. I shook my head with wonder; she'd known I was coming. I pointed her out to Georgie. "She's right there."

He rolled his half-open window down further and leaned on his elbow. "There's a gas station down the road. If you have any trouble, you hustle over there and call me. I'll come back right away."

"I can take care of myself, Georgie, thank you," I said before closing the door firmly. I'd already shot the sideshow entertainers and had a handle on the music scene. Now it was time to talk to Orlaith about penetrating the world of the Irish Travellers. Time was ticking. Though the deadline for the contest was weeks away, there was still so much to do.

I jumped when Georgie hit the steering wheel with the palms of both hands. He didn't like this one bit.

My faced flushed red, but I ignored him and walked away. I

down on the south beach drag

knew he had some kind of date with Cassie, so it was none of his business how I chose to spend my time.

He moved off slowly and crept down a side road. I didn't turn back to check, but something told me he was watching my every move.

As I spanned the fifty yards to Orlaith, her gaze was locked on me. The last time I'd seen her, she'd scared me a bit, but somehow I knew today would go differently. I skipped over to the wagon. She cackled, a wide grin stretched across her face.

When I finally stood before her, she embraced me. After gently rocking me to and fro, she held me at arm's length and stared into my eyes.

"My cousin," she said, her grin settled into a *Mona Lisa* smile.

I reached into my purse and pulled out a wrapped box of chocolates I'd bought at the candy store—the fancy kind that cost a pretty penny. She held the box to her heart and twirled around, making her white skirt flare. It'd been worth the expense.

She motioned for me to follow her into her wagon. She struck a match and lit the flame on a propane camping stove, making a *fwoosh* sound.

The stove hissed when the flame got going, and Orlaith filled a copper kettle and put it on to boil. She prepared her ceramic teapot the way I'd heard they do it in the British Isles: warming the teapot with hot water, then dumping that out and adding tea leaves before again filling the pot to steep the brew.

The earthy smell of tea surrounded us. She patted my hand and murmured, "I love chocolate. But you knew that."

It was true. I did know exactly the kind of candy she would like. But how?

The warmth I felt toward this woman surprised me. I watched the side of her face while she worked; she looked disconcertingly familiar. At our first meeting, she'd indicated that her

backstreets

people were from County Limerick in Ireland and had intuited that mine were as well. Which, of course, they were.

Did we all look similar? Had we been genetically isolated, with the same shade of red hair and the same shape of nose? If I ever ran into another "cousin" from Limerick, would I know them from their ruddy skin and amber-colored eyes? Or was it possible that Orlaith and I really were more closely related than I knew?

A large encampment spread beyond her wagon. There were two other wooden wagons besides hers, and they were equally colorful, but the majority of the people there were living in travel trailers. A few had pitched simple tents.

The sight of it made me itch for an entrée out here among the Travellers. My mission was to photograph disaffected and marginalized people. Who better than them? Their unfamiliar way of life evoked the stuff of fairy tales, and felt rich with possibility.

I sat in a wooden chair at the table. "Orlaith?" I asked.

She held the teapot in one hand, an oil lamp illuminating her face. "Yes, young one." She poured our tea into delicate cups that sat on matching saucers.

"I am here at the shore to take pictures. That's what I'm good at."

I told her about the contest and about the types of subjects I was looking for. In a release of emotion, I found myself telling her that as much as I loved Mom and Pop, they had always thought I was strange. They were trying to put a stop to my work and cut my artistic aspirations short "for my own good," I was sure.

She listened intently, never interrupting or disagreeing with me.

After my outpouring, she took my hand and again locked eyes with me in a way that bored into my soul.

"Those of us with the gift—the vision—cannot be understood by most," she said, stroking my hand. "Only another with the gift can know you as I know you."

A chill of understanding shot through me.

"You must be patient with your parents, Maeve, for you will soar. It's only a matter of time. But before you do, they will fight you. They fight because they simply fear all they don't understand. All the warnings that have been told to them—it is a terrible burden to fear for a child. A daughter most of all."

This was a revelation. She was spot-on that they'd always been afraid—always correcting me, making me feel like a bad person. When I got straight A's in first grade, Mom said, "You need to go out more and play with the other children." I was too driven, too intense, they told me. They criticized me for the hours I spent studying old magazines and movies. When I talked my mother into bringing me to the library, she always tried to steer me away from the art section.

She also admonished my creepy eyes, the way I dressed, even how I walked. Her summation was that I would never attract a man. It hurt that she didn't understand—I didn't want to.

I said none of this, only nodded at Orlaith and sipped my tea. On a tiny and heartbreakingly fragile plate of bone china, she served me one of the chocolates from the box I'd brought. The buttery flavor of caramel filled my senses when I bit into it. When had I last felt this relaxed?

We sat comfortably in silence until Orlaith was ready to continue.

"I can't go to the Travellers and just ask if you can take their pictures," she said finally. "They will want to know what you are seeking in these pictures, what you want."

What I want? The answer rose to my lips before I was aware that I was speaking. "You are all *Travellers*, Orlaith. Please tell them I yearn to know why."

She tilted her head. "Why?! We were born so."

"I want to see the beauty in your life. Surely, it would be easier for all of you to settle someplace; so there must be some reward in constantly moving on. Can you show me the meaning of your . . . nomadic . . . life?"

backstreets

Orlaith quieted. She took a bite of her chocolate and closed her eyes. It seemed she was in a trance. I'd never seen anyone savor a morsel that way, like pleasure was a sacrament.

After a few silent seconds, she opened her eyes, smiled, and winked at me.

I knew for certain she would help.

As luck would have it, the Travellers were planning a wedding. Orlaith, God love her, decided to try to set me up to do the photographs. Of course they wanted pictures of the big event, and I very much wanted to take them. It would be a mutually beneficial arrangement.

Within an hour we were meeting with the bride's and groom's parents at a picnic table under a wooden pavilion at the center of the encampment. The weather had turned since my arrival and rain pelted the metal roof, creating a soothing sound. Barbecued ribs sizzled on an outdoor fireplace constructed from large river stones. I hadn't eaten breakfast, and the saucy aroma gave my stomach pangs. By the time they made up their minds about me, I'd be mad with hunger.

It quickly became clear that Orlaith was something special around here. The Travellers were Catholic, so it wasn't that they treated her like a holy woman, exactly. They had nuns and priests for that. Was she a shaman of some sort? Or perhaps an oracle, because she knew how to read the future? I was still figuring it out, but I knew one thing: whenever she opened her mouth to speak, everyone leaned forward.

They asked Orlaith a question in Shelta, their native language, and waited. She turned to me and in English asked, "How much will it cost?"

"I did a wedding four months ago. I'll charge half as much as I did for that one—eighty dollars—but they'll have to pay for

down on the south beach drag

the prints themselves. There's a good lab in town that can make contact sheets for us. Like this one." I pulled one out of my bag to show them what it looked like. "See? You get this, then pick what you want to make into a full-size print."

A rumbling conversation ensued, and Orlaith raised her voice as they went back and forth.

Many Americans believe everyone speaks English in Ireland, but they also have some faint notion of what they call "Gaelic" expressions, which are seasonally hauled out for St. Patrick's Day. The truth is there are many, my grandparents included, whose first language was Irish. Shelta was derived mostly from the Irish language, but with some English words tossed into the mix as well. I was delighted to realize I could make out some of the discussion, if I listened closely enough. Orlaith said if you really studied it, you would find a little Hebrew and Greek in there too.

"So, only black-and-white pictures?" Orlaith asked. "Can you do color?"

"Yes, I can do color. The important portraits should be black-and-white, though." It was a strong opinion of mine.

More rumbling. It took time for them to simmer down.

My head jerked up. I wasn't good at sitting around with nothing to do. Had I dozed off? They were all staring at me. Apparently Orlaith had asked me something and I'd missed it. She cleared her throat. "They want to know, are you willing to get acquainted with us before the wedding takes place?"

"Ah. That's ideal, really. How would it work?" I was suddenly wide awake.

Orlaith smoothed her skirt, folded her hands together, and looked down at them before she spoke. "I will schedule some visits."

The other four adults murmured their approval. Orlaith nodded as she made eye contact with each parent in turn, receiving and acknowledging their consent.

backstreets

"You can share a cup of tea with them and read letters aloud to them if they wish. You see, when the families return to camp from their journeys, there's usually mail waiting."

Before I could even get my question out, she answered it for me.

"Being on the road so much, not everyone can read. Some can, but many not well. It would be a service that would be much appreciated."

"Can I bring a camera?" Orlaith repeated my question to the others, though I was pretty sure they understood me perfectly. Or had she said something else? Another discussion began.

"If you are always behind the camera, they can't get to know you," Orlaith said carefully. "Surely the knowledge goes both ways. Won't your pictures be better if you understand your . . . your . . ."

"Subjects?" I filled in.

She nodded at me with a smile. The entire group nodded and smiled too.

The bride's mother explained something to Orlaith at length, then Orlaith translated: "In these early days, she will want to know why you stop to take a picture. Since the marriage is arranged, for instance, you may want to photograph a shy scene as the young couple gets to know each other. She says it would help if you explain the thoughts behind your process—the why of it is important to us."

I grinned broadly. The *why* of it. Had anything ever made more sense? It was how I lived my entire life.

chapter 18
the sword swallower's blade

I went to both families' trailers that Thursday and Saturday morning. I read to them. I sipped tea. Played with the children. With permission, I began to collect some shots. It wasn't yet clear to me what these photographs would contribute to my portfolio, or if I would submit any to the contest, but I knew the entire experience was unique. And unique was what I lived for.

During three full days the following week they allowed me to be involved in the wedding preparations. The shots I took filled all my senses: Musicians practicing Celtic instruments. Yards of sequined fabric for the full skirts of the dresses. Barbecue marinating. An ornate cross of heavy gold that would be the groom's gift to his bride. Now the pictures were starting to form a separate collection in my mind.

The Select Six was so limiting. What on earth would I leave out? It was a good problem to have, but led me to more questions. When I got home, I would have to start printing, then lay all the pictures out and make some hard decisions.

How much film should I buy for the wedding celebration? Travellers were coming from all over the East Coast. The O'Hara clan, the bride's family, was renowned in their world, like royalty.

One colorful character after another arrived in their caravans.

the sword swallower's blade

The piles of gifts grew bigger by the day, each offering more grandiose than the last.

Then Seamus Gallagher showed up and eclipsed most of the others—in my eyes, anyway. Seamus and Orlaith were very close; he was a friend of her late father. He wore a felt hat decorated with a long eagle feather, which he claimed to have pulled out during a wrestling match with the giant bird that he described in great detail. As he told it, he'd been camping in Yellowstone National Park and the bird had wanted the fish he'd just caught. Seamus was not about to share.

He squired me and Orlaith around like we were his daughters, and when the music started up at night, he danced with us. He cooked countless meals over the campfire, introduced me to all the recent arrivals, and made quiet suggestions as to photographs I might want to take.

I raced around, trying to capture all the vignettes created by each camper.

One night, exhausted and a bit drunk, I dragged my sleeping bag under Orlaith's wagon and slept there. When I awoke, she was outside frying eggs and bacon on her camping stove.

"There's coffee on the fire," she said.

"Thanks, I need it." I rubbed my temples.

She giggled. "Nothing wrong with having some fun. Fun is our purpose here. Will you come and see me again soon, young one?"

"Yes, of course—but I've got another idea too. Why don't you come out with me one night? Let's go hear some music. Give you a chance to meet some new people. Get your name out there." The coffee made a gurgling sound as I poured it into my cup. I took a moment to savor the aroma.

"Most people don't believe in my gift," she said. "If they do believe, it frightens them."

"All I know is, there are some people on TV who claim to be clairvoyants, and I get the feeling they aren't anywhere near you in terms of ability. I think about the day I showed up here—you were waiting for me."

"Yes. I'd had a dream. It often happens that way." Her upturned face had a lidded look of satisfaction.

I shook my head in wonder. "You like what you do."

"Many's the time I do good, stave off evil doings."

I nodded. "Just come out with me once. Let's see what happens."

The next time Georgie showed up at our apartment, he had coffee, Danish, and jelly doughnuts. We'd both been up late the night before, so ten thirty seemed like the right time for a little breakfast. He insisted we sit in one of the porch swings.

"Where's Cassie?" he asked. The question disappointed me.

"I don't know." I sniffed. "She didn't come home last night."

We scooted our butts into the deep seats and crossed our legs under us. A lazy sun was rising higher in the sky, illuminating every summer bloom. Petunias, geraniums, lilies of every hue. The fragrance of rugosa bushes drifted to us. Morning dew still glistened in the shaded gardens, making red and white impatiens shine. Best of all, the porch was still cool and overhung with inscrutable shadows. I wasn't sure we could even be seen from the street at this time of day.

I put a hand on Georgie's arm to silence him when I saw Father Murphy walking Paddy down the street. In his long black habit, he cut an imposing figure. He was dressed for high Mass, a zucchetto covering his head. Perhaps there'd been a funeral, or would be soon. He must have left for a break to take the dog for a quick stroll. He went right by, totally unaware we were there.

We were silent till he was a block away. I just didn't want to get into the whole "Good morning, Father" thing. I wanted to focus all my attention on Georgie instead.

"How'd the show go last night?" I asked.

"It was okay." He shrugged. "I guess I've done it enough—it just comes automatically. But I really hated to leave you guys at the Osprey just to go to the Hootch."

To leave me. He hated to leave me. I would always rather be with Georgie than without him. Dare I hope he felt the same way?

"How did Cassie do?" he asked.

Cassie again. As quickly as my hopes had risen, they were dashed.

After she sang at open mic night, Cassie and I had gone to The Upstage, an after-hours club where she could have a crack at singing before a different kind of audience. I licked pastry sugar from my fingers and took a sip of coffee. "You wouldn't believe it. She sang her heart out. The audience was all musicians. You'd think they would be a tough crowd, but they loved it. Does anyone besides performers ever go there?"

"Yeah, some. But you have to kind of know about it. All the players like to go after their gigs. It's a great place to try stuff out and show off for each other."

My fingertips were again coated in white. I sucked on one at a time. He was doing the same. "The pictures I got were something. Everyone was there."

"Except me. I missed out."

"It's hard to believe Cassie's the same little girl I grew up with. We had a great time. But then Rickey showed up and—"

"Ugh," Georgie interrupted loudly.

"What?"

"I told you—Rickey thinks he's your boyfriend."

I squinted at him and got close to his face. "He does not. I took his picture. That's it." I didn't want to talk about Rickey. "A couple of us sang backup for Cassie again. It seems to give her the confidence she needs. She was just awesome. Seriously."

down on the south beach drag

I ripped off a piece of my lemon Danish and offered it to Georgie. Fed it to him. "You got a speck of lemon on you," I said, then kissed it off the corner of his mouth.

Now what was I doing? I'd been blaming my newfound boldness in the evenings on having drinks, but apparently this was the new me. The shore me.

"Wait a minute," he said when I pulled back. "Is this really such a good idea?"

"Why the hell not? If you tell me you're in love with Cassie, I'll be sick. You and every other guy she meets."

"It's not that. I just don't know about starting something right now."

When I laughed, the sound of my voice was deep. Husky. Desire swept through me. I pulled a corner of his shirt up out of his waistband and slid my hand onto his naked skin. A groan escaped me.

His eyes went smoky. He was aroused too.

He jumped up and put his breakfast on a side table, took mine from me and did the same, then pulled me behind the wisteria arbor. Draping purple blossoms hid us from passersby on the sidewalk; we were swathed in their sweet scent. As he gathered me in his arms, our eyes interlocked. I was so happy that I would have my first real kiss here. A memory to treasure.

When our lips met, everything but Georgie disappeared. I was lost in him. His gossamer skin. The sweet taste of him. All the blood in my body seemed to rush to my lower half. A pressure grew. I longed to be released from this exquisite agony, but I could have gone on kissing him forever too.

"Shit! God damn you, Maeve."

We jolted apart. While we couldn't be seen from the front of the house, anyone walking to our back entrance had a clear view. There stood Rickey. Fists clenched, muscular. Giant in his fury.

the sword swallower's blade

"You squirrely little dude," he shrieked. "What are you doing with Maeve? I thought you were after Cassie."

I jumped in. "And I thought you were screwing Sandra." How dare he interrupt. "Who do you think you are?"

"We're just having our breakfast here," Georgie said. "Nobody wants any trouble."

Rickey's chin was quivering in an alarming way. His eyes bugging out of his head. He spoke directly to Georgie. "You think you're man enough for her? You're not. Maeve and me? We've just started. She's just young—she doesn't know what she wants yet."

"I know enough to know it's not you," I snarled.

He stared down at me. "Did you tell Mr. Wonderful here about the pictures?" he shouted. "The ones where I'm naked as a jaybird? Just you and me and your camera? It was great, Georgie boy. Really great. I got off like you wouldn't believe. Maeve's no prude, believe me."

What a gut punch. Fear made me break into a cold sweat. Then silence.

A voice from the sidewalk startled all of us. "Is everything all right?"

Father Murphy. He scanned from Georgie to me to Rickey. "You're the young man that was coming up the stairs as I was leaving the other night, am I right? A photo subject?"

If it was possible, Rickey puffed up to an even larger size. "So?"

"These two young people happen to be my parishioners. I've known them since they were children." Father's stance was rigid, cautious.

Rickey never knew when to shut up. "What's your point, *holy man*?"

As if on cue, a police cruiser turned the corner. Father signaled it over. Tires crunching gravel, tar fumes rising with the warming sun, it pulled up beside him.

down on the south beach drag

The car was hardly in Park before the driver jumped out. "What's going on, Father Murphy?"

"Officer Diaz, so good to see you. In the nick of time too. Could you please escort . . . I'm sorry, I didn't get your name . . ."

Diaz put a hand on his holster. "Rickey. Rickey Travers. We've met before. Plenty of times. Looks like it's time to move on, Travers."

Father came up the front stoop and beckoned to me. "Let's go upstairs, Maeve. Georgie? Will you join us, please?"

I set the kettle to boil in the kitchen. We sat at the table and gave Father the basic story of how Rickey came to think of me as his girlfriend. I left out plenty. Especially the part about me photographing him in the nude.

Georgie was aloof. He didn't meet my eyes.

I could tell Father wasn't wholly satisfied with my story, but thankfully the life of a priest is a busy one, and he had to leave shortly for a meeting. Georgie followed him out.

Days passed with no word from Georgie. I held my breath walking to church that Sunday. Prayed he would be there. He hadn't called. I'd left a message for him, but he hadn't phoned me back.

What Rickey'd said had sounded pretty bad. I'd known going that far with him was a bad idea, but I'd gone ahead with those shots anyway. It was a stupid mistake. But maybe the photos would be worth it.

When I entered the church, I dipped my fingers in the holy water and made the sign of the cross. Perhaps it could clean the sin away.

I knelt and put my forehead on crossed hands.

Holy Mary. Mother of God. Pray for us sinners . . . show me the way, please. The real way. What is God's will for me? He made me like this. He knows who I truly am. Will I ever be smart enough to figure

the sword swallower's blade

my path out? Will I be strong enough to do what he requires of me?

Georgie came down the aisle with his mother and father. They had one of the reserved seats in the rows close to the pulpit. He glanced my way and waved, polite but far from warm.

Waiting to say goodbye to Father Murphy, we wound up fairly close together in the receiving line.

"Hey, Maeve," he called to me casually.

His mother went on her tiptoes and whispered in his ear. He bridled and I heard him hiss, "Mom, stop. She's just a friend."

The steamy shower that night felt divine. As hot water pummeled the back of my neck, for the first time in a long while, I exhaled fully. I'd splurged on a bar of Yardley's Old-Fashioned Lavender Soap. Showering was a whole to-do now that I was eighteen, including shaving my legs every day because I couldn't stand the feel of stubble on my calves when I got into bed at night. Washing and conditioning my long hair was now part of my daily routine too.

The amount of work a woman had to put in just to be presentable to the world was unfair. I'd considered cutting my hair really short, in a pixie. Cassie and Sandra had nixed the idea, but had a stream of other things for me to try: Eyeliners and perfumes. Jaunty caps and accent belts. Platform shoes and pleated skirts. The suggestions never ended. And they always cost too much money and more of my time.

Cassie had taken to using an eyelash curler after she applied her last coat of mascara. She used three different layers as a rule. Excessive, it seemed to me. The day she talked me into trying the damn thing, it clamped down on my lashes and wouldn't let go. I'd ripped out some of the follicles by the roots by the time I finally released myself.

I did like the scent of this fancy soap, though. One luxury that was worth it.

down on the south beach drag

When the shower curtain flew open, I screamed.

A naked Rickey climbed in with me. He must have picked the bathroom lock. A furious banshee couldn't have made a louder wailing than the sound that was coming out of me.

My rasping breath was hard to draw in. Tremors shot through my body. Pure reflex made me push him with all my might. Luckily, I caught him unprepared, and top-heavy as he was, he toppled right over backward, over the side of the old claw-foot tub as it caught him across his upper calves.

The curtains and oval rod went with him as he plummeted, and the metal piping hit me in the back of the head. I grabbed onto a towel rack to steady myself.

Cassie burst through the door and stopped dead at the sight of me: completely exposed, bleeding, and shouting obscenities at Rickey. In the middle of all this chaos, Georgie showed up. In what seemed like a microsecond, Cassie produced a big towel and wrapped it around me while Georgie fished Rickey out of the wreckage. Though he was a much slighter man, he put Rickey in an arm hold that rendered him helpless.

Rickey's face was bleeding profusely. He looked like a dangling puppet in Georgie's grasp. Good, he was hurt too.

Georgie must have been a wrestler in high school. Or taken lessons in self-defense. He definitely knew what he was doing.

I recovered enough to turn the water off, though everyone was already soaked.

Georgie growled, "Listen, buddy. This girl doesn't want you. Get the fuck over it."

Sandra appeared in the doorway. As her eyes swept the room, she looked disgusted by all of us. She stared hard at Rickey, having assessed that he was the wrongdoer. "Fuck you, Rickey. You're always the loose cannon."

The sound of her voice shattered something inside of me. I was shaking. It was as if I were watching somebody else when the

the sword swallower's blade

sobs wrenched out of me. Cassie climbed into the tub and put her arms around me.

When she started to cry, too, Georgie lost it. "That's it! You're not welcome around here anymore, bub. I'm going to have to worry about all these girls now, because you are out of your mind. You think you're such a Don Juan? You think you can just pick any girl you want any time you feel like it?"

He dragged Rickey backward out of the room. Sandra jumped out of his way as the boys struggled.

As Georgie slid Rickey toward the front door, he warned him, "You come back here again, you better believe I'm gonna be waiting for you. You might want to ask around and find out who I am, Tattoo Man. Bello is my last name, okay? Georgie Bello. B-E-L-L-O."

Rickey got the picture. "All right, all right. Let me go. I'll walk out. Don't want that kind of trouble."

Scratch the surface of a bully and you will always find a coward.

But Georgie wasn't having it. He opened the door and shoved Rickey right down the stairs.

Sandra clutched at her silk robe. She looked upset—flustered, even. "All right," she said. "Fine. I'll tell him he can't come back. But Maeve's not having any more of her freak friends over either."

"I've still got pictures to take . . ." I protested weakly.

Sandra spat on the ground. "Everyone's sick of your pictures. Your pictures are what got us into this mess. No more photographs in this house." She turned on her heel and slammed her bedroom door behind her.

chapter 19
rosalita

The next morning, I turned to Cassie for support, hoping she'd help me change Sandra's mind.

Instead, she shrugged. "I'm tired of all this too. Why does everyone you hang out with have to be . . . All these characters you've brought home to photograph? Every single day around here is about you and your photography contest. Can you find just one normal person to bring over?"

My head lurched up. "I thought you liked them."

"They're . . . nice. They've all been nice to me. It's just . . ."

My head was pounding. I knew I would hate what she was about to say. "Just what?"

"Come on. Nobody thinks of them as regular people. Georgie must know that's true."

I pressed the palm of one hand to my heart. Thank God Georgie wasn't here to hear what Cassie'd just said. Yes, I wanted his infatuation with her to end, but not at the cost of his tender feelings. In fact, I realized, I'd do most anything to keep him from being hurt.

Sandra came into the hallway with her nose crinkled, like she smelled something bad. She'd overheard the conversation. "What did you expect, Maeve? You got Rickey naked and photographed him like he was some kind of God. I'm sure any guy would be turned on."

rosalita

"But what about you? He wants to cheat on you—with me." I was pretty sure that what Rickey had done to me in the shower was illegal, but I was hesitant to report him. If I exposed myself in that way, my father would come in a heartbeat to take me home. All our goings-on here at the apartment were private, and it was important they be kept that way. As supportive as my father was, I was his only daughter. He expected me to be asexual until I got married to the right man. I not only had to avoid impropriety, I had to avoid even the appearance of such a thing. Sex was only allowed when I wanted to have children. It was what the church *and* my father expected from me.

"If you were thinking about *me*, you probably wouldn't have started this whole thing," Sandra said, tugging on a skirt and high heels. "I mean, you are the one who got what she wanted. You asked him to take his clothes off and you got your precious photographs. By the way, it would have been nice if you'd asked me, 'Hey, Sandra, do you mind if I ask your boyfriend to take his pants off and get hard in front of me?'" She primped in the mirror one last time, then headed for the door. "I'm in a hurry," she called over her shoulder. "I've got a house to show in twenty minutes."

I stood there, my hands dangling at my sides, feeling like an idiot. How had I gotten myself into this mess? More importantly, how was I going to get out of it?

I trailed Cassie into the kitchen. She sat down at the table and put her coffee down. "This is a tough one. I'd love to tell you that you didn't do anything wrong, but honestly, if you're going to play with fire, sometimes you're gonna get burned, Maeve." She scowled as she took a sip, and made a great gulping sound when she swallowed.

"You are not saying I should have done it with him?" I blurted.

"No—geez. Sex is supposed to be fun. But I think you could have let the guy down easier."

down on the south beach drag

I was indignant. "He scared me."

"It doesn't mean anything. If he wanted to actually hurt you, he would have done it. Guys are just immature. They don't know what to do with their feelings, so they do stupid things."

"Not all guys," said Georgie, who had just appeared through the swinging door wearing a black straw fedora with a short brim pushed up all the way around. So cute.

I widened my eyes at him to let him know I disagreed with what Cassie was saying.

"You don't get it," I said. "I really thought he might rape me."

Cassie leaned toward me and looked me straight in the eye. "Maybe you should work on your reaction. If you don't react, he'll probably stop acting like a jerk."

That had been Mom's answer to everything when I was growing up. Stop reacting. Just ignore it. A strategy I'd never known to work. "Cassie, you know perfectly well that getting rid of Rickey isn't going to be that easy."

Georgie looked out the window and asked, "What's *this* now?"

A police cruiser had pulled up to the curb with Father Murphy sitting in the passenger seat. My stomach lurched when Pop climbed out from the driver's side.

The intensity of his stare bridged the two floors between us. *Oh, no.*

"Maeve Margaret."

"Dad."

"Cassie." Pop nodded and tipped his hat to her.

"Hi, Mr. O'Connor." Cassie sounded impossibly young. Innocent. Like nothing at all could be going on. She might make a great actress as well as a singer.

He put his hat under his arm and strode in, his expression far from kindhearted.

I felt the ground giving way. With legs shaking, I plopped down into a rocking chair.

Pop was midway into the room when he saw Georgie and asked, "And who is this?"

"Georgie. My friend." Social convention seemed irrelevant at the moment, yet it was ingrained into me. "Georgie, this is my father, Malachi O'Connor."

"Sir." Georgie grabbed his fedora off his head, but looked pretty calm considering.

"Georgie . . . ?" Pop was fishing for his last name. It was his habit. He always wanted to know if he was speaking to another Irishman.

"Georgie Bello."

My father was clearly taken aback. "Bello. Mafia-type Bello?"

"My grandfather was a businessman. He's retired now." Georgie was bright red.

Pop hitched up his holster. I'd never seen him look taller. "He served time. Ten years."

"Eight and a half," Georgie corrected. "The papers always exaggerate things."

Georgie had once mentioned his grandfather, implying the family had power. But organized crime? Maybe I didn't want to know. Had I deliberately avoided putting two and two together?

Pop looked Georgie over. "And what are you? Some kind of male impersonator?"

Father Murphy jumped in. "I'm afraid you don't understand the entire story, Malachi."

The disgust on my father's face upset me. This wasn't the man I was used to. He looked at Georgie with what could only be described as hatred. Yet he didn't even know him. How could he hate him?

He was staring at me now, though he spoke to the others. "You'll excuse us. I'll be needing to speak to my daughter alone."

down on the south beach drag

They did what he asked. All filed into the living room, leaving the kitchen door swinging behind them.

The kettle shrieked. At the kitchen table, a fierce argument ensued between my father and me.

"My daughter, the light of my life, is not a whore. Or a lesbian. Or someone who would fall for the likes of him. Her. Whatever abomination it is."

"Stop acting like I'm some kind of delinquent. And you, all high and mighty, Mr. Policeman who gets to decide what's right and what's wrong. I don't want to be your enemy."

"Then stop acting like one."

A knot grew in my stomach. "What are you saying, Pop? I have a right to pick my friends, you know. Sorry they're not all up to your very particular standards. But you know what? I learned a few things since I've been away. You and Mom always act like everybody's supposed to be the same. Like there's some giant set of rules in the sky that say you have to conform to your, your . . . suburban . . . *masquerade*. I've figured out that plenty of people don't exactly match up to what you've taught me. Married? A bunch of kids? Not everyone's dream, Pop. In fact, for some of us, the very idea is a nightmare."

Back and forth we went. He was dismissive. Dictatorial. Rigid. I was angry, disputing his judgments, disappointed with his narrow views. And he didn't even know the half of it—about how far things had gone with Rickey.

"I've got a nice place to stay and a good job, I'm living with Cassie and Sandra, I'm going to Mass on Sundays . . . everything we talked about. I don't know why you're so bent out of shape."

"Let's just say I've been hearing some things and I have a bad feeling about it," Pop growled. "That tattoo guy has a record."

He has a record? That was all the ammunition Pop had? Clearly, he didn't know about the attack. The fact I knew Rickey was not enough for him to make me close up shop here.

He muttered. "You're better off among your own people."

"Georgie's mother is Irish. She's a Donovan from Tipperary."

He waved his hand in the air. "Ack. That's so far north, she—"

"She doesn't count?" I cut him off. "That's what you're saying? So far north she doesn't matter? Who died and made you king? You sit here and decide who's important and who isn't? Most of it hinges on being from Ireland. A country you've never even been to."

He flashed those green eyes at me. "You know what I mean."

My face had to be red as a fire hydrant. "I *don't* know what you mean. What about Mr. Katz? He's not one of us. How does he get to be your best friend? I could tell you plenty about that family. I've come to think our whole town just agrees to pretend to be some scripted brand of normal. I bet everyone has their own dirty secrets."

He didn't answer. He looked at the floor. Gotcha, Pop. Lots and lots of secrets.

We were getting nowhere. Both of us needed a strategy to save face and walk away. I had an idea. "Dad, I'm the only bookkeeper for two restaurants now. I gave my word I'd be here till the end of the summer."

Though he pouted at his steaming mug, I could tell this last statement had gotten through to him—he was a stickler for a strong work ethic. "Some brochures came while you've been gone, from the Junior College," he said. "It turns out, they have a bookkeeping program." He sat up straighter. A hopeful smile suddenly beamed my way. There was relief in it.

I didn't get it. I shook my head. "But you and Mom said nursing or teaching."

He smiled wider, so pleased with himself. "Maybe we can talk about it. Seems like another good option to me. You're already getting experience—it would look good on the application. And one day you could do my taxes. You know how I hate it. Every April I go mad."

down on the south beach drag

"I guess that might be okay as a backup plan," I said slowly.

This is how it was reluctantly agreed that he would tell Mom about my job and make the case that I couldn't leave the shore just yet. He was dejected, hat in hand, as I walked him to the front door. But he rallied to make a parting comment. A little jab, just to regain some sense of control.

"If I get another bad report, if Father Murphy tells me you're taking pictures of any more weirdos, I'm sending your mother down," he said. "You can deal with her yourself."

chapter 20
fireworks over little eden

We'd all taken to going to the Osprey every Thursday night, hitting the diner, and then The Upstage after hours. Even Orlaith came. I'd gotten permission for her to set up a card table and tell fortunes on the patio, where people often stepped out to have a smoke. She enjoyed the music and the patrons loved her. She made good money, and many couples started dating based on her prediction that they would have fun together.

The house band had asked Cassie to come to a rehearsal so they could work up a full set for tonight, featuring her as lead vocalist. She was thrilled. The audience was already packed—rumor had it, Springsteen was coming to test out a new song. They said he was going to sign up for open mic during the second set, just like everyone else. People were excited. But rumors like this often were just that. Rumors.

When I arrived about nine o'clock, a cacophony of discordant sounds greeted me. The musicians and Cassie were tuning up. Georgie stood at the bar. I headed toward him and discovered a scotch and soda waiting for me.

He clinked the rim of his glass with mine.

For sound check, the band opened with a killer rendition of an old Chuck Berry song. They'd taught Cassie and me that you have to "start strong and finish strong" when you create a set of music.

When I really thought about it, the same was true for any kind of performance or show. If I were to ever have a book of my photographs published, I would also want to start strong and finish strong. The idea sent me into a daydream of possibilities, but also made me think about my original purpose for coming to Asbury Park. I felt for the cameras I had hanging off both my shoulders. My treasures.

I don't know how long I was staring into space before I realized someone was waving at me. I groaned and leaned way over to whisper in Georgie's ear, "That's Cassie's ex-boyfriend."

"What!"

"Her ex-boyfriend."

"Where?" It seemed horribly rude to point at Bobby. Though I didn't really like him, I'd known him since I was fourteen, and some kind of loyalty I wasn't expecting to feel still prevailed.

Out of the side of my mouth, I said, "The guy in the tan shirt."

I took a sip from my drink. When I shifted my gaze back to where Bobby had been standing, he was gone.

I motioned to Georgie to move closer to the stage. I had my drink in one hand and was clutching my camera straps with the other. The "press pass" Cassie had made for me hung around my neck. The crowd separated and let me slide by. I set my drink down behind the guitar amplifiers and stood on the floor behind the platform, covertly surveying the room through the musicians' legs.

Cassie was in the middle of a song. She'd told me many times that when she was concentrating on the meaning of lyrics, she tuned everything else out.

Off stage left, Bobby was rooted. He was staring at her, entranced, and though he was most certainly unaware of it, Georgie was close behind him. Cassie stepped back when Gary, the

fireworks over little eden

lead guitarist, started his solo. She came over to me and picked up her glass of water.

I jerked my thumb to my left, and she looked back behind the stage where I stood. I shook my head and pointed out toward the audience. I couldn't see her reaction now, as she was facing away from me. But when she went back to the microphone stand and picked the verse back up, she was right on cue.

If anything, she sang her heart out more than ever. Her tone was powerful and confident. I moved to the side of the stage to photograph her in profile. A light with a red gelatin filter beamed directly down on her. She was awash in the intense color.

I focused my lens. *Click.* A big, stupid smile crept across my face and wouldn't let go. The muscles of my cheeks ached a little from the effort. *Click, click.* The sheer joy in her performance was spellbinding. When she pranced across the stage in between the next two verses, everyone burst into applause.

I melded into the audience and continued to snap pictures while I was dancing. Many of the men in the audience were taller than I was. I held my arms up high, camera in hand, and prayed I could capture the view of the stage that shone through the shadows of the other partiers. It was sure to be a cool effect.

Orlaith joined me on the dance floor, and we got lost in the music. Totally gone, till the last note of the last song. Cassie held us in the palm of her hand. When the set finished, she stepped down to hug all of us.

Sandra had developed a thing for Boom, aka Ernest, the house band's drummer. She whispered, "Boom and I were going to go back to our place. Springsteen's not going to show up; I don't know how these rumors get started. But now that Bobby's here, I won't leave if you think you'll need my help."

I pulled her closer to me. "You know Boom is married."

She expelled a puff of air. "*He* is. I'm not. Don't get your panties in a twist. I'll hang out for a while and see what goes on here with Cassie. Bobby's gained a lot of weight, hasn't he?"

I glanced his way. It was true. He had.

He'd been watching us, and when he caught us looking his way, he came toward us.

Before he reached us, Cassie surprised me by turning on her heel and getting back up onstage. She began packing up her guitar and microphone—leaving Bobby with Sandra and me.

"*That's* your boyfriend?" the band's guitarist, Gary, commented just loudly enough for us all to hear. "He's just a fat ex-jock."

Cassie threw back her head in an exaggerated laugh and tossed the length of her honey-blonde hair. There was still a crowd gathered, and heads turned.

I actually felt a little bad for Bobby as he stood there glowering. She was making him sweat this moment out. He deserved it, of course. Yet I found myself taking pity on him.

When Georgie came to stand in the exact spot where Cassie had been moments before, I got nervous. He didn't say a word, just watched Bobby carefully, like he was trying to come to a decision. His "I come in peace" gesture silenced the nearby crowd. You could have heard a pin drop as he nodded at Bobby and announced, "I'm going to take the girls out for breakfast now."

Bobby winced. "Breakfast? It's one o'clock in the morning."

Georgie's chuckle was menacing. "Exactly. Too late for dinner. It's what we like to do. Right, Maeve? It's our thing."

"Yep. It's our thing." I sounded improbably peppy.

Just then, the last-call lights flipped on, stripping the club of any charm it'd had. Ashtrays full of cigarettes littered every table, as did the smudged glasses of hundreds of dead cocktails.

Bobby pretty much ignored Georgie and turned my way. "But I haven't had a chance to catch up with you guys."

It was interesting he was suddenly including me in his little reunion. "Us *guys*?"

fireworks over little eden

"Uh . . . you girls. I haven't seen you in months."

"Cassie hasn't seen or *heard* from you in months," I shot back. "Things have changed, Bobby. She had a rough time when you left, but she's doing much better now. Despite you."

"I know I went a little nuts." He put his hands in his pockets. "I guess I could have handled things better."

I stared at him. "You sure could have."

Cassie still had her back to us; she was fussing with the guitar picks and extra sets of strings in a compartment in her guitar case. Ignoring Bobby was the opposite of what I'd expected from her. I'd thought if she ever had the chance to be near him again, she'd practically swoon. Maybe she was uncomfortable that her new world and old life were colliding. Could it be that she was actually done with Bobby and hoping he would move on? I thought at the very least she would be curious about him.

Though he was staring up at her dazzling backside, Bobby spoke directly to me. "You guys . . . uh . . . girls all staying together around here? You got a phone number?"

Sandra had been waiting for a moment like this. "If you want her number, you can ask her yourself." She sounded angry.

When Bobby said, "Okay, I will," she humphed away with a flip of her lustrous black hair. Leaving me alone with him and Georgie.

Thanks, Sandra.

Cassie was close enough to hear everything that had happened, yet she ignored us and loudly called to some of the band members, "So, we're going to rehearse on Monday? I want to work on that Derek and the Dominos song." She laughed brightly in their direction as she snapped the latches on her case shut.

I heard Bobby let out a soft whistle. His fists hung down by his sides, clearly clenched. He groaned as he stepped up on the stage platform, as though his legs were really heavy.

Georgie's eyes shifted and his lips pursed out. The rest of him seemed to go quiet in a way that put me on high alert. I reached out and laid a hand on one arm to make sure he didn't do anything impulsive. Or crazy.

I whispered in his ear, "In the end, it's her choice. We'd all like to keep her from getting sucked back into the whole Bobby thing, believe me . . . but she'll only be ready to walk away when *she's* ready."

He pressed his lips together and nodded slightly, though his eyes never left Cassie. His intensity was exhausting. As was a creeping sensation I tried to name. Was it once again envy? My new green friend?

Cassie didn't glance at Bobby at all as he hovered near her, not even a casual peek in his direction.

Please let that mean something, I prayed silently.

She pulled her shoulders back, held her head high, and moved away from him. Her impressive hard-body guitar case might as well have been a scepter of royalty. She was a queen, and she making damn sure Bobby knew it.

"I'm ready," she said. "Let's go eat."

As we all swept out of the bar and into Georgie's car, she never looked back.

chapter 21
incident on 57th street

A new show, a Broadway extravaganza, was debuting at the Hootch. I was vibrating with excitement. Georgie had convinced his boss to let me position my cameras on tripods at the back of the stage.

Ever since Rickey told Georgie about the naked photos I'd taken, there'd been no more kissing between us. He remained a fixture in my life, though. As far as my photography went, he was still my champion. My sweet friend. A protector. But not my boyfriend. What Rickey told him had changed everything.

One of the other performers waved to me. A trans woman in a sparkly red mermaid dress. "Maeve," she called, "when are you going to take my portrait? All you care about is Georgie."

"I'm shooting some of the other girls here at four tomorrow," I said. "Come on by."

Not only could I snap pictures of all the dancers as I pleased at the Hootch, but I had both my studio lights and the stage lights to play with. There wasn't anyone running the stage lights on a steady basis, so they always welcomed an extra set of hands. I was around so much, I was kind of working at the theater now. That earned me an extra fifty bucks a week on top of what I was making with my bookkeeping job. I put the second paycheck directly into my savings. Usually.

The spotlights illuminated a tall cone of dusty air that flooded each dancer. If I planned it right, I could make it look like whoever was onstage, Georgie or each dancer, was the only entity that existed in the universe. It was just them, in the cosmos, floating in their feathered and sequined costumes, suspended in their personal column of light, surrounded by a pitch-black that fell off so fast it was dizzying.

I got goose bumps anticipating how the pictures would turn out. My excitement made each simple inhalation of breath take concentration and effort. I wound the film of my medium-format camera forward, and it made its satisfying whirring sound.

Georgie came up behind me, put his arms around my shoulders, and placed his cheek next to mine. I inhaled his delicious scent, taken aback. I liked it, but he hadn't actually touched me in an intimate way since that day on the porch. I blamed Pop's insults when they'd met, and Rickey telling him so crudely about my photographs. And Cassie's ongoing but meaningless flirtation. The fact that I didn't consider myself attractive enough for him mixed in with my doubts too.

He nuzzled my neck and murmured, "You're just so damned beautiful standing here."

Beautiful, huh? Yeah, right. I wanted him to be attracted to me, of course, but I didn't for a moment consider myself beautiful. Not after all the things I'd had to listen to my whole life. I felt a strong need to protect my heart.

"Don't toy with me, Bello," I said. I let myself lean back into his embrace and close my eyes for a moment, but even he couldn't keep me from my work. I looked through my viewfinder, testing different angles for a shot.

He stood stock-still, as absorbed in the choices I was making as I was. I knew he was taking in how I was framing each shot. As was his way, he would probably remember everything and describe the sequence of my pictures to me later in the evening. In great detail. Georgie was a true muse in that regard. The first person in my life who I felt understood me. Feeling understood was a powerful aphrodisiac. My heart raced at his closeness.

I'd overheard him talking about my pictures in the past, and it was flattering. He often told other performers, "You gotta see Maeve about some photos. Believe me, if she takes your picture, you will never have looked better. No corny portraits with her, no—she somehow finds the hearts of people and gets it on film. She'll reveal your *soul*. I'm not exaggerating. I'll show you some she did of me."

When they did call, I felt blessed. Neighbors from his artsy neighborhood, members of the trans community, other performers—rainbows and rainbows of colors and lifestyles.

Sometimes I was embarrassed by his effusive praise, though it also made me feel warm inside. Here, in the theater with him, I was cocooned. No one tsked at me for being too much this way or that. No one reminded me about sin or of the world I would return to when summer came crashing to an end.

I was hyperaware of the minutes ticking by. One day soon, I would be gone. I couldn't run fast enough to capture all I wanted to. A painful reality check that made my heart quicken.

I'd had a terrible nightmare the night before, in which Mom and Pop knew all about my pictures. The looks on their faces haunted me.

If only I could leave Asbury Park and head straight to Manhattan. How could I go back to my old life? My childhood bedroom? And do what? Pretend I didn't know what life could be? What satisfying work meant? What love could be, given half a chance? If only I had more money. If only I knew someone with a cheap room to rent. If only I knew other artists in New York City.

But I had to go home for a while. That's all there was to it. I had all of my pictures to print—many hundreds. Then I would have to choose my six favorites to send to the contest committee, along with an official copy of my high school transcript. An essay was required, too, and it would take me days to write and edit it, to fully express what the opportunity to attend the School of Visual Arts meant to me.

If Pop or any of his henchmen on the local force spotted me here at the Hootch, or at the Travellers' encampment, or even at some of the after-hours events Cassie and I went to with the other musicians, he would drag me away by my hair. But Pop hadn't come back since the day we fought. He didn't know the ways in which I'd changed.

Down here at the shore it had been easy to forget where I came from—and what I would be forced to return to.

Georgie's arms were still around me when he finally spoke. "It's just gorgeous, honey. Be sure to show me the negatives after. Summer's growing shorter by the day."

I was moved that he sounded melancholy about my leaving. In the gardens surrounding our apartment, blazing pillars of Liatris were already blooming. They always signaled to me the end of the season, their beauty bittersweet.

Georgie squeezed me. "Don't you just go off and forget about old Georgie."

I nearly whimpered at the thought of it. "I couldn't ever forget you. I'm going to miss you so much."

He gave me another squeeze and kissed my cheek. "We're both going to the City, girl. I'm going to see you there. I can't get stuck here for the rest of my life. We both have to figure out how to make the move to the Big Apple."

"But how will I find you?" I trembled. "I don't know how this contest is going to work out. Maybe I won't win. Where will you be in the City?"

"You've got the phone number I have now. And in New York? I'll know where to find you. You'll be haunting every gallery in town. I'll go in and ask, 'You seen a tall, skinny redhead in here?

Incident on 57th street

She's always got her hair up with a crown of pencils stuck in it.' How many girls like that you think they're going to see around?" He elbowed me lightly. "I'll find you, don't you worry. And you'll know how to find me too. It's a pretty small circle I run in."

Cassie appeared before us like an apparition, escorted by one of the dancers.

"Look what I found scratching around at the back door," the dancer said with a wink.

Georgie burst out laughing and hugged her.

She'd come to tell me that another patrol car had parked in front of our house for more than an hour. As soon as it drove away, she'd rushed over to the Hootch.

"Do you think it's your dad again?" She picked at a cuticle nervously. "Or maybe another officer doing him a favor by checking up on us?"

"Damn it." I frowned. "You should have been going to church this whole time. If I can drag my ass out of bed on Sunday morning, you can too. Father Murphy must've told them you were skipping."

"I'll go this week. Just say that I've been working on Sundays until now."

I saw two of the strippers talking, their costumes made all the more colorful by the background of black velvet curtains where they stood. One called out, "Maeve, honey, remember you're taking my picture tomorrow afternoon. I got some new wigs for the occasion."

I shivered to think what Pop would make of that.

In a panic, I turned around to hug Georgie one more time. It was a quick embrace, because he had to make his entrance for the first set.

He stroked my cheek, and instead of saying goodbye, he said, "I could just eat you up."

"Go ahead," I quipped. And meant it.

down on the south beach drag

He was already gliding toward the black backstage curtains, click-clacking away from me in his patent leather derby shoes, the sequin band on his black hat sparkling like a clear winter night. I watched every move he made.

Part of Georgie's job was to warm up the audience, so he was always on first. He sang his impressions, danced like a demon, and finished by playing the drums with a trio he'd put together for the new revue.

Cassie, who'd stayed to watch the show with me, was dumbfounded. "You didn't tell me he could play drums." She sounded confrontational. "Or that his vocal impressions were so good—Frankie Valli? Tony Bennett? He nailed them all. That guy sings his ass off."

I snapped a shot, *click*, my concentration on my viewfinder. "You've heard him sing before."

"Just once in a while. Not a whole show like this."

When I finally glanced over, her mouth was still hanging open in surprise.

Georgie was chortling into his microphone. What was he up to?

"I've got a special treat for you tonight," he crowed. "Please put your hands together and welcome *Cassie Olsen* to the stage!"

As Georgie whispered into his guitar player's ear and modeled a tempo for him with an air guitar, Cassie gasped and searched my face, as if I might be able to explain this. I was as shocked as she was. But perhaps I trusted Georgie more than she did. I took hold of her shoulders, turned her toward the open stage, and gave her a little shove.

Through my lens, I followed her every move through the wings. After nearly stumbling, she strode toward the guitarist's microphone, and he stepped away to yield it to her.

Georgie hit his drumsticks together, counting out the beat. I had no idea what they were going to play until a rhythmic strumming started, and the bass player joined in. Just as I identified

Incident on 57th street

the tune, recognition also spread across Cassie's golden features, along with a smile that lit up the theater like a beacon of hope.

How did Georgie know Joni Mitchell was Cassie's favorite? Their impromptu arrangement of "Big Yellow Taxi" was a blast. He and Cassie traded off the verses, and killed it. It was as if they'd been doing the song together for years. When they reached the chorus, he sang a full third above Cassie's notes in harmony—what a range he had!—and the lusciousness of the resulting sound made Cassie sound like a genius. It was better than any performance the real Joni Mitchell had ever done in her life.

I peeked out at the crowd that was, let's face it, a group of creepy men gathered to see a bawdy burlesque review. Still, they got totally into the moment. When they started clapping along, Georgie called out to the players to repeat the first two verses. Some of the guys in the first few rows jumped up to dance in front of the stage. Four of the professional dancers that hadn't yet performed spilled down from the side entrances and joined them, so the band vamped for a while to make the most it. The crowd was having the time of their lives.

Snap, snap, snap went my camera. Once I was out of film, I held the palms of my hands to the sides of my face. I would remember this evening for the rest of my life.

When the last chord rang out from the last chorus, the entire audience jumped to their feet. Even from where I stood in the wings, the applause was deafening.

The embrace Cassie gave Georgie was long. It melted the smile on my face.

When he pulled away from her, his expression was clear: he was a man in love.

chapter 22
we're an american band

It was Thursday. We were standing in a circle in front of the stage. Boom had showed up without his drum kit.

"I'm done with music," he said, sniffling. "All these late nights screwed me up. There's no reason for me to cheat on my wife. No offense, Maeve, but Sandra's not even a nice person. My Debby's an angel. And she's way prettier—even you have to admit that. Geez, we're having a baby. And she left me." He started to cry.

He did seem messed up. It made sense for him to get a grip on his drinking and the other temptations that come naturally on the night scene.

He dragged a hand across his eyes, wiping away the tears. "I think if I really make an effort, she'll forgive me. I hope so. We've been together since high school."

"We gotta play in an hour and a half. Do this one last show at least," Gary begged.

"Can't do it, Gare-man. You know I love you, but I got to bounce." Boom turned suddenly and strode away. He hit the push bar with the full force of his fear and frustration and the door exploded open.

Without missing a beat, Cassie insisted they call Georgie. "We're going out to my car to get my address book and find his number," she told the guys as she grabbed my arm. "You guys figure out the set list and how you think we can teach it to him fast. He's heard us play most of the songs."

Cassie talked nonstop as we walked out to the small sedan her parents had recently passed down to her. "Listen," she said, "my motives are entirely selfish." She was still high from her impromptu show at the Hootch. "Singing with him made me so much better. We killed together."

She dug through her glove box, which was stuffed with papers. "This is serendipity coming at me. Divine intervention." She found her leather address book and began flipping through it. "Playing with Georgie is so easy. He feels what I feel. Maybe more so. I have to be better just to keep up with him."

Turned out Georgie was available. We made a scramble to the Hootch to pick up him, his drum kit, and several other instruments in black cases.

When he emerged from his dressing room, I was stunned. He wore a stretch velvet Mick Jagger–style jumpsuit with a silk scarf tied around his waist. With his hair pushed up into a style like Keith Richards's rooster shag, he was a rock and roll vision of the day.

Serendipity made this happen? I thought glumly. *That's just great. Georgie and Cassie, together again.*

There was a hasty sound check back at the Osprey. Everyone agreed Georgie was very good, and the relief was palpable. A bonus, as far as the band was concerned, was that his talent for mimicry made him a natural for blending harmonies with all of them. A drummer who could sing well was apparently a valuable commodity in the music world—and it turned out he could also play clarinet, trumpet, and saxophone. This I hadn't known.

Gary was already writing his own songs. He had big dreams for the group and had already made it clear he thought Cassie

down on the south beach drag

could help him get where he wanted to go. Now it seemed he'd added Georgie to that list too.

Some of the young men at the club that night were pretty mouthy about Georgie. Even though he wasn't dressed tonight as a man's kind of man, he was clearly less muscular than most, and his suit's deep V-neck revealed no chest hair and a slight cleavage. Some guys openly recoiled from him.

But I could tell some went the opposite way. They were smitten.

The drunker the crowd got, the more they had to say about Georgie's gender-bending appearance. I couldn't stand two guys in particular who continued to make rude comments. I went over to them, introduced myself, and pointed out, "Bowie and Jagger, even Keith Richards are pretty feminine. They wear woman's clothing."

"*No*, they don't," one said, shaking his head.

I tsked. "Blouses, long silk scarves, designer hats . . . I'm not sure where you draw the line, guys. You're all big Rolling Stones fans, right? The suit Georgie has on was copied from Mick Jagger. And what about Led Zeppelin? The lead singer is certainly androgynous."

"What are you supposed to be?" the second guy demanded. "What kind of getup do you have on? When I walked up behind you, I didn't know if *you* were a guy or girl. You're tall enough to be a boy."

There was an uneasiness in my gut—you never knew what might happen when alcohol was poured into some angry rednecks who were out to prove how macho they were. I decided to stop pushing.

"To each their own," I said as lightly as I could, already backing away.

To my relief, they didn't follow.

we're an american band

■ ■ ■

Before Georgie joined the band, the audience was mainly local white kids. But within just a few weeks, the club began to draw in people of color and a small but noticeable minority of gays. The ages of the customers became much more diverse as well. Whatever it was about the new mix of people, the dance floor filled on the first note of every up-tempo song.

I was in my element. Although I wasn't the celebrity that Cassie had become, I was the de facto house photographer. Apparently, that made me somebody to reckon with, and people were suddenly paying attention to me.

The number of customers paying a cover charge swelled. So much so that the owner of the club gave Friday nights, too, to what was left of the house band and Cassie and Georgie. They now called themselves The Asbury Revue.

Georgie would open the show alone until the club filled. He started at five in the afternoon and the full band joined him sometime around nine o'clock. Accompanied only by his keyboard, he did his imitations of famous singers. As it was meant to be cocktail music, he soon added jazz greats like Mel Tormé and Nat King Cole into his repertoire. And the audience seemed to get better used to Georgie's in-between appearance once he started taking requests. You could tell he never tired of singing the songs. "I love the classic American songbook," he'd told me countless times.

So did many middle-aged people in the area, and they had money to spend. They started coming in large groups and lingering for hours. Word had gotten around: you could come to the Osprey for a proper cocktail hour and great entertainment. Georgie's parents even showed up one night.

He had a fishbowl on his keyboard that served as his tip jar.

down on the south beach drag

When I asked him if he was exhausted from putting in such long nights, he waved a hand in the air and told me he was making so much in tips, he had to empty the cash that was jammed into the bowl between sets.

"This is New York money, Maeve," he said, eyes sparkling. "You know my dad won't support my singing career, so this is the money that's going to get me to the City."

The swinging sixties audience was an unexpected bonus. He wasn't about to turn that tip bonanza down.

When it was time for Cassie and the rest of the band to start, Georgie sat down at the drums. Although Cassie was the center of attention, she always made sure that he had some big moments in the show too. In addition to him having his own solo during each set, the two of them worked out some duets. Very *convincing* duets—so romantic. While they made me squirm with discomfort, the audience couldn't get enough.

But the best part for me was the regular presence of other musicians who stopped by and sat in. *Click, click*. I was right there to capture precious moments.

Even in my funk, mooning over Georgie, I was rarely without a camera and plenty of film. One night, I looked up toward the smoky stage lights and saw the audience reaching their arms up to sax player Clarence Clemons as if they were worshipping him. As if they might devour him. An astonished Cassie Olsen stood at his side, a microphone loosely dangling from her left hand. With a flash, I froze that moment for all time. The picture was perfectly exposed, the expressions on their faces priceless.

It was the sort of thing that happened all the time now. Just a day in my new life.

chapter 23
tenth avenue freeze-out

All summer long, the musicians had been fighting over what was the best song of all time. Debates raged. Some of the guys decided to organize a contest at The Upstage Club to settle the matter. Each candidate would present their nominated song, give a little introduction, and then play it over the sound system. At the end, the audience would judge. A vote by applause.

The minute the needle dropped onto the record on the turntable, the crowd of musicians were on their feet. Since they didn't have their instruments, they grabbed something and turned it into one. A little serving station was temporarily looted; fellows were thumping on busboy tubs and playing spoons. They also danced out the parts they would normally play on each piece. It was, in a word—frenzy.

Danny was at the party, and several other players I knew well, including the guy that got the record deal. They joined in with the dancing, which really doesn't happen often with professional musicians. It cast them in a different light. Just cutting loose and having fun.

I, of course, caught it all in a series I couldn't wait to print.

down on the south beach drag

■ ■ ■

It was four thirty by the time I let myself in our front door. Still dark. I took my shoes off so I wouldn't wake anyone else up, but I needn't have bothered. Light leaked out from under Sandra's bedroom door, and I heard her throaty laugh. A man called out, sounding drunk. I thought it might be Boom and I cursed him out for being weak, though I really couldn't be sure it was him.

Cassie must still be out. Gone off someplace to score some pot, which was standard practice for her nowadays.

I padded across the darkness of the living room to the kitchen to get a glass of water. A movement outside the window stopped me. Though my heart was racing, I longed to make sense of what I'd just seen, so I crept to the sliding glass door where the drapes were drawn, pulled open a thin gap, and peered through.

It took time for my eyes to adjust, but luckily the moon was bright. I could make out the silhouette of a man bending toward Sandra's bedroom window. A slash of light from the lamp inside ran across his forehead and down to his chin. Half of his face was tattooed—Rickey. He was watching the goings-on in Sandra's bedroom, smiling in that creepy way of his that made my skin crawl.

I held my breath, too afraid to make a sound, and kept watching him. He was stroking himself. After a time, I saw him shudder; moments after that, he crept down off the rickety fire escape.

When I was certain he was gone, I held onto the doorjamb and slid to the floor. It took many minutes to quiet my ragged breathing.

On trembling legs, I made my way to my bedroom and flipped on the light—revealing Bobby and Cassie lying together, naked, in tangled sheets that looked damp.

"Sorry!" popped out of me as I quickly turned the light off.

I didn't know why *I* was sorry. What the hell were they doing there? They didn't move at all. I grabbed a pillow and my blanket, and headed for the couch.

I didn't sleep a wink that night, jumped at the least little sound.

When Sandra and I crossed paths in the kitchen the next morning, I said, "Guess who was out on the deck last night watching you have sex?"

"I know what you're going to say about it. I know."

"What do you mean, you know?" She knew Rickey was a voyeur, in addition to his many other sins?

Sandra sat at the kitchen table. She was in sad shape, but smirked at me over her morning coffee. "I'm sure you will think it's perverted, Maeve. You love your judgments and all. We dig it . . . Rickey and me . . . we like to watch each other with other people. It's just something we do sometimes."

She never ceased to surprise me. And offend me.

"We agreed he wouldn't come over. We all decided."

Hearing our voices, Cassie had joined us, and I turned to her for help. But her mouth was a straight line. She stared down at the table rather than meeting my eyes.

"So I guess you don't think you're in any position to criticize," I said, annoyed. "At least what you and Bobby did wasn't against the law."

Sandra checked her watch. She sighed and flipped her hair back behind her shoulders. "He was *outside*. He wasn't bothering you. And it's not against the law if you have permission."

"I'm sure Boom didn't give his permission. Things are bad enough with his wife. I certainly didn't give mine. Why would I want Rickey lurking around? After what he did to me? He's lucky I didn't call the cops. Or that our parents didn't find out."

Both Cassie and Sandra started laughing.

"What?" I asked.

"That empty threat of yours has turned into our private joke," Sandra said.

"We're all pretty clear why we didn't call the police," Cassie said, nodding her agreement. "Especially Officer He-Whose-Name-We-Won't-Say."

I put my elbows up on the table and my head in my hands. This wasn't funny. How could I even begin to explain to them how Rickey scared me? I wiped my eyes with both hands.

Instead of comforting me, Cassie glared.

"I didn't sleep at all last night, Sandra." It was the truth. I started to cry. I was wiped out.

She blew on her hot coffee before taking another sip. "You're overreacting." She put her cup down and ran her fingers through her hair, then fished around in the pocket of her robe and pulled out a thick hand-rolled cigarette. When she lit it, its smell made it clear it wasn't tobacco. She handed it to me. "Take a hit off this and you'll be fine. Then maybe you can take a nap . . . that's what I'm going to do."

I accepted it and inhaled deeply. I was so shaken up, I welcomed the numbing effect I hoped it was going to have. As I exhaled the smoke through my teeth, I hissed at Cassie, "Is Bobby gone? I'd like to get some sleep in my own bed if you don't mind."

She shook her head and shrugged, seeming only the least bit embarrassed. "He's not up yet." She giggled. "We had kind of a long night."

"Well, wake him up. You two can figure out some other place to copulate. I'm exhausted. Sandra, you better tell Rickey that you are going to keep your curtains drawn tight from now on. If you don't, I'm going to tell your father—I swear I will this time. Then we'll all be heading home."

Sandra was sucking on the joint. She laughed. Hysterically now. She gulped air before being able to continue.

"No, you won't," she finally choked out. "You won't tell my

father anything. You don't want our parents to know what's been going on around here. Face it, Maeve. You're in it as deep as the rest of us. I very much doubt you're going to leave Georgie before you absolutely have to. And you keep talking about finishing your show? No amount of pictures will ever be enough for you. You're like a junkie needing his fix."

I bristled. Shocked. Surely, she wasn't putting me in the same category as her. Even with the drinking and pot . . . the late nights . . . I was still a good person. If I died, I wasn't going straight to hell. Sandra's trespasses were different. Very different. If I could see her soul, it would look like leopard skin. Stain upon stain upon stain. I hadn't done anything even close to the terrible things she had.

She was right about one thing, though. I never wanted to explain to my parents some of the things that had happened in the last two months. I reached out for the marijuana—just one example of the many ways they would be disappointed in me.

How many others would there be before summer ended?

chapter 24
higher ground

At the very beginning of the summer season, I'd said to my boss, "Give me a key to the exterior door and your office. Leave the cash-out forms and the ledgers on top of the file cabinet. I won't disappoint you." Three times a week, I showed up to work. I got paid for twenty hours but it took way less time for me to complete the paperwork. I only showed up when I could squeeze it into my actual life. Twice a month, my paycheck was there waiting for me, sitting on top of the pile, when I arrived.

It was an arrangement that worked well for both Dennis and me. He took full advantage of my talent with numbers by gradually having me take over all his books for his two restaurants; and I took full advantage of the flexible hours and decent pay. I worked directly with his accountant, so I rarely saw him or the other employees. When I did, I just waved to them and shut the heavy oak door of his office behind me. The work would always be waiting for me, anytime of the day or night I chose to come in.

On this beautiful Saturday, I arrived midmorning to find Dennis making a series of desperate phone calls. It turned out he didn't have a waitress for the dinner crowd, and he expected the restaurant to be busy. He slammed his old black phone into its cradle—over and over again. The noise was jarring, distracting me.

"I tell you what, Maeve . . . I'll pay you double if you'll waitress tonight," he suggested. "You'll make a fortune in tips too. I've

higher ground

got a busboy scheduled. All you have to do is take the orders and serve."

As I didn't have anything planned, it was a good opportunity to make some extra cash. As Georgie had said, I could consider it New York money—*my* New York money. My share of the summer rent had cost me almost all my savings from my high school years, but I was slowly replenishing my account.

All of my young life, money had been a grating problem. A scab that would never heal. When I saved up and bought my first nice camera, my mother decided she didn't need to buy my school clothes anymore. "If you have enough for something frivolous," she told me, "then you can pay for something practical too." Ever since, I'd worked hard and saved up for the next goal, like coming down here, but every time I met one I was left saving all over again.

I stared out the window, over the garbage cans and into the parking lot. Could you ever have too much money? The price of film alone was costing me a fortune.

Sure, I could wait tables tonight.

"I'll do it," I said. "What time do you want me here?"

A short nap in one of the porch swings at home that afternoon refreshed me. A strong cup of tea and a shower helped too. As usual, I'd been out late the night before.

Thunder showers and hard rain had cleared out the oppressive humidity that had plagued us for days. On the walk back to the boardwalk, the breeze brought with it salt spray that spritzed my face. The feel of it put a spring in my step. I swung my purse as I walked along.

Different sequences of photographs I had taken over the summer flew through my mind. The Select Six for the New York Area Photo Contest would only be a teaser. I had so much material, it

down on the south beach drag

was going to take days and days to go through the negatives. I was feeling optimistic about the contest. *New York, here I come.*

With the many hundreds of images I'd collected, I would be in my darkroom printing for a long while. By the time I was done, I'd have enough to do several gallery shows. I had images of all the sideshow entertainers; the many hired men and women who called themselves carnies; dancers from Hootch; musicians, musicians, musicians; the night life; and many of the Travellers, thanks to Orlaith.

I also had shots of local business characters, each deserving of their own sequence, who'd been kind enough to sit for me. Recently, I'd finally gotten around to asking the renowned Madame Marie to let me get a picture of her in her fortune-telling establishment, and she'd said yes. A real coup.

There were colorful restaurant owners too. And the guy that had the arcade surrounded by customers playing on his machines had been fun to shoot.

Then there were my morning and evening beach pictures.

And the night shots of Asbury Park? They were going to turn out great. Miss Asbury was her own character. Her boardwalk sequences were going to be iconic, if I did say so myself. The Ferris wheel, the carousel. I'd found a vintage postcard and re-created the shot: the crowd with their beach umbrellas, the convention center in the background. This would be my first picture of the Select Six. It would firmly establish the setting.

I daydreamed for the whole walk to work.

The "busboy" Dennis had told me about was actually a bartender named Don who'd been made the same double-pay offer that I had. And he didn't look too happy to be here.

I asked him for a damp rag, and wiped down the tables and

higher ground

cleaned off the ketchup and mustard bottles. The salt air could easily clog up our saltshakers. The solution was to add grains of rice into the crystals; I checked each one, making sure the salt shook out freely.

"You sure are thorough," Don called over.

I shrugged. "This place can get grungy. That definitely affects tips."

I joined him behind the bar to help him polish glasses. The place had been kind of a mess when we began, but by the time customers started floating in for drinks and dinner, I felt like we were ready.

At first, Don kept running from the kitchen to the back of the bar, then out to clear the tables, before circling back again. It wasn't an efficient system, and I thought any lag time was going to cost me. I took matters into my own hands.

When he caught me pouring some beers for customers myself, he looked pissed. Before he could say anything, though, I said, "Let's just agree to split the tips. If you're not out here when I need something, I can fix the simple ones myself."

A begrudging nod was his response.

We made up a system on the fly. It was kind of genius. What one of us couldn't get to, the other did.

"It's like we're a tag team!" I called over to him at the height of the rush.

He let out a hearty laugh.

We were rewarded for our hard work with many compliments from our customers—and plenty of cash. We couldn't wait to count our overflowing tip jar.

With a loud click of the dead bolt, I officially closed up the place around ten thirty. Don threw fistfuls of our cash up in the air, cheering. I felt giddy too. When he did a backflip in celebration, I laughed so hard, I bent over and couldn't straighten up for a full minute.

Getting down to business, we sat on two barstools. I counted out the money in the till. Don turned every one of our bills so it was oriented the same way. He smoothed them into separate piles according to denomination. He had the founding fathers' faces staring up at him, with the dollar amount over their right shoulder.

He fanned the stacks when he was done, then paused. "Wait a minute. Let me make us a drink before I count these."

I paused and fixed in my mind the total of the money I was in the process of counting. "Scotch and soda, please . . . sixty, seventy, eighty, ninety, a hundred . . . twenty, forty, sixty, eighty, two hundred."

I glanced over as he pulled out the ingredients for a gin gimlet for himself. He put down a cardboard coaster for each of us, set our drinks on top of them, and danced back around the bar to count his piles of money in earnest.

"Jeez." He shook his head. "This is crazy money."

Don and I had joked around a few times before, and it seemed he enjoyed my company. Still, I was more than surprised when he said, "Let's take some of this cash and go out and hear some music. I heard Bruce Springsteen is playing in Point Pleasant tonight."

It sounded like fun, especially since it was still early, according to the internal clock I'd acquired over the summer. I took off my apron—and remembered I had a huge ketchup splatter on my denim skirt.

He saw it too. "What did you do to yourself?"

It had been frantically busy for a couple of hours. Who knew what had happened?

"I'd love to go with you, but obviously I have to change first,"

higher ground

I said. "If you're okay with taking me home, I'll grab a camera while I'm there too. I've got the first round of drinks when we get to Point Pleasant."

"Sure." He lifted a gym bag up from behind the counter to show me. "I thought ahead and brought a change of clothes. You finish cashing out. I'm going to shower in Dennis's office. We'll stop by your place after."

Dennis had installed a full bath off his knotty pine–paneled room. He also had a single bed in there. He often joked with a wink, "For the nights when I'm in the doghouse with the wife."

As I sipped my cocktail, Don closed Dennis's door behind him. I checked over the numbers I'd entered and heard the spray of the shower start up. When I was done, I thought about the historic carousel whizzing around and around on the boardwalk. It was one thing to see the iconic landmarks, and another entirely to really know this town. Its layers. The different scenes that coexisted all at the same time. Or those that appeared differently in the day versus the night.

Don came back out with his dark hair slicked back and eyes shining. The olive tone of his skin made those eyes pop. What a gorgeous face. As he was still buttoning up his shirt, I couldn't help but notice he was really fit too. Muscular.

Why did the sight of his body, or most men for that matter, hold no attraction for me? Nor did I, I was pretty sure, hold any for him. It was obvious we would be friends and nothing more. I settled that in my mind. You can never have too many friends. I wasn't at all sad about it. Maybe Georgie might fall for me one day.

Did Don have an ulterior motive in being so pally with me? Anybody who went out to see music lately would have seen me up on the stage or photographing the bands. I actually knew most of the musicians in the area. I wouldn't go around bragging that we were close friends but . . . we'd had many good conversations. Maybe Don had seen us chatting. They were fascinated by my aspirations in the art world of New York City, and I was fascinated with them as originators of the Shore Sound. In fact, most of them had gone out of their way to be encouraging. At least that's what I thought their intentions had been.

All the lights were out as we pulled up outside my apartment.

Don opened his car door and stood with both elbows propped up on the roof, scanning the neighborhood. "Power's out as far as the eye can see. For blocks. I wonder what caused it?"

I twisted my knees toward the driver's side as he rooted around in his glove box to find two flashlights. We used them to guide our way up the narrow stairs. No one else was home. For my roommates, it was still far too early for bed on a Saturday night, that much I knew for sure.

I was still spooked by the whole Rickey fiasco. Fiasco*es*, really—him attacking me and then finding out that he was Sandra's Peeping Tom. Could he have been spying on me too?

Thank God Don was with me now. I took a moment to thank the Blessed Virgin in heaven too. I was convinced it was she who'd saved me from being raped. Cassie was merely the vessel she'd used to help me. I'd made a point of finding my rosary to thank her properly. Disaster had a way of bringing me right back to my roots.

While unlocking our apartment door, I pictured Rickey standing on the other side of it. The slightest noise in the apartment was now capable of making me tremble. When I had a nightmare about him, and I often did, I awoke in a cold sweat, sometimes crying. I'd had to learn to live with all my senses on high alert, causing a queasy stomach that no remedy could cure.

Clunk went the dead bolt opening. *Creak* went the door. Despite the darkness, my eyes were staring back at me from the hall mirror. And they looked ghostly.

higher ground

The flashlight I carried was small, the circle it cast narrow, forcing me to keep my search for something to wear simple. While Don waited in the dark living room, I slipped off my skirt and put on a pair of shorts. I pulled my good sandals out from under the bed. My favorite camera was always in its place of honor on top of the dresser, so that was easy to find. I grabbed it. Good enough.

"Let's hope the lights come back on by the time we get back," Don said as I locked the door behind us. "Otherwise, I'll worry about you."

I worried about me too. I often did, lately. Would I always live with fear in my gut now?

As we drove, it became clear the power outage was confined to my neighborhood.

Just my luck.

Introducing Don around the club was a kick. I could tell he was impressed at the easy banter I had with the players. Even the waitstaff seemed like old friends. Several of them bought us rounds of drinks, so it turned out to be a cheap night out. I got some good pictures from the edge of the stage, despite the alcohol flowing through my veins.

Time stopped when Georgie showed up with Cassie. He came right over.

"Georgie, this is Don."

"Hey, man," he acknowledged Don, but wasted no further time on him; he turned to me, eyes brimming with excitement. "We decided to come over to sit in with a new duet we cooked up," he told me. "We're going on at the end of the first set."

You could tell the other guys were happy to have them. Though I waved to Cassie, it was terribly awkward. We'd never talked outright about how I felt about Georgie, but she had to know. And she monopolized his time anyway.

down on the south beach drag

The front man spoke into his microphone. "I'm going to call two people to the stage to do a song. Mark this down, folks. They are going to be famous. You remember someday that I was the first to tell you. Please welcome Cassie Olsen and Georgie Bello."

Polite applause came from all around.

As Georgie settled himself behind the keyboard, he said in the mic, "How about a little nostalgia for a change? I've always loved this old Irving Berlin song."

Cassie stepped up to the main mic while he tinkled the introduction.

"Can we do this, Georgie?" the lead guitarist asked. "Are you sure?"

"Just keep it light," Georgie hollered to him.

Once the drummer found the beat, the rest of the band followed.

Cassie sang to Georgie, "He doesn't look like much of a lover, but don't judge a book by its cover. He's got the face of an angel, but there's a devil in his eye."

It may have originally been Irving Berlin who wrote this, but she was addressing what folks might think about Georgie. So ballsy. The audience clapped and laughed.

Georgie went back at her. "Ev'ryone wanted to know, how she could pick such a beau."

With a twinkle in her eye, she came back with: "He's not so good in a crowd, but when you get him alone, you'd be surprised."

Then Georgie: "He doesn't look very strong, but when you sit on his knee, you'd be surprised."

And so it went. Amusing. Adorable. The sax player perfectly hit his requisite solo. They kept it up-tempo. Everyone had a grand ole time. Everyone but me. If I'd had my own car, I would have left. Instead, I smoldered in the back of the large room.

During the band's break, we were all invited to step outside and smoke some pot. Under the blue streetlight, with the summer smells of hot tar and coming rain, Danny said, "You guys ever been to Jersey Freeze? Just soft ice cream—that was all you could get. Two flavors—one was chocolate and one was vanilla. When I was a kid, I didn't like chocolate or vanilla. I just liked the cones. So the guy used to save all the broken cones for me."

I listened while everyone shot the shit. I didn't have the energy to muster a story of my own after seeing Georgie casually loop an arm across Cassie's shoulders.

Danny was standing right next to me. It was always a good night when he came.

"When do you go to the City?" he asked me. "The big move."

"I hope September. I still have to win—remember?"

"Don't put it all on that contest. You know what you want. You can figure out a way to get it. My father always said"—he wagged his finger at me—"the harder you work, the luckier you are."

Work was all I had now that I was sure Cassie and Georgie were a thing. So I supposed luck wouldn't be a problem.

chapter 25
blinded by the light

At two thirty in the morning, I staggered from the back seat of Don's Ford, half in the bag. The power was still out. Thank God Don was letting me borrow his flashlight again.

"Are you sure you're okay, Maeve?" he called out his car window.

"I'm fine. I'll just take it slow." I burst out laughing. "I admit, you were right. I shouldn't have had that last drink."

Don had met a boy at the bar, and I could tell they wanted to be alone. Not wanting to be a bother, I waved at them to go, and they sped away.

I picked my way up the steep stairs, steadying myself with the handrail. The world was starting to spin. I cursed it. Maybe I was cursing myself. It took a few tries to unlock the dead bolt, but when I did, I was greeted by the warm glow of a hurricane lamp placed on a side table. A pillow and folded blanket sat on the couch with a note on top. I held the paper close to the flame to read it: *Bobby's here. Sorry. I'll explain everything in the morning.*

Damn it. She was still sleeping with Bobby? Where the heck was Georgie? I thought he was her date. And "explain everything in the morning"? If ever I'd needed a good sleep, it was now. But I had no energy to get thoroughly mad about being displaced to the couch again. I was woozy and needed to lie down.

blinded by the light

I'll just rest a minute, and then go brush my teeth, I told myself. But the second my head hit the pillow, I was dead asleep.

Someone was unzipping my shorts. Tugging at them. I sat up in a dazed panic, gasping for air. A hand covered my mouth, silencing me.

I bit down, hard. When I heard a scream, I pushed at the body lying on top of me. I could taste blood.

He flew off, knocking the oil lamp to the ground.

The glass shattered. A flame chased the lamp oil across the floor. Orange ribbons of light tickled the skirt of an armchair. The old afghan that was draped off its arm went up with a great *whoosh*.

Hot already. Hard to breathe. This old house would go up like a tinderbox. We had to get out.

My assailant had not lost his focus in the bedlam and the blaze. God knew what kind of drugs he'd taken that he didn't notice the fire. Or care. He had a single goal.

"Maeve, baby," he slurred.

Rickey. Stinking of stale sweat and hard liquor.

He dragged me back down on the couch.

Though I was kicking my legs wildly and screaming, he managed to poke his erection into the general vicinity of my vagina. But he hadn't gotten my shorts all the way down yet. The thick denim fabric covering my crotch was all that stopped him from entering me. The feel of him, pounding against my bottom, made me want to throw up.

"Cassie! Bobby!" The hand again covered my mouth, making it hard to breathe.

There was no question as to what I had to do. Pop had taught me long ago to use my thumb as a weapon. I pushed mine now into Rickey's eyeball. It was disgusting. But he was an assailant.

down on the south beach drag

Not a person. I distanced myself from the act. Disassociated completely.

Shrieking with pain, he fell to the floor. The old china cabinet near me burst into flame. I watched it all as though from above.

Rickey's screaming acted like a fire alarm. A mad scramble ensued that was hard to follow. Voices. Footsteps. A wall of heat waves and flames hid me. No one could help, as they wouldn't even know I was there.

A sinking sensation grew where my heart used to be. I was alone. It was up to me to get out of here. Survival—all that mattered.

More of Pop's lessons came to me: "Drop to the floor. There's less smoke the lower you get. Crawl to an opening. Get out."

Sandra's room seemed the safest place. The least amount of smoke. If I could just get to it, I'd be able to crawl through the window. To the very spot Rickey used to watch her from. That old fire escape was going to have to come in handy. Rickety or not, ablaze or not, it was my only way out.

Cassie and Bobby had run out the dining room doors to the deck. As I looked out Sandra's window, I could see them already making their way down the shaky stairway. Sandra and Boom must have gone out through the old pantry downstairs; through the shooting flames, the front door was wide open.

My negatives! They were in a kitchen cabinet. If my pictures went up in the blaze, my life would have no meaning. None.

I ran through the swinging kitchen door to get them. The air at this end of the apartment was still relatively clear. I looked out the window by the table at the sheer drop to the ground. I couldn't get out here. I grabbed my filing box of negatives and crawled back to Sandra's room.

The living room was an inferno. I'd wasted precious time. The heat was so great, I'd be burned crossing the room. Even so,

blinded by the light

I ran. A sizzling noise and creeping sensation spread across my eyebrows and arms. The smell of burnt hair engulfed me. But I made it. Sandra's bedroom window was wide open.

Squeezing out of it was harder than I'd thought it would be. When many packs of negatives dropped out of the box and fell onto the bedroom floor, I panicked. I wanted to lean back inside to save them, but the hallway was ablaze and the heat was unbearable; I could barely breathe where I was standing out on the deck. I didn't dare reach in to try to fish them out.

I still had many of my photographs. I was alive. That would have to do.

It sounded like two people were still behind me in the blaze. Two voices. Scuffling. I heard a loud grunt, then a guttural groan, but it was all hard to hear over the pops and cracks of the fire. I was still pretty inebriated, and disoriented. I didn't trust my perceptions entirely.

I clutched the stair railing as I made my way down. Cassie, Bobby, Boom, and Sandra were outside. I ran as hard as I could and threw myself at them, weeping. We huddled on the street, watching the blaze take hold of the old mansion that had been our home.

A blur of movement at the front door made us all freeze.

"What's that?" Boom said.

It was difficult to make out much. The air around the house had become so hot it was distorting into waves as it hit the cooler night air, and our limited angle of sight made it even harder to make much sense of the movement. Was it a person?

"Who is it?" came Sandra's panicked cry.

I thought I caught sight of someone in a long dress amidst the mirage emanating from the blaze. A phantom—a white shape moving along as a human might—speeding away.

The usually cheery sight of the Ferris wheel lit up the distant horizon. It mocked me. Nothing was cheery about it now. I gasped for air, still choking on soot and smoke. Where was the oxygen I so desperately needed? I sucked in, filling my lungs, but the acrid taste of the fire persisted and made me cough again till my stomach muscles ached.

Cassie stepped away from us and threw up. Both men hacked and spat on the ground. It was all so gross.

The apartments on the first and second floors had been rented by the week all summer, Saturday to Saturday, so we never got a chance to know the renters.

"Someone might be trapped inside!" I hollered. *Maybe more than one person*, I added silently. But none of us moved toward the house, too afraid of the fire to do anything but stand and watch.

It was a relief when I heard sirens.

The white shape, whoever it was, had made it out alive. Someone had escaped and didn't want to be around when the police and firemen got here.

I was at the Asbury Park police station, sitting in an interview room. I, Maeve O'Connor, the eldest child and only daughter of Officer Malachi O'Connor, had been brought in for questioning.

I had my elbows up on the scratched wooden table and my face buried in my hands. I couldn't stop crying.

Surely, if I could just get control of myself, I could convince the police that what had happened was all a terrible mistake. Yes, a crime had taken place, but it was not *my* crime. I hadn't done anything except what I'd had to do.

Yet how would I begin to explain how I came to know a man like Rickey Travers in the first place?

When Pop leaned over the back of my chair to comfort me, he let out a strangled cough. I was sure it was the pungent odor of smoke still saturating my hair and clothing that gagged him. He shot back up and paced back and forth behind me.

blinded by the light

Sergeant Glen Martin sat across the table, waiting for me to compose myself. He tilted his chair up on its back legs. It creaked as he did. When he started to pointedly twiddle his thumbs, I pulled myself together and quickly nodded to indicate that I was ready for his questions.

Pop's presence at this interrogation was a favor granted to him because Pop was a well-known policeman. He'd patrolled his beat for twenty-two years.

Apparently, I'd missed the question Sergeant Martin had already asked me. He looked annoyed as he said, "Try to focus," and repeated it. "The boy who allegedly attacked you . . . his parents say you two were an item. They claim that you've been dating for a while. Did you, in fact, take pictures of him naked? They say they have some of them at their house."

My eyes shot sideways. *What is Pop thinking?* I could barely croak out my answer. "It wasn't like that. I've never gone out with *anyone*. The pictures were for an art contest."

"A contest?" Martin let out a barking laugh.

Humiliation flushed through me. "The New York Area Photo Contest. Photographs." The two statements came out rather perky.

He laughed all the harder.

My face burned. How often had I been surrounded by people who thought art was a joke? That *I* was a joke? They had crowded me out, trying to eradicate my spirit, forcibly trying to jam me, a square peg, into a round hole. The same old story.

It seemed all my father caught from the exchange was the word "naked."

"Naked?" he exploded. "Jaysus!"

He'd been upset with me the last time I'd seen him, but he'd never raised his voice like this. My hands grew clammy. Though I told myself not to cry again, my lips and chin began to quiver. *Damn it.*

down on the south beach drag

"It's not like you're Michelangelo painting cherubs on the Sistine Chapel," he shouted. "You can't even paint! You take pictures. Is that even considered art? What were you thinking, girl?"

The sergeant silenced him. "You are going to have to let me handle this, Officer."

Pop turned away and stared out the window with his hands clenched behind his back. The sound of his torn breathing filled the room.

Martin continued, "What about the erotic dancer? I understand that she calls herself Georgie. You were taking pictures of him too . . . uh . . . her too?"

"Georgie's not a dancer. He's a singer and an impressionist—and a very good one. A terrific musician too. He plays lots of instruments. He's the master of ceremonies of the review at the Hootch. He warms up the audience and performs between dancers."

"Hootch is a burlesque theater. They have strippers there."

He had me there. "Ah, yes they do."

Martin looked down his nose at me. "And your . . . Georgie . . . is a girl dressing like a man."

The way he said it set my teeth on edge. "It's way more complicated than you understand. Not everyone is strictly male or female, though for some reason we like to pretend that's the case." I saw there was a watercooler across the room, and I desperately needed a drink. I stood and went over to it, poured myself a cup. The cool water soothed my throat.

The sergeant frowned. "And your point is . . . ?"

"Many kids just aren't born that way." I smiled at the memory of Georgie sitting at a piano. "Georgie just started a new band, The Asbury Revue. They play a lot at the Osprey."

Martin's head snapped up. "He the one that does the jazz cocktail hour there?" Suddenly, he seemed impressed. "He's really good."

blinded by the light

I nodded. "Yes, he is."

Martin was a music lover. What a surprise! But he recovered his tough guy demeanor quickly. "But he's still working at Hootch, right?"

I couldn't catch my breath. "For now. He hasn't been able to get other work . . . because he . . . because of who he is."

"Because of who *she* is. I'm not sure how you came across such a character, Miss O'Connor, but are you aware that cross-dressing in this state is illegal? It's against the law, and you were taking pictures of a woman in men's clothing. That makes you an accomplice."

"You went to see him sing!" I retorted. "Sounds like you loved the show. Why didn't you arrest him if what he's doing is so terrible?"

"My God!" Pop bellowed.

I turned in time to see him rest his forehead against one of the old panes of glass. I thought he might be crying. I felt devastated that I had caused him such disappointment. He didn't understand—of course he didn't. My new life, my friends, how much I loved Georgie. All of my kindred spirits. That for the first time in my life, I felt at home.

In an attempt to erase that pitiful sight, I whipped back around toward the sergeant. A great roaring sound filled my ears. Though I was choked up, I willed myself to speak.

"I didn't know it was illegal," I said haltingly. "I knew it wasn't . . . usual . . . ah . . . or common . . . but I didn't know it was against the law. In Georgie's case, I don't think it's a choice. I don't think you're right." The thought of getting Georgie into trouble was terrifying, as I had some idea of what might happen to him in jail. My face continued to burn.

"Have you lost your senses?" Pop cried out.

Though it was the last thing I wanted to do, I turned back to look at him again. Agony was written all over his face.

"This is going to *kill* your mother," he said. "Two months ago, you were the best daughter a man could hope for. You never stepped a foot in the wrong direction. What on earth happened? What happened to you?" He began to sob.

I'd never seen Pop like this, not even when his own mother died.

Detective Martin let out a deep sigh as his head dropped. The poor man looked defeated. He rested his clutched hands on the table. "I'm afraid it gets worse than that, Malachi. The pornography with Rickey, and aiding and abetting Georgie . . . even the possibility she had something to do with the fire . . . we might have cleared things up and gotten her off with a fine."

Martin locked eyes with his fellow officer—my father, standing by the window—and they shone with what I thought was empathy. There was sadness in them, too, but empathy most of all. He had already told us he was a father. Perhaps one of his children had been arrested at some point as well.

Martin nodded curtly before he went on. "The boy, Rickey Travers, is badly injured. He's got third-degree burns, and one of his eyes is badly damaged."

I let out a wail, though I also wondered where it was coming from. My eyes skittered around, searching for the source of the sound. All I had wanted was for Rickey to stop what he was doing to me. I didn't intend for him to be hurt. I didn't wish ill will to a soul on Earth—

"They don't know yet if they can save the sight."

My father stormed across the room. "No matter what she's done, she was defending herself," he snapped, surprising me. "It's what I taught her to do. How else is a girl to get away from a grown man? And she didn't start the fire, Sergeant. She didn't deliberately burn him or anyone else. The fire chief told me she was lucky to get out with her own life. What's keeping me sane today"—he widened his arms to indicate the room we were in—"is reminding myself that my daughter is lucky to be *alive*."

Once again, Martin held up his hand for silence. "That's not what I'm implying. I don't think she started the fire... not intentionally, anyway. Maeve admitted that she was drunk. When we found Rickey unconscious, he was in the yard outside the house. You can imagine he was easy to identify because of his tattoos. And his size. It's really a pretty small town around here, when it's not tourist season. I knew who he was right away—and that he'd been stabbed in the back."

Two gasps filled the quiet. Pop grabbed the back of a chair to steady himself. Like me, he must be hearing every pound of his huge heart. A heart I was sure would never go out to me in the same way ever again. I'd brought shame to him. Searing shame.

"We apprehended Georgie as he was fleeing the scene." The sergeant stared at me as he shared this information, waiting for my reaction. "If you were in on this, Maeve, you were pretty clever about it. The weapon had a wooden handle that burned in the fire."

How could this be? What knife was he talking about? And I hadn't been thinking when Rickey attacked me, or when the fire started—I kicked into pure instinct. I'd crawled across the floor and out that window. Scrambled down the stairs as fast as I could go.

Why would I have stabbed Rickey when I'd already gotten away?

"Dad, you don't really think I did *that*?" I turned a pleading look in his direction, desperate for him to believe me. "I only did like you taught me. I escaped."

My father stared at Sergeant Martin. He refused to meet my eyes.

chapter 26
thunder road

What with me being the defendant in an arraignment, followed by criminal hearings and the exorbitant cost of a good defense attorney, there was no time or money left over for anything else in our household. All attention was focused on the scandal I had brought to my family.

To say the situation was uncomfortable doesn't capture the friction. Excruciating is closer. Yet I had to live at home. Among them. Where else did I have to go? Tensions were running so high that I kept to my room as much as possible. I often lay on my bed, the only private space I had, slumped over, my chin dipping to my chest, pinning my arms across my stomach.

I'd lost my moral compass in Asbury Park. That must be what had happened. If only I hadn't let Rickey suck me in. He was the problem. And Sandra, too, with how she kept luring him back into our lives. The drinking and marijuana couldn't have helped anything either. My judgment had been clouded by drugs and ambition. If not for that, I would still have Georgie, Orlaith, Cassie, and music in my life. I hadn't really needed Rickey at all.

Hell, as I looked back, I could have walked down to the sideshow tent myself to meet the other performers. It was clear to me now. It might have taken time to earn their trust, but I had the time. They would have sat for me eventually, Rickey or no Rickey. Using him as a shortcut had been my fatal error. A mistake that had cost me big. Cost me all of it. The world I'd discovered and loved had gone up in smoke. Literally. About a third of my negatives had burned in the fire. And now I'd been dumped back here at home.

The minute I'd walked in our back door to the kitchen, I'd practically heard the crash of my sad failure. Same damn peeling wallpaper was all I'd had to greet me.

My mother was bickering with my father at the least provocation, as she blamed him. "If you hadn't catered to her every whim," she often sniped, "we wouldn't be in this mess."

He had not catered to my every whim. No one ever had. What was she talking about? And now that he thought I was exploring my sexuality with unsuitable people, outside of marriage, he was furious with me.

Every time she blamed him, he responded with a broken exhale that tore my heart out. What was worse, I knew it was something I would have to get used to. I had learned something over the summer: I wasn't ever going to be the girl they wanted. Maybe if I'd had even one sister to take the pressure off me. A girly kind of girl. But no such luck.

I was sure Mom dreamt of the white wedding where her only daughter walked down the aisle during high Mass. A passive little wife, mother of her first grandchild. Well, that wasn't going to be me. Ever.

They'd always thought me weird, and they didn't even know yet about my feelings for Georgie. And now he was in jail. A felon. An already difficult situation made impossible by the crime he'd committed. And he'd done it to protect me. *What does it take to stab another human being?* I wondered. *What is the personal cost of such a thing?*

My sensitive Georgie. My loving boy. I longed to hold him. To rock him in my arms. To thank him.

The second he was out of jail, I would have to leave home.

down on the south beach drag

Whether he loved me or not, I couldn't go on without him in my life in some capacity. That decision would be the end of home life as I knew it. Mom would disown me entirely. It was going to be a long road alone. I had to prepare for the worst.

It killed me that I wouldn't be able to see my brothers. Maybe when they were older I could write to them. But Mom would have already poisoned their memories of me by then.

When the boys heard my parents fighting, the younger kids often cried. It was confusing to them. They loved me and weren't privy to the details about my time in Asbury Park. Being little, they tried to make sense of the bits and pieces they'd overheard by asking endless questions:

"We went to see the sideshow last summer. Wasn't I allowed to talk to the Tattooed Man, Mom? I said hello to him."

I wondered if it had in fact been Rickey that he spoke to. I cringed at the thought of him talking to my baby brother.

"So, Mom, Georgie was a singer in a place with showgirls? They have showgirls on *The Ed Sullivan Show*, and we watch it every Sunday. What's wrong with that?"

"Jesus is naked on the cross, Mom. Is naked bad?"

At that last one, Mom took in a sharp breath. "That will be enough questions," she hollered. "We have told you all we can. Just don't get it in your heads that you're going to be artists too. It's all I ask of you. Can I have that one thing?"

They wept all the harder—"We love art class. It's our favorite!"

Mom threw up her hands. They wailed until she ran upstairs to her room and slammed the door.

Since Mom was hunkered down in her room, further explanation was left up to Pop. He sat down with them and got them to color while I did the dishes.

"The kind of art you are working on now is fine," I heard him tell them. "Here at home. A nice activity. But to try to make a life of it, boys . . . it's very hard. Impossible, really. Your mother thinks there are easier ways for you to make a living. I think so too."

I was glad that I had my back to them, because I couldn't help but snicker. Easier for who? Make a living at what? Being a nurse or a teacher, neither of which I cared one whit about? Sacrifice thirty years to collecting a paycheck, just hoping I'd live long enough to get back to taking pictures when I drew on my retirement pension? That was not my future. I didn't know how I would find my way out of this mess, but it would happen. Mom and Pop said my legal bills could be paid off in a year if we tightened our belts. Then we could talk about me starting at community college. That was their plan: me staying here at home.

I didn't openly disagree with their ranting, but figured I could sock away enough money in a year to move to Manhattan. First, though, I had to find a job—despite my currently bad reputation. Though I knew I was still more than competent, I was probably going to have to lower my standards for the kind of work I was willing to do. In the meantime I was stuck here, sealed in our house with my family. With the judgment. The dishonor. The horror.

Cassie called out of the blue. How happy I was to hear from her! She asked if she could come visit. A total thrill. Someone my own age to talk to. And I hoped her presence might also ease Mom and Pop's scorn. They'd known her since the day she was born, and were grateful she remained a loyal friend to me. They thought it was such an honor. The beautiful and popular Cassie Olsen.

Since there was so much to talk about with her, I asked my mother if we could sit in the living room when she came. She hemmed and hawed because it was pretty much a museum of family photos and the few good pieces of furniture that we owned. No one ever sat in there.

"Where else can we talk?" I demanded. "I share my room—if we go up there, the kids will be all over us."

down on the south beach drag

"If it's a nice day, take a walk to the park," Mom said. "If it's raining, we'll talk about the living room." She sounded pretty normal, considering she'd mostly given me the cold shoulder since I'd been home.

In the end, I called Cassie back and told her I'd meet her by the elementary school. "Let's take a walk down memory lane," I said. "But we can't go over by the church. I'm in the doghouse with Father Murphy too. You can't imagine."

No point in him spotting us and questioning our motives.

Cassie and I walked toward the old railroad trestle, just as we'd done when we were kids. I didn't know where to begin. While nothing much had happened in my small world besides the frequent legal meetings and hearings about my case, Cassie had stayed at the shore. She probably had lots of news to tell.

I asked, "Is Sandra still at Cookie's?"

Cassie giggled. She looped her arm through mine, and I slowed down my gait to match hers. "That lasted about a second after you left. Sandra came into her big commission from the sale of the mansion right after the fire. She went out to celebrate, and that same night met a guy. He'd just divorced because he likes to go to sex parties and his wife didn't. It was a real problem. Sandra says he calls himself a swinger."

I stopped short and stared at her. "My goodness."

She nodded, then shook her head. "I don't know how that's going to work in the long run, but for now she's got her own money, a group she loves to party with, and a new boyfriend who's moved in. She's in heaven."

"Sandra with a steady boyfriend? Now I've heard everything." I couldn't imagine it.

"It's a different kind of relationship. Open. I guess it works for them. I don't know if I could ever do that—not be jealous of the man I love. How about you?"

I thought about it as we walked along. Not long ago, I'd thought there was a solid line you could draw between right and wrong. But now I knew there were lots of shades of gray in between. An infinite number of them.

"If I'm ever actually in a relationship, I'll let you know."

Cassie squeezed my arm. "You're only eighteen, Maeve. And you have . . . maybe different tastes than an average girl?"

I was glad we were both facing forward. I didn't want to look directly into her eyes. "So, you know?"

"Know what?"

"Know about me. That I don't like most boys."

"When have you ever liked boys? Except for your brothers, and even that is touch and go." She hugged me like she was putting her whole heart into it. "If I don't know you, Maeve, nobody ever will. You're wonderful. Fun-loving. You see things that most of us miss—and we get to have those experiences because of you. Why would I want you to be any different?" She pulled away and faced me.

I put a hand over my mouth. I was trying not to cry. "I've been so afraid to tell you. Afraid it would change our friendship."

She looked angry. "I know what you think. Just because I was supposedly popular in high school, you think I was doing you a favor being your friend. It's always kind of pissed me off."

My eyes widened. "I'm sorry."

"So many talents are random, you know. Because I could do some gymnastics, I wound up a cheerleader. Do you think I thought it made me better than you? I'm going to be a musician now because I work hard at it. A lot of that is because of you. And you know what? I'll never be half the artist you are. Not if I live to be a hundred."

down on the south beach drag

"Cassie..." I was stunned.

"You inspire me, Maeve, that's why I like you so much. You inspired me to be a better student too. To take my God-given talent seriously. To shoot for something better than the same old life in this crappy little town."

I put my hands over my eyes. Tears rolled down my cheeks anyway.

"Did I say the wrong thing?" She rubbed my back until I could pull myself together.

"No... it's just... now *I'm* stuck in this crappy little town."

"It's only temporary. You were voted 'Most Likely to Succeed.' Everybody always knew that nothing can keep you down."

Her compliments were starting to embarrass me. "Oh, I never got to ask you. What happened with Bobby?"

"Ha." Cassie giggled. "It turned out there are plenty of other guys who are way better in bed. I don't think of sex as a big mystery anymore. Or that it automatically means true love. Some just try harder. Dealing with Bobby and his big ego? It got old pretty fast."

Both Cassie and Sandra had skated away from scandal unscathed. It wasn't fair.

Our whole town was pointing their finger at me—I was the Jezebel, but I hadn't slept with different men. Or *any* men, for that matter. Cassie'd had sex with a guy when she was high on acid. And Sandra? Come on. She was totally amoral and hadn't paid any kind of price for it. Likely never would.

Neither of them was wasting time worrying about mortal sin, like me. Was it all bullshit? The whole Catholic thing?

We were in the deep woods now.

Cassie got a nervous look on her face. "Georgie's grandfather is a powerful man. You know that, right? He really wanted Georgie to go to college. That's probably not going to happen now, with his felony charge. They'll make a plea deal on the stabbing, but with a record of any kind, the good colleges..."

"How do you know all this?" I stopped walking and studied her face.

"I've been visiting him in jail."

A punch to the gut. I would have done anything to see him. The conditions of my parole wouldn't allow me anywhere near that jail.

"How is he?" I asked.

Cassie went pale. "Not great." Her voice broke. "It hasn't been easy. He says it's the only time in his adult life he was happy to be mistaken for a girl. You know, at least they put him with women. It's been hard, even so. But"—her face brightened—"his family decided, given the circumstances, to support him in trying to become a professional singer. They're finally getting behind him in a big way. Once he's out, they're going to bankroll a group of the Asbury Park musicians to travel around the country and tour. They're going to buy us two white vans. He's designated me as the lead female vocalist." She let that sink in, looked up at the sky. "He's sure I'll land a record deal."

A chill went through me and I stomped away, shaking with anger. This was *not* happening. Not on top of everything else.

I wanted to kick something. Smash something, hard.

Cassie followed me but kept her distance. "It only makes sense," she pleaded, her voice tender.

"You bitch."

"Stop." Her voice hardened. "Don't say anymore. Don't say things like that, 'cause you can't take them back."

"You and Georgie," I spat out. "*My* Georgie."

This was the straw that broke the camel's back. I fell to the ground sobbing.

She sagged under the weight of my fury. "Think about it this way—it's a good opportunity for both Georgie and me. It's not like we're never coming back. It's not like Georgie and I are dating."

down on the south beach drag

I groaned toward the sky. "It's worse than that. You're going to get all Paul McCartney, John Lennon kind of bonded. The Sonny and Cher kind. Simon and Garfunkel. How can I compete with that?" Brutal. Cassie was *my* best friend. Georgie was the man *I* loved.

She cast her big blue eyes toward the ground. "Simon and Garfunkel broke up two years ago."

"Aaaaaaah!" I screamed. "The worst of it. The absolute worst. I'm in prison here, and Georgie asks *you* to go with him."

When she shrugged, I started to run.

chapter 27
long walk home

Cassie knew better than to chase me. I howled as I sprinted my way back home. I wanted to run until I threw up, purge myself of all my foolish notions, admit it was time to surrender. I was never going to get what I wanted. It just couldn't be done. There would be no New York, no great love, not even a life I could tolerate.

Days somehow passed. I stumbled around at home, trying to be of some help. Cassie left messages, but I didn't return her calls. I overheard Mom telling a friend I was a ghost of my former self. Father Murphy came to counsel me and my parents. He had softened his opinion of me, and wanted to help us weigh options for my future. The neighbors began saying hello when I stepped outside our house. Father must have spoken to them too.

All that was well and good, but it didn't make a difference, now that any possibility of ever living my real life was over.

Pop came home one night and said he'd seen Sandra's father. Mordy was so relieved that she hadn't been hurt in the fire, he'd been happy to let her use his credit card to buy a whole new wardrobe. Pop was shocked and, I think, very disappointed in his friend.

"I'm starting to see how all this happened, Maevey," he said. "You girls were too young to be on your own. It should have been clear to me that you couldn't control the others. We shouldn't have asked you. I'm sorry, my girl." The regret in his voice melted me.

Pop also informed me that Sandra had sold another luxury house through Katz Real Estate. With her family's help, she'd used her commission and what was left of the money she'd made from her last sale to put a down payment on her dream home, and secured a mortgage.

All the while, I was still sleeping in a twin bed, sharing a room with my baby brother. Sandra was the one who'd brought Rickey into our lives to begin with and then kept him coming around for the kicks it gave her, never giving a thought to the danger she was putting us all in. The injustice of it all was intolerable. Since all of my cameras and cash had gone up in smoke, I didn't even have photography for comfort.

The provisions of my bail agreement, and Mom and Pop's rules, meant I couldn't even return to the apartment in Ocean Grove to look through the wreckage.

I had nothing but the shirt on my back.

We sat down as a family every night for dinner. Mom and Pop insisted, though they stared at their plates in hostile silence the entire time. The only sound was utensils scraping the china, sometimes punctuated by the baby crying.

It didn't help when a reporter found a portion of one of my black-and-white negatives that had somehow survived the fire, then convinced Rickey to lend him one of the color prints I'd taken of him in the nude. A scathing newspaper article was printed in both Bergen and Monmouth Counties, which included my hometown and Asbury Park. The title was "Lewd Voyeur Apprehended." It sounded like they were talking about someone else, someone I didn't know. Certainly not a good little Irish Catholic girl like me.

A companion piece, an opinion article, asked the inflammatory question, "What is happening to young people today?" The essay concluded that parents weren't doing their jobs anymore.

Mom took to her bed in shame after the pictures were published—leaving the household chores to me.

Adding to my torment, a representative of the committee for the New York Area Photo Contest called and sent a certified letter that I had to sign for. She was quite rude when she informed me that my preliminary application would no longer be considered. In the event I still chose to send prints to them, she said, the envelope would be stamped return-to-sender and sent back unopened.

I was left with absolutely nothing to lose. So, I wrote a letter.

The Bergen and Monmouth Reporter
Editor Patrick Maloney
185 Woodland Street
Fairlawn, NJ
August 16, 1972

Dear Mr. Maloney,

I am the alleged "voyeur" referenced in your recent article, "Lewd Voyeur Apprehended in Asbury Park." It's clear to me that the reporter isn't aware there is a difference between an artist and a voyeur. Unfortunately, neither were the police. Perhaps a dictionary can illuminate the fine point: An artist is a person whose work exhibits exceptional skill in the arts. A voyeur is a person who gains sexual pleasure from watching others when they are naked or engaged in sexual activity.

Since 1797, when Goya painted The Nude Maja, *many artists have aspired to create a nude rather than merely represent the naked. Their intentions are sometimes misunderstood, as mine certainly were. Yet I can't help but recognize that I'm in good company. Mark Twain once called Titian's* Venus *(1538) "the foulest, the vilest, the obscenest picture the world*

down on the south beach drag

possesses." I'm sure you have seen it. It's actually one of the most beautiful paintings ever created.

In his 1956 book *The Nude: A Study in Ideal Form*, Lord Kenneth Clark draws a difference between the naked body and the nude. He says nakedness is someone without clothes, causing embarrassment, even shame. A nude, on the other hand, as a work of art, has none of those undertones.

My photographs of the performance artist Rickey Travers were the culmination of the work of a sequence of three artists. There was the subject himself, who is a second-generation performer; his tattoo artist, Charles Howell; and me. Under my studio lights, my photographs captured the moment and the man. I am very proud of them.

While I have no doubt the charges against me will eventually be dropped, the entire experience has caused my family a great deal of suffering. They were terrified to find out I'd been caught in a fire, mortified when I was arrested, and are drained financially by my legal fees. I'm sorry to say, being only eighteen, I have very little money of my own, so I can't really help them. It's my only regret.

Any readers who are also lovers of art and would like to help, please drop a note of support to Officer and Mrs. O'Connor, 87 Brook Street, Avalon Park, New Jersey. Yes, my father is a policeman. Can you imagine what he's going through?

Art lovers unite!

Sincerely,

Maeve O'Connor

Defending myself, I felt better than I had in weeks. How I hoped that they would print my letter, and some readers would understand.

In the meantime, I had to find some way to take a break.

long walk home

Reading had always been an easy escape for me. Though there were some who were still shunning me, I decided to risk the ridicule and walk down to the library for a good novel to lose myself in.

The problem with the library was that I hadn't returned the last two art books I'd borrowed many months ago. They were hidden in my special box, my hiding place, up in the loft of the garage. I also didn't look forward to the expression on the librarian's face when I handed them over; they included some pretty risqué shots. If she was someone who already felt scandalized by my behavior, my choice of books would surely inflame her opinion of me.

No matter. It was the only way I could get another loaner.

As I climbed the ladder to the partial loft where I kept the box, dust fell from the joists and made me cough. A cluster fell on my white shorts as I ascended. Kind of disgusting.

But as soon as I reached the top, relief flooded through me. The box was right where I'd left it.

I grabbed it and carried it down under one arm.

The workbench in the back of the garage was covered with tools. I cleared some space off the top so I could lay the box down. It took both hands to slide the carton's top up and off.

Something . . . something about the contents was different. I gasped as it became clear.

On top of the library books were three stacks of negatives, secured by rubber bands. I released some and held them up to the light coming from a window. These were the pictures I'd lost in the fire!

There was also a brief note, written on the charred remains of a page from my old notebook.

> *If your father knew we had been spending time together, he would be even more upset than he is now. Though we are related, he never approved of me or my family. I thought I*

down on the south beach drag

would just leave the pictures here for you to find. So you see, my dear girl, this is one of my gifts. A dream woke me and made me run to help with the fire. It showed me right where the negatives would be, and where they should go. And once I had them, I ran so the police wouldn't get ahold of them. I'm afraid I've had run-ins with cops before, and don't trust them.

The bastard deserved getting stabbed; you are not to blame. Call me at 201-646-9321 and leave a message. Better yet, come visit. There is always a place for you with me. Just don't tell Malachi until this all simmers down.

It was signed, *Your Cousin.*

I walked on air to the library and returned the books. Glared the librarian right back in the eye. *Go ahead, judge me if you want—I no longer care, you old biddy.*

Feeling evil, I asked, "Where might I find a copy of Phillip Roth's *Portnoy's Complaint?*" That novel had been banned by the church three years earlier. Just for good measure, I added, "I'm eighteen now."

No more notes needed. Not for me. I thought she would pass out.

The novel was about a lust-ridden, mother-addicted young Jewish bachelor. It had a scene where the main character masturbates, which was a sin in the Catholic Church. The irreverence entertained me for a few days. I went back to the library and borrowed three more banned books. It was an interesting study, thinking about why they were forbidden by the church.

When I was halfway through the last novel, cards came pouring into our mailbox as a result of my letter, which both newspapers actually had deigned to print.

long walk home

Mom displayed them on the fireplace mantel. It *was* heartwarming how many cared about my arrest. Others had written their own letters to the editor to defend me, too, and that certainly helped with Mom and Pop's attitude. My shunning had taken its toll on them. I think they memorized all the kind words. I could just imagine Mom quoting some of these famous people to formulate a retort to the snide comments she'd been getting. Her saying, "Well, Joan, you've heard of the Rockefellers? Yes, well, Happy wrote to me personally. She said artists are born a certain way. There's only so much a parent can do other than honor their gifts and their work."

I was poring over them when Mom answered the kitchen wall phone. It was only when she said, "Maeve, it's for you," that I was pulled out of my stupor.

I stretched the cord out as far away from my brothers at the kitchen table as I could get, took the receiver into the dining room, and sat on the bare wood floor, holding my hand over my other ear to hear over the kids' racket.

No one except Cassie and the photo committee had called me since I'd been home. "Hello?"

"Hi. Is this Maeve O'Connor?" The voice was a strong one.

"Yes, it is." *Who is this?*

"It's Robert Mapplethorpe calling."

A prank call. Someone trying to play a trick on me. Though the very notion of someone local knowing about Robert Mapplethorpe tickled me.

"Very funny . . . and I'm Mickey Mouse." I lay back and giggled. The coolness of the oak planks felt good.

He laughed too. "Ah, really, Maeve, it's me, Robert. I'm trying to think of some way to prove it to you . . . I've never had to do that before. Let's see . . . I just had a pretty big show. You may have read about it."

My heart stopped. I started to hyperventilate, sat up straight, and eked out, "Robert . . . why?"

down on the south beach drag

He chuckled. "I read about your arrest—pretty wild—and I admired the pictures they included with the article. They cropped the black-and-white, right? I'd love to see the whole image."

An audible noise escaped me, unintelligible though it was.

"Then your opinion piece. Good for you, putting yourself out there. Don't take no shit from anybody. Am I right? The letters to the editor in response, they floored me. Peggy Guggenheim. The Vogels! Hollywood stars. Professors. You're a cause célèbre, Maeve O'Connor."

Still wowed about Robert Mapplethorpe calling *me*, I said, "I can be in New York in a couple hours. I'm coming from Jersey."

"No need . . . slow down, Maeve. I've got so many questions for you. Did you get a lot of mail? After the article?"

"Yeah, we did. I'm looking at the cards now, actually. My mother put them on the mantel."

He laughed, sounding delighted.

"The best part—the biggest relief, to tell you the truth"—I was babbling now—"a benefactor paid my legal bills. I couldn't figure out how I was going to pay my parents back. I would have been, like, an indentured servant, forever. I've received enough donations now that I'm going to be able to get some new equipment too."

He laughed uproariously. "You're going to find there's a lot of money hanging around the art world. Rich people can't do enough for you, once you hit. So . . . tell me more. You had the tattoo guy sit for you—both the photographs I've seen are of him. What other kind of work did you do while you were down there?" I heard what I thought was him inhaling a cigarette. "How's he doing, by the way? The guy you stabbed?"

I would never live that down. Probably be best to let it become legend. I told Robert the whole truth anyway. "He's okay. It wasn't me who did the stabbing, despite what you may have heard. Or read. He's going to be fine. My lawyer thinks they're going to dismiss the charges against me soon. I'll have to pay some fines."

I thought about the film negatives I'd found in my box. They were now securely wrapped up and hidden with the others, where no one besides me would ever find them.

"I've got a couple of hundred photos, maybe closer to three hundred, thirty-five millimeter and medium format, but I haven't had time to make prints yet," I told him. "Getting through the police inquiry and the court process has been pretty all-encompassing."

"Sure"—Robert hissed as he exhaled—"I can imagine." Might be he was smoking pot.

Where the energy to pitch Robert on my collection came from, I don't know, but in a heartbeat I went from surprise that this conversation was taking place to being blinded once again by my ambition. The quickest of turnarounds. Head-spinning. Here I was—me, still mired in the muddy bottom of my young life—and here he was, a famous rising star of the art world. Yet I knew I sounded confident when I said, "Yeah, so I have the various sideshow performers from the carnival circuit. Diane was my hero—I'm sure you can tell. Tons of sittings with a wonderful group of trans women. Many of them are performers at the same club, so I've got them in glamorous stripper costumes and some in street clothes. Their master of ceremonies—we became really close—he was raised as a girl, but he's really a boy. He's the sexiest androgynist type you've ever seen. You think Mick Jagger is something? You got to lay eyes on his pictures. So much confidence. Singer, mimic, musician."

I heard Mom moving around by the doorway, and assumed she was listening in. I cupped my hand over the receiver to muffle the sound of my voice.

Robert grunted. "Nice. You sound smitten."

"Completely. You don't know the half of it."

He guffawed. "I don't, but I bet I can imagine."

down on the south beach drag

"Then there was intensive work I did with a fortune teller's community. A large caravan of Travellers."

"You got real Gypsies on film? No kidding. I'd like to see those pictures." He fell silent. "You know, my girlfriend's from South Jersey . . . you catch any music down there? I've been hearing a lot of buzz."

"Sure. My best friend Cassie's a musician." *She is still my best friend. Nothing can stand between us forever.* "She introduced me to everyone. We should go down for a night and see the bands. Before they all leave and go on tour."

"Yeah? That could be fun. You seen that guy everyone's talking about? Bruce . . . ?"

"Springsteen?" I snorted. "Of course. He's great. But it's not just him, Robert. You can't believe the scene at the shore. The bars are jammed. I did a really interesting sequence outside The Upstage Club as the sun was coming up and most everybody left on the sidewalk was coming down. I'd love to show you. A lot of the players I met are in it."

"Let's do this," Robert said. "I have a particular gallery in mind for your first collection. Bring your prints and we'll grab some takeout and have lunch with the owner. What do you think? Saturday at noon?"

What do I think? "I'll see you Saturday. What's the address?"

I looked across the room at Mom, standing by the kitchen stove. My stomach sank. I didn't need her to remind me that, as far as she was concerned, I was grounded.

I was eighteen now, of course. A legal adult. She was going to have to learn that she couldn't control me anymore. But I didn't want to be cruel. This ordeal had been awful—hardest on her.

What to do? What to do?

A light bulb went off in my head. I'd learned many things from her. My current state of affairs notwithstanding, Mom

long walk home

was the master of her own destiny. She knew exactly what she wanted and let nothing stand in her way. I simply wouldn't take no for an answer either. Just like her. We'd have to work it out from there.

chapter 28
here i am

As I came barreling into the room to hang up the phone, Mom's face was flushed from the boiling pot she was stirring. She looked me over slowly, trying to discern what had changed in my demeanor.

The second I put the phone into the cradle, it rang again. I thought it must be Robert, that he'd forgotten to tell me something.

"Hello?"

"Is this Maeve?" a man growled.

"Yes, it is."

"Jesus, Maeve. If you're supposed to be some kind of pervert, what does that make me?" There were multiple guffaws in the background. "It's Big Danny."

I laughed and leaned against the wall. It was so good to hear his voice. "Who's there with you?"

"Everybody. They can't come to the phone right now because they're too busy catching up on some back issues of the newspaper." A crowd's laughter eclipsed everything. How many people were there? I was convulsing against the wall. Laughter feeding laughter. Contagious.

Even Mom was smiling, although I don't think she knew what we were talking about.

"You got celebrities and scholars taking up for you in the

letters to the editor," Danny said. "Damn. You started something. Just remember, there's no such thing as bad publicity. You got to ride this wave. Wait a minute, Boom wants to read you something he found particularly intriguing."

Boom spoke in a proper manner, enunciating each word carefully. "The Tattooed Man, Rickey Travers, said the female photographer went so far as to photograph his genitals." More gales of hooting from the crowd.

"The tree of life, Boom," I whispered. "It grows!"

"The tree of life, guys!" Boom hollered. "It grows!"

Everyone in the background applauded.

Danny took the phone back. I could hear him fighting for it. "Care to share more, Maeve?"

"My mom's standing next to me," I said, sending a covert glance in her direction. "It's not a story I can tell you in its entirety right now."

"Your mother—put her on."

He sounded so sure, I just handed the receiver over. She took off one of her clip-on earrings and held the phone up. "Hello? Well, hi, Danny. You're one of the Belmar Gallaghers?" She whooped. "Oh, I know your mother."

All I could hear from the other end was mumbling.

"Yes, we are related if you go way back, but my people aren't from the same town as yours. The same county, though."

Mumble, mumble.

"All right. I'll tell her. Just hold on one second." She put her hand over the mouthpiece. "Maeve. The kids are going to make a record. I guess there's a recording studio just over the New York border from us."

I held out my hand for the phone and took it back. "Danny, how come you're not recording in the City?"

"No budget for that, girl. Our studio's not that far from you, right?"

down on the south beach drag

"No, not far." My stomach fluttered.

"Can you come take some pictures for us?"

At the studio? You bet I can. "I'll bring several cameras, Danny. And I'll get some new lights too. God knows what it will be like in there. I just need a few days to get ready."

"Here's Cassie," he said. "I'll call when we have a firm date. It should be the first part of next week."

Tears filled my eyes. "It will be wonderful to see all of you again."

"Maeve, it's me."

Cassie.

A sob escaped me. "I'm so sorry. Jealousy made me lose my mind."

"It's okay," she said. "We're going to see each other soon. It will be fun."

Cassie must have held the phone up in the air, for a great chorus of "Bye, Maeve," rang out. With a click, they were gone.

Feeling inspired, I opened the cabinet and dug out the phone book. After finding the name I was looking for, I dialed each number carefully, allowing time for the dial to rotate back to the original position.

A receptionist answered on the first ring.

"Hello," I said quickly, "I'd like to speak to Mordy Katz, please."

"Who's calling, please?"

"Please tell him it's Maeve O'Connor."

He picked right up. *Right* up. "Maeve! How are you?"

"I've been better, Mr. Katz."

We were both silent for a beat.

"I didn't do a very good job of being in charge, did I? I'm sorry."

My mother was listening to every word.

He cleared his throat. "It's a miracle none of you got hurt.

Houses can be rebuilt. There's insurance for that. This, too, shall pass. If I know you at all, you're going to land on your feet."

Mom winced but kept on stirring what was in the pot.

I murmured, "Thanks." This was harder than I'd thought it would be. "You're not going to believe it but, after all that's happened, I'm going to ask you for a favor."

"Okay." He suddenly sounded out of breath.

"I need a car next week," I said. "I was wondering how much it would cost to rent one from you."

Mom turned toward me with a hand on one hip.

"I'll *give* you a loaner, Maeve. I'm not taking money from you. Listen. The summer didn't work out perfectly. That's a given. But Sandra has grown up a lot. She told me some things. I'm not going to speak for her, because I know that one day she'll tell you herself. All I'm saying is, take the car. I don't think any less of you for how all this played out. Hey, I was eighteen once."

I bit my trembling lip and choked up. My eyes met my mother's.

"Pick it up Monday, honey," he said. "I'll have it clean and ready to go."

"Thank you." When I put the phone back in the cradle, I hung on to it with both hands for a few seconds. People could be so kind.

Maybe everything could turn out okay after all. Maybe, just maybe, there was reason to hope.

In a quaking voice that sounded almost awestruck, Mom asked, "What is all this? What's *going on*, Maeve?"

"You're going to have to unground me," I said, my voice only slightly steadier than hers. "At least on Saturday. And then most of next week. I have to go to the City this weekend. I only have three days to get ready for my meeting. It's at a gallery. I'm going down to my darkroom now to print, and I'm not coming up except to sleep."

down on the south beach drag

She shook her head and let out a great sigh. "At least tell me that you're not going to do anything crazy. Promise." Her eyes filled with tears.

"I won't. I promise." I took her by both shoulders and turned her so I could look her in the eye. "Mom, I promise."

We held each other until the pot started to boil over.

I must have sounded convincing, because Mom didn't argue with me. In fact, that evening she left a plate of food on a little chair outside my darkroom's door instead of insisting that I join the family at the table. I ate it when I took a five-minute break to use the bathroom.

By midnight I knew I was on to a really important show. It had all the elements I'd struck out to find and record for posterity. I crossed my fingers and silently thanked Orlaith, wherever she was now. For her entrée to the Travellers. For saving the lost negatives. For helping me to understand my true nature.

I knew she'd heard me. And that I would see her again.

I pinched my tongs to lift a picture of Georgie out of the fixer tray. As I rinsed it with water, I stroked his image with my fingertips. My Georgie. No matter what, I loved that knucklehead. If all I got was friendship, I would take it gladly. What made it so simple was that he was worth it.

Maybe he would come to see the show at the gallery if I really had an opening and he'd gotten out of jail by then. That could be fun.

Some light had appeared in my life. Dim light, maybe, but it was definitely there at the end of the tunnel I'd been living in. The meeting with Robert Mapplethorpe might come to nothing. Big Danny might never call me again. But hope—hope was something worth living for.

A knock at the door made me jump. I was in the middle of

developing another print, and shouted, "Pop, I can't open it right now," though he could have heard me fine if I had spoken in a normal voice.

"Tomorrow's another day, Maevey girl," he answered quietly. "Go to bed."

"No can do." I picked up the front of the developing tray and violently swooshed the solution back and forth across the photo paper. My voice-volume still on high, I said, "I'm going to New York this weekend and you can't stop me."

I thought he must have laid his forehead against the door, because he sounded muted when he spoke next. Lately he had a way of laying his forehead against something when he was upset. "You just might want to keep in mind that the world has changed an awful lot since your mother and I were young," he said. "I went to war, Maeve. I have some idea of the world."

"I know you do, Pop."

"We've made mistakes, your mother and me. We know that. You see . . . we really weren't ready to be parents. You just came along. We were left to figure it out."

I'd always thought it strange that my parents didn't celebrate their wedding anniversary. When I asked about it, they claimed it was an Irish thing. Yet other families I knew did. A chill went through me.

"Pop," I almost barked out. "On what date did you get married? You've never said." I stood frozen, the tongs in the air.

He put on his father voice: "No need to get into all that."

"You didn't want me to find out, but you know I'm not stupid. How long do you think you can keep a thing like that secret?" They'd always acted so superior. Examples of morality, supposedly. "What kind of Catholics did you two turn out to be? You married Mom because she was pregnant!?"

My father scrambled to recover. "We didn't want you to think you weren't wanted. Yes, your mother was pregnant. Scandalous for the time, I admit. And she's maybe gone too far to make sure you don't suffer the same fate. But the world has gone mad. With all the hippies and yippies now? Everywhere I look, I see drugs, sex, and rock 'n' roll. It's an anthem. They act like it's something to be proud of."

I lost track of the amount of time I'd left the paper in the fixer solution. I panicked and had no patience for his rant as I tried to figure it out. "Well, at least the world is opening up. Especially for women."

"Women's liberation?" he scoffed. "A bunch of lesbians. Not that homosexual acts are even criminal in some states anymore. Lord . . . and all the narcotics I'm seeing on the job? It's horrifying. You just wouldn't believe it."

I moved closer to the door and leaned my forehead on the panel too. I wanted him to hear what I said next clearly. "I'm only eighteen, and I already feel like so much has changed in my lifetime. I'm sure it must be hard, Pop, but I'm busy trying to find my own way. I can't take care of you and Mom while I try to figure things out. And I'm not watching your kids anymore. I'm not their mother." There was only two inches of wood between us.

I regretted that last part. About the kids. Things inside me were percolating, and I was taking it out on him. I wished I could reach through the door and embrace him. Just for one second be his little girl again, when things were simpler. But the photo waiting in the tray behind me compelled me to stay. My work was more important. It was more important than anything I had done before. That realization gave me some comfort.

It wasn't that I *wanted* to be a photographer, that I was indulging myself in a whim. I was *born* to it.

"We just always hoped to be good parents," Pop said. "If you love us at all, Maeve, I will continue to expect you to explain yourself." He wanted to make sure I was listening.

"Yeah? I don't know how that is going to work." I put my

hands on the door, spread out and high up, and pressed my full body against it. "I'm not a child anymore."

"Now, this fellow you are going to see in the City," he said, switching gears. "Is he famous?"

I looked up at the ceiling and sighed. "Well . . . I know who he is. All the artists know him, if they are paying attention. I think he's going to be a household name someday soon. So yeah, he's pretty famous."

"We always knew you were different from the other girls," he whispered.

"You did?" All my attention was now focused his way.

"We thought it would pass. That if we discouraged you, it might be a phase."

My eyes filled with tears. "Maybe I don't want it to pass."

"You just haven't met the right man yet. Until you do, it's my job to protect you. Even if it's from yourself."

"Orlaith told me that. That you would fight me." I fumed. I'd been a good daughter, hadn't I? More than good. A good sister. All the responsibility they had heaped on my little shoulders. All that had been required of me. Still, I wasn't good enough for them. I wasn't the girl they had wanted.

A moment of silence stood between us.

"Orlaith?" he finally murmured. "I've a cousin Orlaith. A distant cousin, but those people have intermarried so much, the gene pool is pretty . . . concentrated, I guess you would say. There's some way you remind me of her as you've gotten older." I had already figured that out.

"Pop. I've got to rinse this paper."

For a few minutes, my focus blanked out everything around me. The next sound I heard was the basement stairs creaking as he made his way back up.

chapter 29
no surrender

Saturday morning, the sun was shining down on a crisp October day. I wore an embroidered Chinese silk blouse and a cardigan with a standing collar, both of which I'd found at the thrift store. The contrast of my red shirt under the black sweater filled me with boldness.

I piled my hair high, as usual. In it, I secured one of the Japanese ornaments Todd and Martin had picked out for me. Ribbons of tiny cascading flowers danced whenever I moved my head. I slid a single pencil under it, just in case I needed it.

My mother had surprised me—shocked me, really—earlier that morning with a portfolio case that had a shoulder strap. An olive branch? She'd stopped short of wishing me well. Yet her eyes had filled with tears when she presented it to me, meticulously wrapped in turquoise tissue paper and ribbon. It smelled brand-new. As I walked to the train station, feeling nervous about my big meeting, I rubbed its buttery leather for good luck.

The train was on time for once. That alone felt momentous.

Here I go.

I window-shopped in Manhattan as I walked to the subway station. I'd left myself plenty of time, for good measure. My long

no surrender

legs felt loose as I ambled along. So many beautiful things to see. Such hip stores. High fashion.

Though I usually dreaded the crowds on subway platforms, I found the station nearly empty, and that, too, seemed significant.

Exactly at noon, I approached our designated meeting spot in SoHo. Robert Mapplethorpe was waiting for me. I recognized him immediately.

Robert Mapplethorpe, I marveled. *Who would have thunk it?*

When I introduced myself, I stuck out my hand, but he gently pushed it aside and hugged me. An affectionate embrace.

"The outlaw girl in the flesh," he said. "You made it to the big city." He held me out at arm's length. "Maeve O'Connor, I like your style."

"You do?"

"What's not to like? Different, but in a good way. I think I'm going to need to photograph you." Now, that was something I didn't hear every day.

He took my arm and started walking. His pace quickened as we reached a corner. He let go and dove ahead of me into the crowd that swarmed the sidewalk.

"Robert," I hollered. "Robert! Stop."

He turned around and let the pedestrians stream around either side of him. Waiting. Smiling.

I ran to catch up to him. "Could you just . . . just let me take you in for a minute?" I begged. "Meeting you is a pretty big deal."

He just kept smiling at me.

In that moment, looking into his eyes, I knew. There was no doubt in my mind. Something big was coming for me.

Who knew Big Danny was so organized? Georgie, newly out on bail, had hired him as production manager. We would be sleeping

down on the south beach drag

in two camper trailers and a big green army tent pitched outside 914 Recording Sound Studios Inc. Billed as *the* place to record on a budget, it was an old, converted garage. Just a squat cement building painted white. The overhead doors of the two mechanics' bays were left wide open.

Georgie's two new tour vans were pulled inside, to get them out of the sun. The vans were used as conference rooms as well as places to live and sleep.

The lot didn't have any grass—it was all asphalt pavement. Heat radiated off it in waves and made the Indian summer sun feel even hotter than it was. My hair absorbed the tar fumes.

We had only one real bathroom, through the back door of the studio. It was surprisingly nice, with a real tub and shower. A nearly constant parade of people streamed into it, so Danny had a porta potty put out back, too, just in case the bathroom was otherwise occupied with showering.

Blauvelt, New York, was in Rockland County, right on the border of Bergen County, New Jersey. My home. I could easily have gone back to my parents' house every night, but I didn't. And wouldn't. I didn't want to miss a thing.

The overarching rule that Danny laid down was that everyone had to be on time and hard at work all day. Sure, he was a gentle giant, but he could still be commanding. Six foot, six inches tall, he had to weigh more than four hundred pounds. He'd been a bouncer in Asbury Park for years, at The Upstage Club. Danny knew how to motivate people. How to talk to them. It was also well known that Springsteen was his roommate. That fact alone commanded respect. So, when he decreed no drinking or pot during working hours, everyone followed the rule. No groupies hanging around, either. Danny's schedule for laying down tracks ticked along like clockwork.

But once the sun went down? Another story entirely.

no surrender

When he first called me to be their house photographer, I hadn't focused on the fact that Georgie was involved. Yet it made perfect sense, as his family was their investor. Cassie had told me that day in the woods that his family had come around, and everyone knew they had money. Georgie said he wanted to get into the music business, and now he was doing just that.

I had a renewed respect for the guy—he did what he said he was going to do. This tour Cassie had told me about was going to support the recordings they were making. Georgie the businessman. Savvy.

The second he saw me, he took me aside and whipped out his signature roll of money. He looked at me steadily. "Whadda you need? Name it."

It wasn't money that I wanted from him. "I still got some money from donations. My patrons." I was embarrassed that he'd asked. "Did you know Big Danny wanted me to come?"

"I would have called you myself, but I was otherwise indisposed." His eyes twinkled.

"And I was under a court order," I said. "Couldn't even call you. That's what the judge said."

"Talk about a sight for sore eyes. Not as sore as Rickey's turned out to be. But still."

We laughed so hard, I grabbed on to both his hands to keep upright.

"It's only funny because Rickey's all right now," I said, wiping happy tears away. "I'm surprised he didn't have permanent damage to his eye. I gave it my all."

"As muscular as he is, I thought I'd better push hard with that knife too." He put his arms around me. A tender hug.

"I admit, I passed out drunk when I got home that night," I said. "Where were you?"

"On that chaise lounge in the far corner. When we all came

down on the south beach drag

in, Cassie told me to go ahead and crash. I was in rough shape too." The way he looked at me made me shiver. He whispered in my ear, "Thank God I was there."

"I think I'll thank you instead of God, since you were the one who stopped that lunatic."

"You're welcome." He clapped his hands together. "All right. Time to talk business. How do you *want* to get paid?"

"Save your cash," I insisted. "I have a different idea. You let me be in charge of all the photographs. Take as many shots as I want. I get exclusive access to every room in the building. Whenever." It was a ballsy request. A lot to ask, since there would surely be other photographers who were interested in taking pictures. I had to look away, afraid I might burst out laughing.

He noticed and smiled. He didn't miss anything. "Access to everything . . . including the about-to-be-famous Cassie Olsen?"

I nodded, my faced flushed. "And, Georgie . . ." I couldn't go on. Really. Where was I getting the nerve? "I want the album cover."

He held up one finger, lost for a moment in thought. "You don't want to get paid now, but you want us to use one of your pictures for our album cover?"

"Yeah. You pay me for the cover and any pictures you'll want for publicity. Magazines. Portraits. Stuff like that."

He shook a finger at me. "You really are something, Maeve O'Connor. So, I don't incur any incidental costs right now, but you get to jump-start your career." One of his eyebrows was raised. He was impressed.

"Something like that."

He held his hand out. "Deal."

We shook on it.

"But, Maeve, we aren't going to know for a while whether we'll want the cover to be in the studio or live onstage. That means you're going to have to come out on tour. At least part of

no surrender

the time. I'm going to be in and out too. I still have to show up for parole hearings. You can catch rides with me."

Hmmm, on tour with Georgie? Music to my ears. A satisfied smile spread across my face.

He rubbed the back of his neck. "And, uh, I got a brand-new silver bullet camper being delivered today. A gift from my grandfather. Kind of a bon voyage present. I wonder if you might consider . . . staying in there with me? While you're here."

I pursed my lips. I was going to get some answers before I agreed. In the end I would cave, no question about it. But I had to know. "Did you ask Cassie first?"

"Why would you think that?"

I threw my hands in the air.

"Okay. Okay. It was just the music, Maeve. When it flows between Cassie and me, it's magic. You've said so yourself. I mistook that for something else. I knew it upset you. I'm sorry—"

"About your love affair?"

"My crush. A flirtation is all. People make mistakes." His eyes locked with mine.

Arms crossed, I could feel a stubborn frown pulling at my face. "How do I know it's really over?"

"Over?" He shook his head. "It never really started. She was still schtupping Bobby. And then that other string of guys." He grabbed my shoulders and pulled me closer to him. I dropped my arms to my sides. Eyes locked on mine, he said, "Jail has a way of making priorities clear. When I was in there, I thought about you. I pictured a life with *you*."

I nodded, hearing the truth in what he said. Believing every word.

I fake-scowled at him. "I still want the cover."

He pulled me to him, laughing.

chapter 30
one of a kind (love affair)

Cassie and Georgie were working on their first album; at the same time, the larger Asbury Park group was making their anthology. It was to be a double package. The working title was *Arcade Sounds*. Sort of a Mad Dogs and Englishmen meets the Jersey Shore kind of thing. It wasn't a live recording, like Mad Dogs, but all the songs would be performed live as part of the show.

Georgie and Cassie came floating in from a different room to lay down some guitar, piano, or vocals when they were called to do it. The other players on *Arcade Sounds* did the same for them. It worked out well for everyone. The whole place was steeped in mutual admiration. For me, as well. I was proud to be the one they called to document these early days, sure that soon we would look back at the kids we'd been. Before we all made it big.

Georgie and Danny had conceived the show they'd be taking around the country, so most everyone was onstage at all times. Just the headliners rotated downstage when it was their turn. There would be staging rehearsals when the recording sessions were completed. These would happen in an old theater in Manhattan that had a hotel next door. In the meantime, we were camping out here in Blauvelt, New York.

As the first full workday came to a close, I found my bag and

one of a kind (love affair)

headed toward Georgie's silver bullet trailer. He'd given the whole crew a tour when it arrived, so I already knew that the couch in the living room folded out to become a full-size bed. I found him making it up with crisp white sheets and a summer quilt.

I stood quietly, admiring him. The cut of him. His gentle manner.

He looked up, and I motioned for him to give me one side of the blanket so I could help.

"This is a beautiful quilt," I said. "I've never seen anything like it."

He smiled. "My grandmother made it. She invented the design. Everybody in the family has one. When she gave this one to me, she said it was my wedding quilt."

Naturally, I was moved by that. I didn't know what to say.

He fluffed the pillows. "Lie down for a minute. Try it out."

I sat at the edge, then flopped backward. For a fold-out, the bed was surprisingly comfortable.

He reached into a storage compartment above us and pulled out a box. Shiny and silver, tied with a sheer silver ribbon.

I sat up and put my hands to my face. "What's this? What have you done? It looks like a fairy gift-wrapped it."

He was obviously pleased. "Open it."

"I can't. It's too pretty to wreck." I threw my arms around him and gave him a grateful smooch.

He had a comical frown on his face. "Come on, honey. Please."

Carefully, ever so carefully, I untied the bow and opened the box. In it was a gold hair clasp with claw-like combs that would easily secure my topknot, crazy curly hair or not. On dainty chains, tiny moon and star charms cascaded down. I reached with my fingertips and fanned them out, taking in the attention to detail that had gone into each piece. My breath caught, for there among the many charms, so subtly you had to look closely, one read, "Maeve and Georgie."

down on the south beach drag

I cried. He held me tight.

"A special gift for my special girl. Custom-made, just for you."

We kissed. Then made love as if it were the most natural thing in the world. The exquisite newness made every caress almost painful in its intensity.

I don't think I really slept afterward. I was too aware of the feel of his naked flesh. His intoxicating scent.

At some point I must have dozed off, as I awoke to the perfectly matched aromas of fresh coffee and bacon frying.

He saw me rousing. "There's my princess," he said. As if he had no doubts at all.

By some miracle, my parents' house was empty when Georgie and I came through the back door, our arms stacked with cardboard boxes.

"Let's start in my darkroom." I pointed to the door leading down to the basement.

Georgie nodded and led the way. He was so cute in his blue-checked shirt and red sneakers. So casual. He had to duck to make his way down the old stairs.

It was Sunday. We had a few hours off from recording, and had thought to make the most of it by getting my things while the family was away at Mass.

"This isn't going to take long," I said. "I never really settled in when I got home from the shore. That would have made it all feel too real. Like I was never going to get out of this place."

He reached over and patted me, then set to stacking my sleeves of organized negatives like he was handling paintings by Rembrandt.

As if I'd known this day would come, I still had the original box my projector had come in. It was folded and tucked between the wooden studs of the wall framing—still in pretty good shape,

one of a kind (love affair)

even after eight years. The chemicals I'd mixed up would be good for a while.

Seeming to read my mind, Georgie said, "Just put the bottles in an open carton. We'll only be moving a few boxes in the front entrance at a time . . . but I have to say, I still wish you'd called your parents before we came over. I feel like we're breaking in. Like thieves."

"I knew they'd be at Mass," I protested. "It was such a last-minute thing."

"Still. The way your father spoke to me last time—it would have been better for everyone to have a heads-up." Footsteps made him look up at the ceiling. "Uh-oh."

I winced. "Sounds like someone's home."

It sounded, in fact, like an army: Scuffling. A thud. The baby starting to whine.

"I hope you're ready, Georgie." I shot him an apologetic look. "It sounds like it's the whole passel of them. Brace yourself."

The first few moments would be the worst. Mom didn't know anything about him, aside from what she'd seen in the papers after the fire. Naturally, meeting him here, like this, would come as a shock. *Please don't let her say something awful*, I sent up a prayer. I knew how insulting she could be. But she wasn't going to get away with that. Not with my sweet man.

I took Georgie's hand and went up the narrow stairs ahead of him. When I stepped over the threshold and into the room, I had to yank him to come stand beside me.

All five of my brothers stared at us silently. It was as quiet as the grave for a few moments.

"Hey, everybody." My voice came out falsely cheerful. I heard the dissonance, but didn't know how to stop. "This is Georgie." There you go, family. Deal with it.

I met Pop's stare and glared back, fighting the urge to stick my tongue out at him.

down on the south beach drag

Mom, to my shock, was unruffled. "That's a lovely shirt, I must say, Georgie. May I ask where you got it?"

"Gimbels. They're on sale." His voice was steady and smooth. Cool as a cucumber.

How was everyone pulling this off but me? My heart could have belonged to a hummingbird. "So, Georgie, this is my mom and dad. Uh . . . I guess you already met Pop."

"Mrs. O'Connor; Mr. O'Connor," Georgie murmured, nodding with each name.

I continued with the pleasantries. "And here are, in descending order according to their age, my brothers: Mike, Terry, Seamus, Brian, and baby Tommy."

I said the list fast, to get a laugh from my parents. It did, but the boys were unimpressed. All but the baby gave a wave to Georgie and scowled. They looked like they were dying to be dismissed.

"All right, boys," Pop said, and they all scattered.

All but Mikey. He sat down at the table instead. "You won't believe what just happened," he said. "Father Murphy stood up at Mass and announced he was leaving."

I shook my head. "What do you mean, leaving?"

As Mom filled the teakettle with water, she said, "He says he's taken a teaching job in Manhattan. At New York University. What can it mean? That's not a Catholic school."

Hmmm. Was this why Mom was behaving herself? Because she was distracted by Father's news? But it was all so odd. Priests could teach at Catholic schools; everybody knew that. But at NYU? What *did* it mean that he was leaving Our Lady of Victories?

"After the concluding rites and the blessing, when he came down the aisle, everyone descended on him," Mom said. "At least your father and I had the decency to stand back and wait. But we could hear what they were saying. It seems he's rented an apartment right there in Greenwich Village." She whispered the

one of a kind (love affair)

location like she'd said a dirty word. Her eyes skittered around the room as though checking to see if anyone had heard her.

I locked eyes with Georgie, and we laughed. We couldn't help it.

Unlike Mom, who seemed perplexed, Pop went ramrod straight at the sound and shot us a look that squelched our obvious amusement.

I didn't dare look at Georgie for fear I'd crack up again. "We'll have to find out where he is and go visit," I said.

Mom's mouth dropped open. "I wouldn't do that, dear. We don't know anything about his . . . his . . . neighborhood."

In a singsong voice, Georgie whispered, "Yes . . . we . . . do."

His voice rising on the "*do*" made me double over. Peals of laughter sent tears streaming down my cheeks. When I started to cough, he patted me on the back.

As I wiped my eyes, I said, "Look. We have to get back to the studio, but I needed some things. Robert—he's taken really good care of me. You know that he helped me apply for that grant, New Dimensions for the Arts? He called me at the studio and told me he's got a room arranged at the Chelsea too."

"The Chelsea Hotel?" The infamous Chelsea Hotel. Pop grabbed the back of a chair before he toppled over, then sank into it with a sigh.

I'd never really believed that people swooned. Apparently, I was wrong.

"I would be furious if you moved in with any man without marital vows," he said in a low voice. "But this? This?" He shook his head, more to himself than at me.

I decided to act like I didn't notice he was upset by the idea. I wouldn't give him the satisfaction. "Yeah, so, I've got the car one more day. We'll move my stuff in tomorrow."

Pop nodded and looked at his folded hands. Not at me. Or Georgie.

down on the south beach drag

"How will I be in touch with you, Miss Goofy?" Mikey asked, using my old nickname. I'd played a lot of silly games with him when we were little.

Mom was hugging Pop from behind as he sat in the chair. "She's dead to me," he murmured. "Dead. I don't have a daughter."

I staggered a few steps backward and Georgie caught me. Mikey let out a loud groan. In our culture, this was a statement saved for children who had committed the most egregious sins.

"Dad, for God's sake," Mikey said. "This is Maeve you're talking about."

I went and put my hand on my brother's shoulder. "I'm going to write you every week. Okay? Can you read the letter to the other boys? Please? If you don't get them, if Pop doesn't give them to you, go down to the library and find out the address of the Chelsea Hotel on West 23rd. You write to me and we'll figure something else out. Or just get on the bus and find me. It's not a great neighborhood, but I know you can handle yourself."

He stood up and hugged me. I started to cry. I tried to wipe the tears away.

"Mike? Can you grab my two suitcases out of my room? We're going to get my darkroom stuff."

Downstairs, Georgie whispered, "It's so sad. Why do you have to leave everyone behind? What is the *matter* with them?"

"It's the Catholic thing," I said, stifling a sob. "Sex is only allowed in marriage, and only if you are trying to have a child. You know that. Add to that, only regular boys and girls are allowed. The rest of us are supposed to hide in the shadows."

He took my hand in his and held it to his heart.

Packed up and ready to go, I slammed the trunk of the car. Georgie pointed to the picture window. All five of my brothers stood there, waving goodbye.

one of a kind (love affair)

Mikey cupped both hands around his mouth and hollered "One, two, three . . ."

The other boys shouted, "Bye, Maeve!"

"One, two, three . . ."

"Bye, Maeve!"

"One, two, three . . ."

"Bye, Maeve!!"

Georgie put his arm around me. We waved back at the boys.

Just as we were starting to enjoy the revelry, Pop appeared. He picked up the baby and shooed the others away. Then he turned his back on me.

The gallery was a relatively new establishment: a nonprofit cooperative at 143 Prince Street, the first photography gallery in SoHo. A second-floor loft under renovation, it was called SoHo Photo. The greatest thing about it was that young and old, Pulitzer Prize winners and unknowns, could all hang out together. There were workshops and classes, a group that gathered for coffee. Sometimes, at night, there were impromptu parties. The artists I met there had tremendous influence on my first real show.

As always, money was an issue for me. It was terrifying that my entire career was held in the balance and I couldn't hire professional framers. But there were eighty members of SoHo Photo, and many helped me, contributing their leftover equipment and materials. By necessity, all the picture moldings were mismatched—sometimes within the same piece. Much discussion was had about what worked and what looked trashy, how to make the most of what we'd been given and make it all look purposeful. Corny versus reimagined, visionary, fresh. The presentation of the hangings was decided by committee. I was happy to have the help.

Orlaith agreed to come to New York to do readings at the opening, kind of a party favor for those willing to come to my show. Mysterious Orlaith of the Travellers; I knew she was the real thing. There were many who walked away from her table shaking their heads, saying something like, "How did she know that? Did you tell her?"—only to turn the corner and find a cluster of portraits of her at the wedding in the encampment. "That's her—she's a real Gypsy!"

Not a Gypsy, a Traveller, I corrected them silently, shaking my head and smiling.

As people milled around, Georgie played his keyboard. Basically, he was doing his cocktail hour sets. Always a hit.

Mom and Pop arrived the moment the doors opened. They were already worried about driving back out of the city and across the bridge at night. I felt a little sick about Mom seeing some of the photos of Rickey. It would have helped if there'd been more people around—a big crowd would be a buffer of sorts—but they were so early that barely anyone had arrived yet.

Rickey's photos were presented right up front, and before I could even get to the door to greet my parents, Mom walked up to them.

I followed. Better to get it over and done. *Call me depraved if you must, Mom—get it over with.*

"Of course they are going to hate it," Georgie had told me. "The show's not art to them. All they care about is how it's going to make them look—'What will other people think?' and all that. You've got to be stoic. The only thing that matters today is what the critics think and whether your work sells. I'll tell you one thing for sure: You get good reviews? And make some money? Eventually they are going to come around."

As I approached my mother and the wall where the portraits of Rickey hung, I heard a woman say, "Hello, I'm an art critic for the *New York Times*."

Mouth hanging open, I watched as she shook my mother's hand.

chapter 31
because the night

"A critic for the *New York Times*—imagine," Mom said. "And a woman too. Your mother must be so proud of you."

The younger woman had thin, sandy-colored hair cut short, in the style Vidal Sassoon had made famous. She was shorter than my mother, so she spoke up to her.

"My mother? She would rather I'd been a secretary. She doesn't approve at all."

Mom clutched at her necklace. "Oh, my."

"I'm Stella. And I want your opinion." She pointed to a photo of Rickey that I'd shot as he swung his penis.

I expected Mom to faint dead away. Instead, she hung on Stella's every word. Someone who worked for the *Times* obviously had sway with her. Good to know.

"The artist used a longer exposure, as you see. The movement blurs his phallus. So well done. At once blunt, because he's naked, but more palatable because we're not left staring at his genitals. Instead, what we focus on is the rest of his body language. The images on his skin that she chose to capture. The expression on his face. So . . . I'm sorry, I didn't get your name."

"Sheila."

"Oh, I love that name. And you're so pretty too."

Martin went by with a tray of champagne; he and Todd had insisted they be waiters. Stella took two glasses and handed one to

Mom. The wine had been a gift from Georgie's family. His parents would be coming to celebrate after they had dinner nearby. They'd invited us, too, but I would have been far too nervous to eat before the show.

"So, Sheila, who is this man before you in the photograph? Is he brutal? Or is he jubilant? What's your take?"

"I think he's, perhaps, misunderstood," Mom said slowly. "A man who has chosen to become an outsider, one painful inch at a time, so he must suffer greatly. And maybe no guidance. Maybe alone in the world." She looked like she was going to cry.

Stella clinked my mother's glass with hers. "Cheers. A very interesting point of view. Thank you. Ah, here's the artist." She waved to me; I'd stopped just short of my mother's attention. "Bravo, Maeve O'Connor. Bravo."

I stepped to join them. "Thank you. I heard what you said, Mom. He's actually very close to his family. They are sideshow performers too. I don't know about him suffering. He's totally self-absorbed."

"But why would he choose to be abnormal?" She frowned. "Doesn't that isolate him?"

"Lots of people are born a certain way, Mom. They don't choose it."

"You must tell me what happened to him, dear," Stella said. "Your model."

I laughed. "Last I heard, he's taken up preaching. He talked a little church down there into letting him say their services. The Tattooed Preacher."

Stella's mouth formed an O. "Absolutely amazing. What do you think the parishioners are like?"

"Probably folks from the carnival life on the boardwalk. You get many outliers at the shore, that's for sure."

Stella moved on to the next section of prints, and Mom turned to me with a gasp. "She loves your work." This was the first time she'd ever referred to my pictures as work. "Maeve. Do you think you'll be in the *Times*?"

I shrugged. "You never know. Maybe."

She grabbed my arm. "I always buy the Sunday paper. If you're mentioned, I'll call you."

I could just see her at the kitchen table tomorrow morning. Poring over the Arts and Leisure section. "I'd like that."

She turned back to the photos of Rickey and just stood there, shaking her head in wonderment.

When I walked away from her, I was smiling. How about that? For once my mother had been stunned into silence.

Next to Georgie and his piano, a second microphone was set up. When Cassie arrived, she did a few duets with him, classic hits to get the crowd going. "Dancing in the Streets." Motown. Disco. Right before they took a break, they did a song from their new album. It was politely received, though it wasn't the best setup for an audience to accept original music.

"After our break I'm going to turn this over to Georgie," Cassie announced after their last song. "But first, can we please raise our glasses to the woman of the hour? My best friend and the artist we are honoring tonight, Maeve O'Connor."

When the crowd toasted me, I choked up. Things like this didn't happen every day. Or any day, for that matter. I wanted to remember every moment.

The gallery director hustled over as Cassie stepped away and spoke for a moment too.

"We are so thrilled to be hosting this event, and I thank you all for coming," she began.

The room was teeming at this point. Loud with conversation. It was tough to get their attention. She waited patiently until things quieted down.

down on the south beach drag

"I just wanted to introduce myself and let you know that we are almost sold out. If you are interested in investing in the first important works of the photographer Maeve O'Connor, please find me and I'll let you know which pieces are still available. I'll be at the desk. Thank you."

Georgie raised his glass to me from across the room and mouthed the words, "A triumph." When I blew him a kiss, he winked.

Where was Pop? I desperately wanted to know his reaction.

Jaysus. He was still standing by the door. Right where Mom had left him when she first walked in. I'd never seen a man look so uncomfortable. Had he even looked at any of my pictures?

Orlaith walked over to him, and what seemed to be an argument ensued. It was probably about me. What else?

I didn't want anyone overhearing, so I scurried over to try to make the peace.

"You always were a smug little son of a bitch," Orlaith was saying as I walked up. "You think you're better than everyone else? For you, there was always only one road. And it was the straight and narrow. Especially the narrow."

"These pictures are profane, Cousin," Pop said. "Disgusting. How this kind of thing could be produced by my little girl is an outrage. An outrage."

"You can't see her gift, Malachi?" she demanded. "Even a blind man could see it."

I saw Pop's stone facade crack just a little at those words. Though she was so small her face was tilted up to his, above her, she was having an effect on him.

Father Murphy walked through the door just then—*Good timing, Father*—and hugged me. When he pulled away, his eyes crinkled lovingly. "You're such a brave girl. Always have been. You have inspired me."

"Thank you, Father." I flushed. Why was he so emotional?

because the night

"No, no. No more of that. You are an adult, and I am . . . well . . . defrocked, I suppose. Though I prefer to think of it as retired. You may call me Francis now. My given name. I wish you would." He was wearing slacks and a soft summer sweater in pastel green.

Pop was standing close enough to overhear the exchange. Apparently, it was the final straw for my father, as he stormed out, muttering, "Blasphemous."

Father—Francis, rather—remained calm. Serene. He was still the same man. Perhaps more so. He seemed to shine.

"How's the teaching going?" I asked.

Orlaith drew closer to us. It was much too crowded to consider any more readings this evening, though she had a fistful of business cards from people who wanted to book her at their events. She looked very pretty in her long, cream-colored dress. It had a plunging neckline and was fitted to reveal her lovely figure. A narrow sequined scarf was woven into her hair. Her eyes shone with interest when she glanced up at Francis.

"It's going well," he said. "I love working with college-aged students. Can you believe someone is paying me to opine on all I love most in the world? Art history, the greatest painters and sculptors—they actually give me a budget to buy art books and materials to prepare my lectures." He slapped his leg and laughed out loud. "I feel like a thief taking a paycheck for that."

We laughed, too, delighted for him.

I was a bit surprised when Orlaith laid her hand on his arm. She had a certain look on her face. The serious one. We both went silent and leaned toward her. She closed her eyes.

"On top of this new happiness," she intoned, "you will find love as well."

"Will I?" He put his hand over hers. "I'm an old man. Are you sure?"

She opened her eyes and smiled at him in that way she had, looking directly into his soul. Anyone that had seen her do it

down on the south beach drag

couldn't deny it had happened. Francis sputtered something incomprehensible.

"Yes," she said. "One of Maeve's people."

I was fascinated and had to know more. "My people? My people how? A family member? A friend?"

She removed her hand and shrugged. Her eyes looked dreamy. It was as if she'd been away and was slow in settling back into the here and now. "I only tell what I'm given. I never speculate beyond what I'm told."

Francis smiled. "Well, I am delighted to hear it. Finding love would certainly be a bonus." He offered an arm to each of us. "Can you take an old man on a tour? Judging by all the people outside talking about this show, you're a smash hit."

Danny burst in the door carrying large speakers. "Maeve," he called out, "wait a minute. Where do we set up? Hey, Orlaith. Father."

I pointed over toward Georgie and whispered in Francis's ear, "I'll tell them all later to call you by your name. It's going to take some time for everyone to get used to it. Don't you think?"

He shrugged. "Some never will. They will see my defection as betrayal. A sin. That's why I must surround myself with those who love me—exactly as I am. Whether they agree with my decisions or not."

Francis wanted to see the pictures of the sideshow entertainers. Though he didn't know much about the technical part of photography, he sure knew the other visual arts. He was a font of knowledge.

"The sword swallower," he mused aloud, studying the image. "Give me a minute to take it in. I like that you have him backlit from the small square window. Since all is shrouded in shadow, it's also steeped with mystery. I feel compelled to move closer. To examine the areas of the highlights."

"This is so interesting for me," I told him. "So helpful,

informing my work like this. What else do you see?" I, too, moved closer.

He folded his arms across his chest. This must be how he looked at his lectern. "Authority" was the word that came to mind. Just by his bearing—his self-assurance, that spark that leapt from his eyes and swept across his face—you knew he was an expert.

"Well, it's very Christlike, isn't it?" he said. "The only thing we see of the actual sword, when he's done swallowing, is the top of the shaft and the handle. It creates a cross at the top of the image. His arms are stretched out to his sides in complete surrender. Like Jesus on the cross." He cupped his chin with his thumb and forefinger, silent for several minutes.

I could hear Georgie playing "Come Rain or Come Shine." A lump rose in my throat.

"Having the sword all the way down his throat like that . . ." Francis glanced over at me and took my arm. "What must he be feeling? There is fear. I see it. Great tension. But in the end, I suspect a wave of sadness. A sadness I wouldn't think I could bear. Yet here he is, bearing it, only proving—so can we all."

He wiped away a tear, and so did I. Then he put an arm around me. "I'm so proud of you."

"Well, I have to tell you, I'm proud of you too," I said with conviction. "You were a great priest. Teacher. Mentor." I put my hand to his cheek. "But to think you would seize the day so—can I say it?—so late in life. To be fully yourself, accepting all the gifts you were given in the first place, no matter what others say. It's really something." I patted his arm.

He changed the subject, lest the two of us start bawling, and gestured toward my pictures. "Such unusual framing; it might appear haphazard—but it's clearly a community effort. Oh, I wish you'd have let me help you, too, when you were preparing the show. It must have been so much fun."

"I'll introduce you to the director of the cooperative," I said

down on the south beach drag

eagerly. "You can join tonight. Then you can be part of a lot of projects."

I had to leave him then, for there were so many others seeking a word with me. But I saw him taking his time, standing before each image, savoring them all like a fine French cheese.

Most of the members of The Asbury Revue were setting up by the time Francis was done with his walk-through. They were organizing themselves into a classic rock band format, deciding who would play what part, who would sing lead, and who would help on harmony. All to celebrate me.

The show was totally their idea. Each musician wanted to tell about the first time they'd seen me or noticed I was taking pictures of them. Almost all remembered the song they'd been playing. The set list had been compiled as a walk down memory lane. Didn't that say so much about them? How could a person be more honored?

Mom begged off, as Pop was still skulking around outside, complaining about the drive home. But I did get the chance to introduce her to Georgie's parents.

The champagne had really started to flow once they arrived. Mom took a glass from them happily. Turned out she liked her drink. I laughed and kissed her on the cheek. She dared to keep my father waiting. A new day.

The Bellos, Georgie, Orlaith, Mom, Francis, and I stood in a little circle. Mr. Bello raised his glass—to me. Such a joy! He had that emotional warmth so many Italian Americans I knew possessed.

"Between Maeve and Georgie, the sky's the limit. Look at these kids. It just took us old folks a while to figure it out. If I'd had my way, poor Georgie would have gone to a snooty Ivy League school. Wound up an accountant. All his talent stuck away in some cubicle office."

The group around him furrowed their brows, clearly trying

because the night

and failing to imagine Georgie as an accountant. We all started to laugh.

Mr. Bello shrugged. "I've learned my lesson. We need to let these kids do what they do best. This opening here is really something. Am I right, Sheila? Just spectacular."

Taking another sip of her wine, Mom nodded, though ever so slightly, and even shot me a proud glance from the corner of her eye.

Tiny as the gesture was, I saw it. And it mattered. But she wouldn't indulge me by wallowing in it. That was not our way.

Mrs. Bello knew how it was, her being Irish and all. She called for yet another toast before Mom left.

Mom emptied her glass and pulled me with her as she walked over to a tray stand and set it down. "If I leave your father alone any longer, he'll explode," she whispered. "It's a shame, really. I'm sorry to miss the band."

She went back to the group with her hands clasped high, between her breasts, in the manner of an old-fashioned singer in an operetta. Her idea of a proper lady out socializing? I had to cover a laugh.

"Goodbye, all," she said. "So nice to meet you. And, Georgie, you sounded wonderful. I could listen to you all night."

He caught my eye and lifted one eyebrow, a question in his eyes.

How would I know what to do with her comment? I shrugged back at him.

He took advantage of the moment and took a chance. "Mrs. O'Connor, I wonder, how would you like it if Maeve and I came and did a sing-along for your family sometime?"

She trilled with delight. "Oh, that would be so much fun. Could I invite my sisters? We used to love to sing together."

What? This power of show business. Of music. Of art. An inherent power to change people's minds about things. A renewed sense of responsibility to use this power wisely, and with courage, surged through me.

It was my hope that both Mom and Pop would eventually come to see how these other artists felt about me. The critics too. Whether they did or didn't see it, however, wouldn't change a thing. I was on my path. No stopping me now.

Mom didn't seem to know how to slip away and leave; perhaps she was intimidated by going out to the city street alone. So I walked her out, holding her hand. I couldn't remember ever having held her hand since I was a child. It was sweet. A new chapter. Except now I was taking care of her instead of her taking care of me.

Pop stood under the closest streetlight. I barely recognized him, slouching as he was. A far cry from his usual ramrod straight posture—and, Lord help us all, he was smoking a cigarette. I prayed it was tobacco someone might have let him bum off of them, and not something else. He'd said he'd smoked in the army, but I'd never seen him do it before.

I didn't go over. Didn't want him off on another rant. It was fine with me that they were leaving now. They'd seen the show. Or at least Mom had. At this point they were kind of bound to cramp my style. I wanted to get back to my friends.

I put my arms around my mother. "Thanks for coming, Mom. It was fun hearing your thoughts about some of the pictures."

She squeezed me back. "I'll call Sunday after the paper is delivered."

"Talk to you then. Bye, Pop." But he didn't say a word.

The speeches were just starting when I went back in. Gary's words moved me beyond belief, telling of the first night we'd met. He said he'd been playing "Proud Mary," and went off on a rollicking cover of the song on his guitar. Before leaving the mic, he made it clear that the past summer had been life-changing for many of us. Not just me. "Maeve is our scribe," he said. "Our keeper of the moments. We love her."

Leave it to Georgie to know enough to bring a pile of clean handkerchiefs to wipe away happy tears. He had one for me, for Cassie, for Big Danny (who played "Let's Stay Together" for her as she gave her heart to the vocals).

All these memories of our meetings. How we all became friends. The *why* of it, as Orlaith had once said to me. What landed us here.

Following the speeches, we all jumped on the dance floor. Including Georgie, who was, of course, an incredible dancer.

He leaned over. "Look out now, Girl. There's more to come."

chapter 32
free bird

The ultimate moment. My Georgie onstage, telling and acting out the story of the night we met in front of the Hootch. All of it. Down to the tap dancing challenge I'd offered him as he leaned against that brick wall.

He then sat down at the piano and sang what was probably my favorite song of all time. A hit made famous by Bobby Darin, then Frank Sinatra. "Summer Wind."

Who could even imagine how I felt standing before him, hearing him sing that song for me? Boom came over and put an arm around me. He was crying, too, so taken was he with Georgie's rendition. I handed him the pile of handkerchiefs and he sobbed, "Geez. He's killing me here."

I blew Georgie a kiss when he was done.

As we walked home that night, I don't think my feet ever touched the ground. I sure don't remember what time we got in.

I would learn the next morning that champagne is kind of a bad hangover, but it had all been worth it.

Things weren't the same with Pop after that night at the opening. I didn't understand his problem. I knew what he thought about us, but after all I'd experienced, I didn't buy it.

Georgie wasn't a drag queen or anything similar—though I

free bird

knew plenty, and was clear that, just like the rest of us, some were good people, some not. Human, was all.

Georgie was not a male *impersonator*, as my father accused him. He was just in between; born that way, in body and mind. And he came down more on the male side. Mostly.

Mostly turned out to be exactly my type. He took my breath away.

To say that Pop didn't like this at all would be an understatement. As the weeks went on and he realized I wasn't coming home, he banned us from his house forever. He didn't really know what to call us, but he was sure we were deviants of some sort.

Mom told me Pop called us names. It was upsetting her.

I wasn't exactly a lesbian, was I? We had close friends who were, but I didn't think what we had was exactly the same. Georgie wasn't a woman.

Whether Pop liked it or not, in fact, my boyfriend was usually the sexiest dude in the room. Something I noticed early on. He was attractive to many people—men and women. Not all, but many. They all said the same thing: You couldn't miss his charisma. His confidence.

Was that threatening to Pop? What I knew for sure was that it riled him up. So much so that he pushed us away. Far away.

The holiday season was hell. I couldn't set foot in my family home. My town, even—at least, I felt that way. I had to mail my handmade gifts to my brothers. They were photographs, of course. In creative frames. Precious moments I'd captured of each of them. Moments I treasured.

Not getting to see their faces when they opened their presents was a rip-off. I anxiously waited for a thank-you note to make sure they'd received them. It never came. I was living in hell.

Georgie supported me as much as he could. I kept a brave face. We made the best of it together.

On Christmas Eve we had a lovely brunch at the home of our

"new" friend, Francis Murphy, and his acquaintance Brian Folger. Brian was a member of SoHo Photo too. I knew him pretty well. They walked us to the train station afterward.

Francis kissed me goodbye and shook Georgie's hand. Waved to us till the train pulled away and we were out of sight. I was sobbing by then, feeling overly emotional about not spending time with my own family during the Christmas season.

We took the South Jersey line to enjoy a huge second meal with Georgie's extended family. They'd invited us to spend the night. Although it was very festive—red wine was flowing, meatballs and lasagna were set next to the roasted turkey and stuffing—I was melancholy. Homesick as hell.

I made a call to wish my family a Merry Christmas, and Mom whispered, "I'll tell them you called."

"Can't I speak to the boys?" I held my breath.

"Your father has forbidden it. Give it time, sweetheart. Honestly, he can be such a turd sometimes. As if we were perfect when we were young. I wish he'd own that it wasn't me who wanted it."

"Wanted what, Mom?"

"Ack. You know how teenage boys are."

A great silence rose up between us—filled with the mention of her getting pregnant with me, and not wanting to be.

"I'll tell them you called, I promise," she finally whispered. "And I'll keep working on him."

The early months on the road were a distraction from my family troubles. Georgie focused on getting the show just right before taking it to the major city markets. I was obsessed with capturing the perfect album cover. It had also been decided that the double album would include a glossy insert of photos with captions—my dream job!

Every day came to seem the same: Van rides to the next

free bird

destination. Late-night arrivals and early-morning radio talk shows. Most days, an appearance on local television. On good days, a short and desperately needed nap. Sound checks. I was insistent upon a light check at every venue, too, so the pictures would be perfect. Then, the meet and greet. The concert. Georgie and Cassie performing. Me, recording the shows for posterity. The press-push afterward. An after-party in many towns, often inescapable because they were thrown by sponsors who were patrons of the smaller but iconic theaters.

Food?

On a good night, we ate well. On a bad night? We subsisted on the cheese-and-cracker plates in the dressing rooms.

Georgie and I fell into each other's arms at night, an exhausted tangle. We worked hard. We also enjoyed the honeymoon we were living. Work. Fun. Work. Make love. Work. Play.

It was hard to believe it was all real.

As summer neared, Georgie proposed the idea of a vacation. An exotic idea to me. When I was a child, we barely took day trips. No money for that. Mom was constantly pregnant, and we perpetually had a tiny infant in the house. No time.

We took Mikey with us when we rented a cottage out on Fire Island. We instantly felt at home there. It was a dreamy week on the beach. A different kind of beach, with a different crowd than we were used to.

Then back to the drill of touring. Months drifted by. Labor Day signaled the end of summer; Halloween passed.

Mom called me every Sunday if she could get a hold of us. Some of these new conversations with her were enlightening.

"I have been praying and remembering," she said during one. "Can you imagine, I was seventeen when your father and I made you? You think the church is restrictive now? Maeve, imagine what it was like twenty years ago. We were such a scandal."

I thought I knew. "I'm sure it was hard. But people get pregnant all the time."

"Not back then. It was ruin. I kept my eyes downcast for ten years. I barely raised my voice above a whisper." To my astonishment, she started to cry. "Me, with the scarlet 'A.' The worst was my worry about how it would affect you. We married, of course. Without ceremony. In the office of the rectory." Now she totally broke down.

"Take your time, Mom. I'll still be here." I felt her pain as if it were my own.

"All those old biddies at the church gossiped. I could hear the names they called me. Sanctimonious bitches. The nuns were the worst of all."

It was so sad. "Mom. I'm glad you're talking about this."

"They treated you like a love child. A bastard. When you were born red haired, they said it was the mark of the devil."

My eyes welled. My mother's revelations explained so much.

"But you see what I did, Maeve—though I'm not saying it was right or that if I had it to do over again I would—I decided to out-pious them. Wait them out. You may not know it, but I'm pretty smart."

I was embarrassed, because I often dismissed her ideas. "Well, I know that. Apples don't fall far from the tree and all."

"I signed up for every committee there was. Worked my butt off for the parish. By the time the boys started coming, I was a fixture of the church. So many of the old people have died off, it seems no one remembers the scandal anymore. But I do, Maeve. I know what it is to be convicted for the sin of loving someone."

I looked across the room at Georgie and nodded, though I knew Mom couldn't see me.

"And how can that be, Maeve? The kind of love that sticks? How can it be wrong?"

free bird

■ ■ ■

Mom was insistent that we come for Thanksgiving dinner. She'd been chipping away at Pop. "This cannot go on forever," she said. "He will just have to make peace with the fact that you are in love."

She sent Mikey all the way into the city to get us on Thanksgiving morning. To make sure we showed up, I suppose. Georgie and I were both nervous. I mean, really, who wants to make a scene?

When we came through the back door, Mom said—exclaimed, really—"Oh, thank God you are here. Georgie, darlin', could you sit down and peel those potatoes? The rest of these fellows are useless."

Yet Mikey came in to help too. "Hey, George. Maeve." He grabbed a knife out of the drawer and sat next to Georgie.

Pop and my other brothers were squeezed into the tiny den, watching football.

"Maeve, dear, could you make the gravy? Mine is never as good as yours." Mom poured us each a glass of white wine and handed Mikey a beer.

"Mom, since when do you drink wine?" I smiled at Georgie.

Mikey laughed. "Or let me have beer?"

"This estrangement has terrified me," she admitted. "There were times I thought I would never have Maeve in our home again. It's our first holiday together in a long time—it's something to celebrate. And to answer your question, I've been treating myself every so often since your show's opening. I'd forgotten how much I enjoyed having a drink."

The boys in the other room all cheered, drowning her out. We had to wait till they settled down to continue our conversation.

When their roars faded, Mom held her glass up in a toast. "I told your father it's the antidote to all the testosterone this house is steeped in. He has his beer, believe me, and now I have my wine. Cheers."

down on the south beach drag

We held our glasses up, though Georgie and I exchanged surprised glances.

Whatever team the boys were cheering on, something had gone wrong. The five of them groaned in unison. Detailed, loud commentary followed. Once again, we waited.

Mom pulled the bird out of the oven and basted it. She picked up her glass and took another sip. "I told your father, without Maeve here to joke around with while I'm cooking, I feel like the hired help."

Georgie was cautiously trying to get my attention, pointing to something.

The article the *New York Times* had printed about me was beautifully mounted, framed, and prominently displayed on the wall over the table. What had my mother paid for that? How could I have missed it?

Mikey saw us looking and laughed. "Oh yeah. She tells everybody about you."

"Not everyone," Mom said. "But I did want to ask a favor. Do you think you could find the time to come out and speak to the Women's Auxiliary?"

I was aghast. "Me? What do I have to speak to them about?"

She held out both hands to me. "Oh, Maeve. All by yourself. With barely a speck of help. Look what you have done with your life. It seems there are all kinds of new freedoms for us women. There are many in the club who want to get out there and start exploring. We're asking some speakers to come in and give us ideas how to do it."

It took me a moment to take this information in. *The Catholic women are interested in new freedoms?*

"I would be so proud if you would come and give a talk," she said. "We'll learn a lot—and I'll help you find the right thing to wear."

There it was. Her days of trying to turn me into the girl she wanted me to be were not yet done.

free bird

"I'm not wearing a taffeta dress if that's what you're thinking," I said firmly.

Georgie held up his glass in a toast. "I'll drink to that!"

Mom pursed her lips but refrained from arguing with me.

I was skimming the drippings, my back turned, getting ready to prepare the gravy. So I didn't see why the room had gone quiet until I peeked over my shoulder.

My father stood near the table. He nodded his head to Georgie. "Hello, son."

Son. The hair on the back of my neck rose up. He had called Georgie *son*.

I turned and stared into Pop's green eyes.

"Father Gastadello said I was to ask you for some time, Maeve," he said. "Time to figure this out in my own head. How to be a family again."

Mom threw up her hands. "Well, thank the Lord. I never thought I'd live to see the day you would apologize for anything."

"I didn't exactly hear him apologize, Mom," Mikey said.

"Close enough," I said. And in the nick of time too. I couldn't imagine how I could have possibly gone on without my father. "Pop, do you know how many times I have started to pick up the phone to ask you for advice about this thing or that?"

I threw myself in his arms and we both cried. It felt so terribly painful. When we let go, Georgie was there with tissues for both of us; Pop patted his shoulder tentatively. It was a start.

Tommy came running into the kitchen. He was a toddler now, a real little man. "Poppa, Maeve gonna smile again now?"

Out of the mouths of babes.

Dad swept him up. "Let that be a lesson to you, Tommy. In the end, family is everything." My other three brothers heard him say it. They were jammed in the doorway, listening.

"Finally, we can get back to normal around here!" Terry hollered.

down on the south beach drag

We laughed so hard we were all bent over, wiping our eyes, a little punchy now that months' worth of tension had broken.

I took Georgie's hand. "Well, you're in it now, George. Part of this crazy family."

Pop was quiet at the dinner table. Stiff and contemplative. The boys were just the opposite, so boisterous I could hardly hear myself think. Georgie and Mom might have been a little tipsy.

My mother grabbed his hand before we began eating. "I want you to invite me out to your next show. I want to dance to every song."

They giggled and shook on it. Apparently, it was a done deal.

I had to laugh. Neither of them could hold their liquor all that well.

Dinner turned out to be delicious. If I do say so myself, that gravy was the best I ever made.

acknowledgments

I get chills thinking about certain songs that touched me so deeply I can remember exactly where I was the first time I heard them. They are the soundtrack of my life. As an Irish Catholic Jersey Girl, the Jersey Shore Sound of Frankie Valli and the Four Seasons, Bruce Springsteen and the E Street Band, Southside Johnny and the Asbury Jukes (with Steven Van Zandt), and The Drifters spoke to my soul. Thank you all for changing a culture, where New Jersey was the butt of jokes, into the coolest place on earth.

Gratitude always to my husband Tom Mehuron, who works so hard to hold down the fort of our lives while I am lost in my stories. And everywhere we travel he makes sure I have a spot where I can write. I have known no greater love.

Also, to my three sons who are my biggest fans. On this, my fourth novel, I must single out my director-son Jonathan C. Hyde. It's a special day when your child turns around and becomes your teacher. He helped shape this book in a true collaboration. Thank you, Jonny.

My lifelong friend Carol Omstead Kroner, who has cared about me for fifty-nine years. Look how far we have come my friend!

My mentors and best-selling authors James M. Tabor, Kris Radish and Marley Gibson. What you have taught me cannot be measured.

Hida Viloria, author of Born Both: An Intersex Life, and activist for those born intersex. Thank you for teaching and mentoring me.

down on the south beach drag

The Savannah College of Art and Design, where I attend classes in the graduate writing program. It is there that I learned, though I am much older than the other students, they think I am relevant and have great stories to tell. That makes me feel like jumping in the air and clicking my heels together.

The people of the Mad River Valley of Vermont, who root for our own.

And, finally, many thanks to the folks at She Writes Press and SparkPress, especially Brooke Warner, Krissa Lagos and Addison Gallegos. Your faith in me keeps me writing books.

about the author

Mary Kathleen Mehuron lives in a ski town in Vermont, where friends call her Kathy and she and her husband raised three sons. She has an almost weekly column in her local newspaper, *The Valley Reporter*, and is the author of three other novels: *Fading Past*, *The Opposite of Never*, and, most recently, *The Belonger*, which is set on Grand Turk Island and Providenciales. Mary Kathleen was born in Chicago and raised in New Jersey. She takes extended time to write on Grand Turk Island, Vermont's Northeast Kingdom, and Savannah—but for the last forty years she has called Waitsfield, Vermont, her home.

Looking for your next great read?

We can help!

Visit www.gosparkpress.com/next-read
or scan the QR code below for a list
of our recommended titles.

SparkPress is an independent boutique publisher delivering high-quality, entertaining, and engaging content that enhances readers' lives, with a special focus on commercial and genre fiction.